I DICED WITH GOD
The Life of Henry VIII
As Seen By His Majesty

Dorothy Davies

I DICED WITH GOD
The Life of Henry VIII
As Seen By His Majesty

Fiction4All

From
Preludes 1921-1922 by John Drinkwater
Sidgwick and Jackson Ltd., 1922

I counted evil twenty different ways,
And none of them plain evil. I diced with God,
And the dice fell as often to my hand,
It seemed, as His, but falling so the whisper
Was ever shadowed at my ear, unheard.
And ever as this new intelligence,
This pride of thought, crept over me and filled
My dawn and noon and sleep, a hunger grew,
A dreadful hunger for that self denied,
And every word I spoke for righteousness
Turned bitter on my lips, because I knew
That every word was righteousness undone.

From Immortality
Olton Pools, Sidgwick and Jackson Ltd.,1917

There in the midst of all these words shall be
Our names, our ghosts, our immortality.

"I have no fear but when you heard that our Prince, now Henry the Eighth, whom we may call our Octavius, had succeeded to his father's throne, all your melancholy left you at once. What may you not promise yourself from a Prince with whose extraordinary and almost Divine character you are acquainted? When you know what a hero he now shows himself, how wisely he behaves, what a lover he is of justice and goodness, what affection he bears to the learned I will venture to swear that you will need no wings to make you fly to behold this new and auspicious star. If you could see how all the world here is rejoicing in the possession of so great a Prince, how his life is all their desire, you could not contain your tears for joy. The heavens laugh, the earth exults, all things are full of milk, of honey, of nectar! Avarice is expelled the country. Liberality scatters wealth with bounteous hand. Our King does not desire gold or gems or precious metals, but virtue, glory, immortality."
Lord Mountjoy to Erasmus, 1509

The Moving Finger writes; and, having writ,
Moves on: nor all thy Piety nor Wit
Shall lure it back to cancel half a Line,
Nor all thy Tears wash out a Word of it.

Rubaiyat of Omar Khayyam.
Included at His Majesty's request.

Author's note:

Why Henry VIII, when there are so many books on his life and/or his many wives? Because it feels as if the books consistently miss the essence of the man and the man himself knows this. He wanted to write his life as he saw it and lived it. For most authors he is either a bluff jovial king or a tyrannical despot, murdering all in sight. The truth lies somewhere between the two.

Henry VIII is a combination of his ancestors, his cautious, quiet, diplomatic politician father, his quiet, beautiful, obedient mother, his equally beautiful grandmother, Elizabeth Woodville, his grandfather, the soldier king, Edward IV, the ambitious Margaret Beaufort and even further back, to the Valois and Welsh ancestors. All that heritage came together in one virile, woman-loving, power-hungry, ambitious and very clever man who was able to manipulate those around him and get his own way by sheer force of his personality.

He is often eulogised in film and on TV only for his sexual exploits but this, like so many 'facts' about this extraordinary king, is just another myth. Some historians seem to get no further than his six wives; others want to portray him only as a mass murderer, albeit with all the killings done second hand. Few, especially novelists, have managed to capture the man himself.

This is Henry as he was; a giant among men. It is also our effort to put right many of the 'errors' made by film makers and others who do not let historical facts get in the way of what they want to see on the screen, starting with the colour of his hair... and to rectify comments such as his being a 'murderous cripple', comments which bother His Majesty a good deal. This book is his observations on his life and on the way he has been - and still is - portrayed.

I know, from being regressed several times, that I was once Katherine of Aragon. The first two occasions were with a hypnotherapist. Both times I went back to the lives of the same two people, in the same order, too, Katherine first and then someone in the 15th century. The regressions were very vivid, even without the prompting of the tape I can remember the words I spoke and the sensations I experienced. The 'Katherine' life was also confirmed by a leading psychic when I asked her about another past life.

So it was no surprise to find His Majesty coming to me, calling me Katherine and asking about writing his story. It is a great comfort to know that when the book is done, unlike the majority of the other authors who are awaiting their turn, my liege lord will not be moving on. He says he will stay with me for the remainder of my natural life and help me in every way he can. This is a gift and an honour; I do not consider myself worthy of his attention and devotion, although he insists I am.

Here then is the eighth person to hold the name Henry and become King, in his own words, as told to the person who was once his Queen, Katherine of Aragon.

Dorothy Davies, Isle of Wight

DEDICATIONS

Dedicated to the memory of
His Majesty King Henry VIII
28th June 1491 – 28th January 1547
'God And My Right'

This book is also dedicated to HRH Charles, Prince of Wales, at the request of His Majesty King Henry VIII. His comments are as follows:

This fine Prince has been maligned, misunderstood, misquoted, caricatured and at times ignored. He has suffered much at the hands of the press, has been through grief, great loss and heartache as well as periods of great contentment and happiness. He has my every sympathy for I have known such feelings myself. But I know and the country should know that his heart and mind are in the right place, that he has the welfare of the people of what you now call Great Britain at the centre of his thinking. He should be accorded respect for the work he does and the example he sets in his devotion to the work of the Royal Family and the many organisations of which he is patron.

In particular I wish to thank him for his patronage and interest in the raising of the *Mary Rose* and in the ongoing work of the Museum dedicated to preserving my favourite ship and all the artefacts discovered with it.

I also wish to remember every person who helped resurrect what was left of the *Mary Rose* and to all who created and those who continue to maintain the Mary Rose Museum in Portsmouth. You do me a great service in preserving my ship. I will not forget it.

Henricus Rex.

For my part, grateful thanks go to:

Mary Holliday, devoted friend;
Lynne Mulrooney, who knows how much help she has been;
Terry Wakelin because he is Terry Wakelin, my rock and my anchor as always;
To everyone in my spiritual 'inner circle' for support, love, laughter, guidance and for always being there.

I would also like to mention Jane Owen for her ongoing contribution in keeping the Tudor connection to Appuldurcombe House alive and kicking.

Henry and I also wish to mention a special person, our daughter Mary Tudor, who is now in this life. She knows who she is.

A percentage of the royalties from this book are to go to the Mary Rose Trust, to ensure the work of the museum and care of the artefacts continues. If we can play a small part in funding the work of drying out the hull so it is preserved for future generations to visit, view and learn from, it will be worthwhile.

Quote: Samuel Butler (1835-1902)
It has been said that though God cannot alter the past, historians can: it is perhaps because they can be useful to Him in this respect that He tolerates their existence.
(*It is to be hoped He will continue to tolerate me for a few more years...*)

Prologue

"Katherine, this nonsense on what you call TV, what is it all about? Tudors! What do they know? For a start, I had blonde hair; did they not know that? What is this dark-haired person who looks nothing like me doing leaping into - or onto - bed with women who look nothing like my wives? I mean, my dear wife, you were beautiful, that one, well ... just plain unattractive, to me, anyway. Now, shall we tell it like it really was?"

"My liege lord, I am ready and waiting. Where do you want to start?"

"Ha! That is a question I have been long pondering, ever since you said you would write my story and chose that title. By the way, how did you know that would sum up my life so well?'

"Simple. You diced with God from the moment you laid eyes on me and probably a good deal before that, too, before I arrived in your life, my Lord. I would need the ability to travel the Realms and find each and every nursemaid, tutor, stable hand, falconer, tailor, courtier ... need I go on... to find out what you were like from the moment you first drew breath until I saw you myself. I do not have that ability, more's the pity but I can go with what I know of you."

"Hm. This might be more difficult than I anticipated. I had visions, you know, happy visions of walking the floor of this room, your office I think you call it, hung with moons for some reason that still escapes me-"

"You asked me about them the first time you came, my Lord. You stood in typical majestic pose, hands on hips, and said "Katherine, what is all this stuff?" and then swept the air with a kingly right hand. I said then 'just moons, sire, because I like them.' No more than that."

"As I said, walking the floor dictating my life story to you, to undo the dreadful impression given by that – that autobiography – yes, I know, before you say a word, I told you to buy it! But I did not think the author would be so foolish as to put grown up words into a three year old's mouth! And then this – this television thing – in the name of God…"

"Too many mistakes, it seems to me. Not that I have watched it, as you well know. I would not bother with something that is so erroneous as not to be true. And now the film…"

"Do Not Under Any Circumstances speak to me of the film, Katherine! That is an outrage and an abomination and a disaster! How could they do that to a book?"

"Quite easily. Hollywood has a talent for wrecking books."

"So I see, so I see. Well, shall we get on with the *real* book?"

"You have had time to consider the outline of the book, my Lord, where you really want to begin. At least, I thought you had, but I might have taken you by surprise in deciding to write three books at the same time, one of them being yours."

"Yes! Damn woman! I – oh, what's the point? Women always get their own way! Why don't we do what that dreadful author did, begin at the beginning?"

"And end at the end?"

"Of course. Need you ask?"

"Which 'end' would that be, my Lord? The one where you were, with great difficulty, lowered into the grave alongside Jane Seymour, or the 'end' that is now apparent, you as a spirit companion and guide to this lowly writer?"

"Ha!"

"Are you aware how much of a Plantagenet habit that 'Ha!' is? You are your grandfather's descendant, for sure!"

"Hm. The less said about him the better, I think, Katherine. A most unsavoury time, most unsavoury. So much gallivanting going on. So many battles, so much fighting and killing."

"You, of course, never indulged in such things..."

"No! Of course not! Well, perhaps..."

"Before this slides into conflict, my Lord, should we not begin the story?"

"Yes, Katherine, let us begin! We will take the sorry tale of one man's life as King of this thrice blessed country and set it aright. We will dispel the myth that I lived solely for women – but what true man would not do just that, if they were paraded in front of him? Endlessly paraded, I would add! – And dispel the myth that all I sought was money. Oh, and that I was fat and old and tired before my time. No, I was fat and old and tired *because* of my time. Too many banquets, too little exercise. Ah, but I was a fair prince...

Enough! We have a book to write!"

Chapter One - Beginnings

28th June 1491 was a momentous day for England. Sadly England did not realise it at the time. I came kicking and squalling into this world, full of vigour, full of strength and hearty of lungs. God be witness to this, what was the first thing they did? Put me to the breast. Now I ask you … what chance did a man have of growing up to be indifferent to women when they did that!

You are going to ask 'how do I know that?' I will tell you that it was the habit of the time. Birth the child, clean the child, console the child with the breast of the wet nurse to stop the inevitable bawling that comes of being thrust head first into a world that does not always appreciate your arrival, then turn to the mother and deal with the after effects of what was and is a most dangerous act – delivering a child.

Why was I not appreciated? Because I was a second son. And because I was one of the 'rich', with servants, maids, nurses and physicians in attendance when so many of my fellow countrymen – and I say that without a hint of condescension, by the way – fought for survival in the most pitiful of conditions.

There is nothing more useless than a second son until they are needed. The 'spare'. The 'might one day be useful' being who hangs around, getting under people's feet – often literally, especially when small – given lessons because lessons are needed, instruction on how to behave, how to conduct oneself at the table in the presence of the Great and Good of England and any other land, come to that. Taught to do these things because even in the most well-run household, where we were all prayed over often, given the best food, the best medicine when ill, the best of everything all the time, accidents, illnesses and death could happen. And did, on a regular basis.

It is hard to imagine me, this giant of a man in every way, being a helpless child swaddled and cradled and fed and taught the basics of life: control your body, your movements, your stumbling feet, your inability which soon becomes an ability to converse, if only by single words for a while. The forming of sentences comes later. Speaking English comes with the milk you are fed. Speaking any language gives you an advantage; you can ask for that which you need or simply want.

To be philosophical for a moment, a child cannot form the concept of 'love' in their mind so cannot use the word to ask for it. Love should be freely given. In my case it was not. Perhaps the nursemaids had a love for the little boy Henry; the tutors did not, that I can assure you. My father, of which much more later – unfortunately – did not. My mother did as she was bid but did she, in her heart, hold a love for her son who soon grew big and strong and determined not to be outdone or overshadowed and showed it in his attitude? I would like to think so. But I cannot prove it and have no way of giving myself concrete evidence on which to believe it.

Your century is a million years from mine; your last century went through changes that happened so fast it is hard to keep track of them. Back then, in my time, everything changed slowly. Even fashion took some time to be adopted. The books say that the court copied Anne Boleyn's long trailing sleeves, yes, they did, but not immediately. At first they simply pointed and stared. Now a look is advertised, I think you say it thus, and every young person appears to be wearing it the next day. No matter if it is ugly, unsuitable, ridiculous or any other word you wish to fasten to it, that is what happens. We moved much slower, we took our time to make changes. Were you to visit a castle in the 15th century and again in the 16th century you would find little change. Maybe an additional building here or there, maybe a few more tapestries, more glass, but not much else. So I tell you that the procedure on the birth of a child was the same for many centuries. A newly born living child was something to be rejoiced over and if the mother survived too, even more rejoicing. Aristocratic children were put to the breast of the waiting wet nurse and so I repeat, I was put to the breast - and never left it.

That's made you laugh, Katherine, something I have not seen for a while! At last, a laugh! But enough of that. What we are to one another is not for the world to know, is it? Or would they want to know? This day I am full of questions, for myself, for you, for the world at large. I am getting few answers; your entire mind is dedicated to writing my words as I send them from my spirit to yours. Sometimes you falter, as if the words are not clear, but I believe you falter only to make sense of them before committing them to your screen, that light which shines before you and magically displays the words which you somehow put on to it. Just as well, with the speed of my thoughts and memories, no quill or parchment would tolerate the rapidity of the words!

To return to the subject - me. I have to comment that few biographies, few historians mention my early years. They tend to begin when the crown was placed on this fair head of mine but my formative years were just that, forming my character so that what came after was a result of what I lived through then. Is this not always so? Are people not formed by what they had/endured in early life and did that not colour their personality for the remainder of the time?

Remember this always, you who judge me even now, you who call me monster and tyrant and despot and a hundred other derogatory terms – I know full well who some of them are – you did not walk in my shoes. You did not live my life. You did not have to cope with all that I coped with in the way of deception, treachery, double dealing: the power-mad potentates who would have liked nothing more than to see me fall from my glorious pinnacle, the self-seeking families who put their women, young and not so young, in my life so that I might see them and perhaps toss a few scraps of honours their way, when they were not scheming to place the bitch in my bed, that is.

I am aware Katherine hesitated long before typing the word I gave her, but it is true. Mostly they were bitches. Fortune-hunting schemers who had no love for me, none whatsoever, but a tremendous lust for that which I could offer them: a position of power and prestige. But my Katherine loved me and I walked out on her and that I regret more than I regret any death, any execution, any act I did in the remainder of my reign.

What a diversion I set up there! I have to say, in truth, many of those who schemed their way into my life and into my bed were doing precisely what that clever title indicates, they were dicing with God – I was God at that time - and they lost. I can load dice as well as any trickster. I did, too.

Enough! I have a deadline; I must work to it! A set amount of months for Katherine to scour the books, take my memories, write my words, ensuring I do not miss anything or anyone in this overall view of a long, violent, bloody, golden, power-ridden period of history. The choice of words is deliberate: the overview will be truncated here and there, of necessity, there is not enough paper in the world for me to write every word, every conversation, every plot, every treasonable act … and have a book that can be held in the hand and read comfortably. You readers today do not sit at desks to read, but hunch over a book in a train or bus or before that thing, that time-gobbling monster you call television or whilst you eat. You are not allowed to throw bones over your shoulder any more, by the way … I would wish I had actually done that. It would have been interesting to see the reaction of those who ate with me and those who were struck by the bones. Would they have kept them as relics or would they have quietly thrown them to the dogs immediately? Ah, can you believe the stupid pathways my thoughts take me these days? Am I getting old or something?

Katherine assures me with your words: 'no, you are not, you are just shaking off the shackles of royalty and being yourself.'

And what am I? A better Fool than the Fool I had, for sure. I employed him at first because I felt sorry for him and he amused me, sometimes. Later he became invaluable. I know I could have done a better job than he did as Fool, but it was beneath a king's dignity to make jokes. Or so they told me. You do know I threatened to kill him once, with my own hands? He took on a dare and cast aspersions on Anne. I wanted to kill him that day. I am glad I didn't, he became a most valued helper and nursemaid in my later life. He is a fine Fool, helper and nursemaid to me now, not that I need nursing but it is nice to be pampered occasionally.

A larger than life monarch in English history? That is how many view me and obviously why there are so many books on my life and so many films and programmes and lectures and assumptions. I like the idea of being a larger than life monarch but I do disapprove most strongly of the many mistakes and wild assumptions they have been making over the years which have somehow become fact. I am grateful for the chance to put my side of the story and perhaps straighten out a few of the more conceited, arrogant and pontificating historians you seem to have around you at the moment. Katherine does not own, nor would I encourage her to have it, the latest book on my life. Already she reads that there are badly written passages in it. Of course there are, he rushed it to coincide with the anniversary of my coronation, as if that matters a jot to anyone but the publishers. This book has been revised several times already and by the time it is delivered to Katherine's publishers, we will have gone over it one more time to ensure that every person named here is named in a way that the reader will understand who they are and their place in history. We will also watch for awkward sentences, unless I ask for them to stand. Not everything can be left to editors, I have to say, although I also have to say Katherine happens to have a superb editor for her series.

What else am I? A despot, killing all who stood in my way. Yes, it would seem that way but there were reasons for every execution, something I will go into later.

A much-married man with an eye for the women? I think, if you look at some of your film stars, you will find there some much married men - and women, too. One has been married eight times, if I remember correctly. Why should I have been any different? Read the book; find out why I was much married. There were reasons, just as there were for the executions.

Chapter Two - Growing Up

I am asked what I remember from childhood, from the early years.

I remember many people. Tall, elegant people, small hunched over people, as in servility, you understand, not hunchbacks. The tall, elegant ones were loaded with gold and silver and wore richly embroidered clothes that shone in the light, either the sun or the many lamps and candles we had around the place. It was as if they were unnatural beings that glittered as they moved. I speak from the child's perspective.

You see, wherever I was there were people. No matter which home I was in, Greenwich, Whitehall, Richmond, wherever, there were people. I never knew what it was like to be alone. There were the courtiers, the servants, the pages, the squires, the nursemaids, stable hands, cooks … an endless variety of people to do an endless variety of tasks, from washing the clothes to writing Father's letters and then conveying them to the people for whom they were intended. Then there were the visitors. They came from other lands to confer with Father. There were counsellors, archbishops and other dignitaries I had to learn to recognise, greet and to whom to be polite. So, I grew up listening to many languages and came to understand them, too. This gave me an advantage few others had, especially when it came to lessons and in my future life, then I would and often did fool them for few remembered how many languages I spoke and how often I overheard snippets of gossip that were not intended for my ears. That, together with a network of spies and informers, guaranteed few things got past this Tudor.

In truth, I grew up in a hothouse of politics and double-dealing, of power play and paranoia. I have the distinct feeling Katherine has used those words in another of her books. Am I right?

I am right, or words close enough to those.

I was an inquisitive, tough little boy, apparently, or so my nursemaids complained to my parents. My father was disinterested; his attention was on Arthur, the heir, the future king. If God had willed it, we would have had a real King Arthur on the throne. Ha! A real King Arthur! Listen to me, as if the original were not real! Of course he was, but he has been wrapped around with legends, myths and mystical mayhem. Poor man doesn't know his Merlin from his Merry Men, oh, sorry, another legend, another time!

Let me start back at the start again.

Right. People, lots of them. A court full of people. Mostly I didn't know who they were. I recognised servants and nursemaids but some of the others, I didn't know if they were important or merely hangers on – the good Lord knows I had enough of them in my own court – as to me they were grown up beings who just about managed to pat a small boy on the head and, if I were really fortunate, find me a sweetmeat from the table or a sugared fruit or confection of some kind. If I were really very fortunate, they would even hand me a gold coin which I would secrete in my room.

Banquets - I remember banquets. Not because I attended them, author of my dreadful 'autobiography' please note! Children did not attend banquets until they were more than old enough to sit through countless courses, to be polite, not to wriggle, scratch, chatter aimlessly, score the trenchers with knives or tip wine or sauces over the table. Find me a three year old who can do that and hold a sensible conversation with a grown up sister and I will show you a paragon that exists only in the imagination of those who write.

I remember banquets for a different reason. My father, whom I vaguely recognised as someone important – due to the fact he sometimes wore a gold crown and fur trimmed robes of fractionally better quality than others around him – would apparently ask my mother to arrange for me to be brought into the banqueting hall and displayed to the visitors, so I learned later when I asked about those times. Arthur would already be there, sat at the table, bored, trying not to become inebriated and lose his dignity, such as he had. Poor Arthur never could hold his drink. My arrival was very much a 'look, I have an heir and a spare!' boasting attitude. The problem was, I was too strong for the nursemaid and would wriggle out of her arms, dive under the table and there scurry around, investigating that part of the grownup world which I regularly saw – boots and shoes and slippers and pattens and all things to do with feet. I rarely saw past knees and thighs at that young age, so my world was leather boots, decorated with silver and gold and fancy trimmings, delicate shoes with embroidery and trimmings, satin slippers – need I go on? Someone would reach out, grab my arm and pull me out from under the table and there would be gales of laughter, then that someone would hand me a sugared fruit or comfit of some kind and the nursemaid would be hastily bid to take me away again. It was a moment for me, an occasion, an 'I am here!' scenario which I played to the full, even then. Second son I might have been, this I knew in the deepest recesses of my young mind, knew full well that Arthur was favoured over me as he was older, but I knew that I had a place in life too and was determined to show them that I lived, that I was not someone to ignore.

My mother was a remote figure to me. I knew she was my mother for that had been told to me by nursemaids and servants, "My Lord Harry, be still, let us wash and robe you, your mother wishes to see you!" and I was scrubbed and dressed and taken to be presented to a pale, serious, unhappy person who did not seem at all pleased to see me, no matter how hard I tried to believe she did. I have been told, and in truth I have read, she was said to be a loving mother. If she was … I saw few signs of it. My belief is this - and I will make it exceedingly clear that this is only my belief – that my mother married my father because it was politically the best thing that could be done in the circumstances. I do not believe it was a love match. I believe instead that they were married to legitimise his claim to the throne, which was weak and constantly under scrutiny from those who would see it collapse. She was dutiful, subservient, biddable in every way. She produced children, sons who would inherit, daughters who would make dynastic marriages. She obeyed her mother in law, my formidable grandmother; she obeyed her husband, my formidable father. I saw love light up her face when my brother Arthur was with her, for he was the first born and the first born is often the loved one, particularly if he happens to be the heir to the throne.

I spent my formative childhood years with her in the London homes we had but could not say I knew her as a person at all. I do not recall a loving arm around me. I do not recall kind words. I do not recall praise when lessons were well learned or some new skill was conquered. All that came from those who were far below my mother: servants, courtiers, squires and tutors.

I remember lessons. Ink splattered paper; ink splattered Harry, as everyone called me back then, when they weren't calling me fool, imp and many other names that would not be suitable for the pages of my book.

Here I have to say I hated being called Harry. I found it demeaning and would often ignore the call if they used that diminutive. I would no more call this Katherine Kate or Katie than I would call Charles Brandon Charlie.

Remember it well, those who write of me! The last work of fiction Katherine tried to read on my life depicted me calling my wife and beloved Queen Kate. I know not where the woman did her research but she and all others need to know I never diminished anyone's name, ever.

Katherine says, quietly "Will Somer?" When he came to me he told me his name was Will. If it were William he never said. If he had, that is the name by which he would have been known. It was a rule of mine; I stuck to it all my life.

Back to being a child. Ah, I wish… no, perhaps I don't. Later years were better for me.

I was into everything and everything was into me, if I could get my hands on it long enough to try it. As I absorbed the languages of those who spoke around me, so I absorbed the sights and sounds, smells and physical things of the castles, homes, courts and anywhere I happened to be. I knew the particular smell of my bedchamber and its hangings, its linens and its chests of clothes. I knew the feel of the panelling and tapestries of the great halls, I knew the sense and rhythms of the kitchens and laundry, all from exploring as soon as I was big enough to explore – which meant escaping the nursemaids and servants set to take care of me. It was easy enough to do; they were far more concerned with the Prince of Wales, my brother, than they were with me, my other brother or my sisters. I seemed to go missing fairly regularly, my absence being noted when it came to mealtimes, then a search party would be sent out to find 'the missing child.' If I happened to be covered in dirt or dust or smuts or grease or just about anything that a boy can find to get into, there would be a lot of harsh words and a few harsh smacks, too, not that it stopped me. There was too much to be learned, seen, experienced, felt, appreciated, to be conscious of 'not doing it again' instructions, no matter how many times they tried to drum it into my head. Only later did the 'whipping boy' come into my life, before then, irritable and irritated nursemaids and squires sent to find me would, if no one was around, hand out a slap or two for the trouble I had put them to and would put them to ensuring I was tidy enough to sit at the table – for of a surety I could not go there covered in smuts and dirt, although to me it was a natural state for a boy to be in. There was time enough for ceremony and quiet, for decorum and politeness. Outside of those times there were places to explore and people to watch and annoy. With many of them I could exert authority from a very young age. So many deferred to me because of my status, royal prince, that I thought I could get away with anything from anyone all the time. It became a habit…

What I learned on these escapades was invaluable.

I learned that things are not permanent, that people do not last forever, that knowledge is a commodity like any other but worth more than any gold or silver. I learned that someone's word cannot always be trusted, that if smiles didn't reach the eyes, that was someone to watch out for in the future. I learned that it was good to compete, to win if possible, to ride better than the next man, to fire a crossbow faster and more accurately than the tutor, to out-shoot the archers at the butts, not because I wanted the praise, but because I wanted – needed - to be better than the others. It was my only weapon as the second son, as the next in line 'in-case-anything-happens-to-the-firstborn' so I would not be dismissed as being of no consequence. This boy, this otherwise overlooked child, was quietly determined not to be overlooked, not to be ignored. And I wonder still why biographers generally do not begin at the beginning, where it really starts, where the character is formed, where the drive and impetus and thrusting desires have their birth. I was determined not to be ignored or forgotten. I was not, never have been and never will be.

You should know I am not forgotten just because I had six wives and killed a few people – all right, a lot of people – but because of my committed determination to that one thing, not to be ignored. There are kings in English history some people do not know, have never heard of, have managed to overlook in their lessons because those kings did not have that determination. As an example, how many people know about King Stephen? How many books are there on my father's life, compared with mine? I do not diminish King Stephen by saying this, I know Katherine will write his story for him in the fullness of time, but few know of him and the terrible civil war he fought with Queen Matilda. Now do they? Be honest with yourself. Have you known of that quiet but forceful king? And my esteemed father, what do you know of him other than he 'won' the battle of Bosworth?

I rest my case, to use an expression from the legal profession that never fails to amuse me.

I feel as if I have overlooked something, have I?

Oh yes. Father. Apart from the occasional mention… I have not spoken of him, have I? Now tell me, how did I manage to overlook the monarch in writing out my childhood memories?

Because he was not there. Because he was ever in this meeting or that, travelling here, travelling there, presiding over this council meeting or that. Endless meetings, endless diplomacy, endless banquets and conversations on matters of high state. A thin, narrow minded, colourless man, devoid of emotion as far as the world was concerned, or so it seemed. I was shocked beyond belief that he displayed open grief when Mother died. 'The man feels emotion!' I told my squires and they looked at me as if I had gone mad. Then one smiled at me and said 'yes, my lord, he does. Sometimes.' I have no doubt that Arthur's death cut him to the very heart but he displayed nothing but his granite face to the world. It took Mother's passing to show me that there was a real heart beating under the austere robes. Not for him the bright colours, the display of wealth, but work-a-day clothes, the darker colours, the sombre cloths. The brightness was for state banquets and the like. Not for every day. It was then I decided that bright colours were for every day.

Why be royal and look like everyone else?

Chapter Three - Siblings

Why did I want a break there? I have no idea, but I have asked Katherine to break the book there and to resume with a new topic. I know full well she is bursting with questions. So ask me!

What were my brothers and sisters like?

Arthur. Yes. My brother, the heir, the Prince of Wales, the quiet one. Arthur was a quiet studious boy/man. He was slender of build, fair of face and hair, lighter than my colouring, with large sad eyes and long fingers. He never did enjoy the cut and thrust of the tourney, the thrill of the hunt, the political manoeuvring, the high level discussions and the thought of power. He wanted to read and plan gardens and build homes and chapels. He had titles, Prince of Wales, Earl of Chester; he was Knight of the Bath and Knight of the Garter, the whole panoply of royal encumbrances. He didn't really care for any of them. Ceremonials bored him, banquets were a chore to sit through, he could dance but had no real sense of rhythm and little appreciation of music. He was a pious, studious, quiet person entirely unsuited to the life of royalty. Unfortunately history is littered with 'unsuitable' people who ended up in the role because of being the first born, or in some cases, the second born and were not really right for 'the job.'

He disapproved of my pranks, my high spirits, my need for constant movement and tried to curb it. Well, he could try all he liked. Arthur had an intellect but it was sadly lacking in some respects. I think, and consider this well, it was only my opinion, that Arthur's intellect would not have befitted him as King. He was not worldly wise, he did not engage in debate, in discussion, in anything to do with political power play. Had he lived to be king, he would have been manipulated by those around him without his even realising it. He needed to live in the real world but the real world would have been too much for him. The real world swallows up innocents and spits them out as so much charnel meat. The real world needs to be confronted, taken by the throat and shaken hard so that it gives up its secrets to those strong enough to take it on and get at them. In some ways Katherine was an innocent back then and she is an innocent now. But she is now an innocent with some worldly-wise knowledge to help her fight back when necessary. I respect that in her.

Again I divert. I spoke of the many titles given to my older brother. I was equally encumbered, being made Constable of Dover Castle and Lord Warden of the Cinque Ports when my only experience of castles was running wild in them and my only experience of water was splashing all in sight when I had a bath. Somewhere between birth and four years I was made Lord Lieutenant of Ireland and created Knight of the Bath. What an ordeal that was! Quite how anyone thought I would manage the night of contemplation and all that went with it, I don't know. What I do know is that I lost out on a later initiation when it would have meant much more to me. They added Duke of York to my titles the day after that celebration, of which I remember so little, and then made Lord Warden of the Marches of Scotland. If at that age I knew such a place existed, then I would indeed be the paragon my 'autobiography' makes me out to be. I wasn't. This I confess to you openly and without shame. I was a boy, as fit and as energetic and as mischievous and as difficult and as contrary as any boy today. Finally I was made Knight of the Garter and that was it, for a time anyway. It was a bit like over-decorating a Christmas tree in your time now, it was a lot of baubles and ceremony for a small boy. All that mattered to me was listening to and obeying the tutors, at risk of serious displeasure if I did not do so, pleasing my mother, for the same reason, trying to learn to be a royal prince as Arthur was and Edmund was trying to be and having as good a time as I could.

Oh, how easy it is to go off the subject! Not that Katherine is trying to drag me back to it, she kindly lets me ramble on, her fingers flying over the keyboard. You see, I do know modern terms, don't I?

The only person I truly respected in my childhood for his intellect and his abilities was my tutor, Mr. Skelton. He was the only one who could control me, to some degree, for his word was law.

We were discussing my brothers and sisters. I must of necessity revert to that question.

My sister Margaret was next in line. Now she was – how do I say this without seeming overly pompous or overly critical? – she was … a living reincarnation of Grandmother Beaufort. There, I said it. I have wanted to say it for many a long year, about 500, give or take a few. Sharp tongued, sharp mind, sharp angular body to go with it. Middling to brown hair, features that showed the lines of her skull, dark eyes that pierced through you and nailed you to the wall, Margaret was not one you went to for consoling hugs or quiet words. Margaret lectured, Margaret censured, Margaret blamed. Do this, do that, do it this way, do it that way. Often she contradicted Mr. Skelton and that did not go down well, as he did not tolerate dissension. He mostly ignored her, though, and continued to teach me deportment as well as all the other lessons it was felt necessary to inflict on me, everything from how to reckon to how to speak in reasonable tones in different languages.

I was next and then my sister Elizabeth. She was a quiet one, not overly pretty but attractive enough when she smiled, which she did often, as she found pleasure in small things: a butterfly, a flower, a bird chattering from a branch, a kitten clawing at her dress or her fine white hands. I remember her slender hands and long fingers more than anything. She had dark hair; I recall that, too, which she wore in long curls trailing over her shoulders. There was great sadness when she died; she was not much more than three, if my memory is correct. I do remember her funeral; the grief everyone was showing was almost too much for me. Poor little Elizabeth. One moment playing with a kitten and chasing a butterfly, the next confined to her bed and then her coffin. It made me glad I was strong, or I felt strong then. I felt invincible, truthfully. It's something we all do when we are very young, we think we are going to live forever. It isn't a conscious thought, it's something that bubbles inside, something that says 'I will live forever!' and the shock comes when Death stalks into the room, his skull features grinning, his bony hands reaching out for your soul.

Katherine reads horror books and I also know she did not think this would be a horror book but – this is just the beginning of some of the horror we must write about sooner or later. I will confess here that the image of Death coming, all skull and bony hands, was the source of a week of nightmares until it settled in my mind. Elizabeth's death did that to me. She is well, she is living in the Realms, she has not attempted to reincarnate or even visit the earth plane. She has her work, caring for the animals which have passed over and which are awaiting their owners. It is enough for her and in truth it is valuable work, in its own way.   Ha! There I go, dropping spiritual talk into my life story! Will the readers accept that, do you think? Or shall we say it doesn't matter, they bought a book on my life written by me and as such they will get that which I give them? But then, I see the look Katherine wears, I read her thoughts: it was ever thus, sire. Am I right?

Of course I am. When it comes to her, I am rarely wrong!

The next child, as it were, was Mary. Now there was a sister indeed! All woman from the earliest age was Mary, full of life, of spirit, of energy, of everlasting inquisitiveness. Pretty, yes, very pretty, russet brown hair that tumbled everywhere, slender of figure, graceful and ever on the move, with eyes that captured your gaze the moment you saw her and drew you in to her world, Mary's world, acquisitive, inquisitive, endlessly charming. I adored my sister Mary the way I never did my sister Margaret, who was too much like Grandmother Beaufort who, I freely confess, I could not love, no matter how hard I tried.

Then came Edmund, a handsome little dark haired boy who lived no more than a year and a few months.

Finally there was another Katherine, spelled the way I spell this one's name, because it pleases me to do so –and because it is right - a baby so tiny, so perfect, the priest said she could not possibly stay on the earth side of life. She was born alive, she died immediately.

There, a review of my family.

I grew up with Arthur being venerated as Prince of Wales, with Margaret endlessly lecturing, with Mary endlessly learning such things as dancing and embroidery and arranging the flowers for table and prattling on about girl things in such a charming way that I actually took pleasure in her company. Later that ability to listen to a prattling woman who was charming with it became a weapon in my seduction armoury, a most valuable one. Ah, the secrets I am revealing… and we have not even begun the story of my life, or rather as she may see it, my observations on my life. I am not entirely comfortable with the fact that once again she is right…

Chapter Four - England, My England

What was England like at that time and how much did I know of it. Now there's a question if ever there was!

I knew only those London homes we went to, Eltham, Richmond, Greenwich, those great palaces. I knew only of the beautiful gardens which I confess I did not appreciate at the time. They were just areas where I could run, hide, play ball, terrorise my dogs, inspect the stables and choose a beast to ride at the tiltyard, an essential part of my training. Luxury came as standard, to use a modern phrase. I do so like your modern phrases, they say so much in such a minimal amount of words. If there was suffering and deprivation among the people of England, I never saw it and no one sought to enlighten me, either. Those who came into my life were either rich, powerful, influential men or paid servants who did not dare do anything but show me total deference. I know the sense behind the words 'absolute power corrupts' and it is possible that in my case it is true. The problem is, from a very early age I was elevated above most people, not only in a social sense, as a duke and a knight, but by size. I grew very fast and was taller than most of the children around me at that time. Yes, I know that servants' children were not given the same rich diet as I had, or such medical attention as was given to the royal children, but for all that, I grew taller and stronger than they did. In rough and tumble games, wrestling, tag or anything like that, I won by size, weight and ability, not because of their deference to me. I loved physical challenge; the tiltyard was a favourite 'lesson', more a pleasure than a lesson, as was practice with arms, archery, crossbows and the like. If anything was damaged in a game, there was always something to replace it or someone to repair it. The advantages of such a life meant you wanted for nothing, no matter what it was.

That kind of luxurious lifestyle has its drawbacks, in that I did not have to consider others or possessions and that carried into my adult life.

Hell and damnation! I did not expect to be this honest, this open, this truthful in this book of mine! What am I doing? Why am I confessing all this? Do I need the approbation of the English that much? Perhaps I do. So many of them consider me nothing more than a tyrant, a despot, a monster of some kind, that it would be – pleasant, can I say that? - to have a little more understanding of my personality, my needs, my thoughts at that time. You all view me at a distance of several hundred years, the same way you view my ancestors. You make judgements on my grandfather, Edward IV, from a distance. You cannot recreate the thought processes of the time, what quickened his thinking, what made him do this or do that. You make judgements on my grandmother, Elizabeth Woodville, and her family. You do not know them. You think you do, from reading books, but how many errors are found in books! You make judgements on my father and his treatment of my Great Uncle Richard III and that is one subject I am going to refuse to discuss, for many personal reasons.

A long pause there. I wonder what Katherine wants me to say. Why? All right, I will tell her why – because the truth hurts. Is that enough for her? I can tell by her face it is enough, whether it is enough for those who will read these words is another matter entirely.

Let me return to the question she asked. We keep diverting … all right, I keep diverting. This is my dictation, after all. So, let me return to the question, having caused my own extensive diversion and revealed a few thoughts that perhaps should not have been allowed to slip through the net of my mind. I will say this to Katherine …

That was for her ears, her mind, her spirit to retain.

England at that time was in the aftermath of the so-called Wars of the Roses. That was not the way I was taught to view them. My understanding was that they were a series of skirmishes, serious, blood-drenched, vicious, cruel skirmishes, when many good men died for no reason apart from the need for some Lord or King to be the upper dog at all times, or so it seemed to me as a child. Remember we are talking of my childhood at this point. It is difficult for me to go back and remember how I felt then, because my later years coloured my thinking and my remembrances, there is no avoiding that, no matter how hard we try. What I am doing is placing my life in the historical context of the time; post Wars of the Roses, post battles and death of a king and the assumption of the crown by my father. Right or wrong was not given to me at the time, just the facts. 'Your father won the battle of Bosworth, he is King of England.' I found out the rest later and formed my opinion on what I learned, not on what I was told by those bowing to my father's supreme authority.

Right now I am trying to remember how it felt to be eight years old, at Richmond or Eltham, given the task of entertaining visitors, working at being as charming as only I knew how to be to impress and dazzle the adults who had come a-calling. I needed to show the world, my world, that is, that I was as capable, as diplomatic, as assured, as knowledgeable as my older brother and my equally all-knowing sister. It seemed to work, judging by the comments the family received afterwards. The family, please note, not me. As always, I was the last to know I had done well. I also need to try and go back to that time and remember how the lessons seemed to me then, not coloured by my later understanding, or partial understanding. For I too viewed my grandparents and their brothers and sisters from a distance, not knowing them at all. They were - and are - names to me. Their lives were known only by what I read and what I read had been biased by the minds of the persons who wrote it or the persons who commissioned the writing of it.

Chapter Five - Katherine of Aragon

Katherine could have said, 'what about me?' for this next section, but she didn't. She occupied herself with checking dates, confirming that I was ten when Arthur married Katherine of Aragon. Or her, depending on how she looks at it.

This is sometimes a little difficult. She was Katherine of Aragon in that particular past life, Katherine spelled with a K, for all those who consistently and persistently use the C instead. Why? It is a known stated fact that my court was covered in tapestries and embroideries linking H with K. Not with C. Not ever with C. So why do you spell my Queen's name with such a letter?

I am diverting once more but that is a cause of intense irritation and I needed to say it.

Back to the life of the greatest King England ever had, bar none … ego, me? Never!

I knew, of course, that there had been much diplomatic coming and going, messengers, envoys, all sorts of people, including my Great Uncle Edward Woodville, arranging a political marriage between my brother and the Princess of Spain. Everyone, when the subject came up, talked of the wonderful treaty that would be signed, sealed and delivered on the occasion of the wedding, of the great alliance with Spain, how it would solve all our problems. Well, that last bit was probably a bit of a wild exaggeration on several people's part but still, it was all romantic and interesting and – foreign. I knew where Spain was on the map, I knew nothing of what the country was like. It had to be warmer than England as it was nearer the Equator than we were and that in turn probably meant exotic plants, foods and wines. I was intrigued. I spoke Spanish but had no sense of whether my inflections were right, whether I would sound Spanish or English when speaking to a Spaniard. Despite the courtiers and envoys being in our homes at times, chances to speak with them, apart from Good Morning and such-like, were very few and far between. I found myself stupidly excited about this Spanish Princess's arrival, having visions of someone of startling beauty, dressed in silk and lace, draped in jewels, someone who was bringing with her a hint of the exotic, the different, the exciting. I never said this to anyone, it was not something I would have thought of doing; these were my thoughts, my imaginings, not to be shared with others. It was something I learned from a young age, even younger than I was at the time of the wedding. I once made the mistake of sharing something with someone in one of the royal palaces, only to have it come back to me through a completely different person within a day. I never did it again.

So I awaited the coming of the Spanish princess and was measured, checked, measured again for my new outfit, tutored in my duties, even insofar as being taken to the great cathedral of St Paul's and allowed to walk the central aisle as I would with the bride on the day. My task was to escort her to her future husband. My task. Ten years old, thrust into the full light of ceremonial pomp. I had little to no memory of my being given the titles I carried with pride, I knew of my abilities within the homes I shared with the family, but outside, in the 'real' world… that was a different matter entirely. I was bursting with pride to be given this important role. It was my first real chance to walk the world's stage, to show the gathered dignitaries what Henry Tudor could do, no matter how young he happened to be.

And I waited on the arrival of Katherine of Aragon. Even her name sounded exotic to me. What I saw, when she finally arrived, was a travel worn, tired, probably homesick (although that didn't occur me until much later) young girl. She was golden haired, I found that out eventually, for she wore a Spanish head-dress. She was serene of face, which was perfect, no blemishes, no ugliness, just perfection, as if crafted by some talented sculptor, and quiet in her manners. She was slender and elegant, with graceful movements. She spoke English with a heavy accent which made it sound charming and Spanish with all the lilt I hoped for and tried to achieve myself. I remember hoping Arthur was in love with this delightful person, because I was, even at that young age. She mesmerised me. It was November, that bleak month of falling or no leaves, of grey skies and dew-heavy lawns, dead flowers and pruned shrubs. There was no incentive to go outside apart from hunting or hawking, no incentive to walk in the gardens and appreciate the Great Outdoors. Katherine's coming was like sunshine falling into that bleak time. It was probably why I fell in love.

The court was all of a dither, full of Spaniards and English trying to communicate with one another, frantic preparations for the wedding, guests arriving and having to be accommodated in various quarters, servants dashing here and there, courtiers busy with messages and translating duties if they spoke even a tiny bit of the language. Banquets were held, meetings were held, life seemed to be lived in a rush from the moment we were roused until we finally got to our beds at night. Arthur seemed bemused by everything and tried to carry on reading his books as if pretending nothing was going to happen. Father actually smiled once, not at me, at Katherine of Aragon and she executed such a perfect graceful curtsey to him in response I almost applauded. And I was consumed with jealousy. I had seen the Spanish princess and wanted her. I knew I was too young, I knew I was not the heir to the throne, I knew

the treaty and all the other important waffle was for
Arthur's benefit, not mine, but that made no difference.
With all the arrogance the duke of York was entitled to
display, that title being second only to the Prince of
Wales, I wanted. I could not have. I went off my food,
my stomach was constantly in knots of fierce tension,
wanting, needing, everyone trying to do their job and
most of that job meant ignoring me, outside of making
sure I got the right outfit and had the right moves in my
head. What did they think I was, a child?

So, because of all that, I remember well the
wedding. I wore a gorgeous outfit of black and silver, a
new jaunty cap with a large silver feather, new boots,
new gauntlets and best of all, I had a new white horse
bedecked with silver harness and rich black velvet
trappings on which to ride to the cathedral. I realised I
was almost as tall as most of the men at arms who
escorted us.

Katherine wore cloth of gold with black lace over it,
pure Spanish lace of the finest quality. She had black
shoes with large gold buckles and the most delicate
pendant hanging over the dress, a large black stone in an
ornate gold setting. She rode in a horse litter, with a
canopy of cloth of gold held over her by riders.
Dignitaries of the court took the canopy and held it over
us as we walked into the cathedral. I remember bursting
with pride as I escorted her down the long central aisle,
aware of the minstrels, the soaring voices reaching the
huge vaulted roof and the musicians playing their
delicate airs. I caught the scent of a hundred different
perfumes as we walked, mingled with the occasional
posy of flowers. I saw the dust motes hanging in the air
as reluctant sunshine split the darkness here and there. I
recall the congregation turning as one to look at us, saw
my brother waiting for his bride and can still remember
me, at that age, reluctant to hand her over to him.

One thing I have to say, for fear this conjures the wrong image in the reader's mind, Katherine, is this: she was six years older than I but I was taller than her, so we did not look mismatched or foolish. We were probably the handsomest couple in England at that time, in truth. I looked but saw nothing in her face when she caught sight of her husband-to-be. I had wondered if she would be disappointed. But the gracious Princess had the perfect bland look royalty learns to assume at all times.

The ceremony was solemn, enchanting in its rhythm and stylised grace. The incense added to the perfumes already there, it became quite heady for a while. I was glad when we were able to leave and breathe the fresh, if slightly damp, November air. I was more content on horseback than anywhere else at that time and was soon back on my new horse, anxious for the procession to get going so I could get back to the food, the company and my Fool, who no doubt had plenty to say on the occasion. His name was John Gossand, something like that. I called him John Goose and that is how he appears in the records of my household. It was he who began my lessons in wrestling, winning four bouts out of five until I grew strong enough and skilled enough to outdo him. His lessons, like everything else I learned through those formative years, were invaluable.

Father excelled himself with the wedding celebrations, as much for the benefit of the visiting Spaniards and other European high ranking courtiers as for the court itself. England rejoiced at the wedding, London in particular was full of cheering crowds. They were overdue for something to celebrate, anyway. This was a good thing to celebrate, the marriage of the Prince of Wales to the Princess of Aragon. They knew naught of the treaty, of the dowry, of the many discussions, they would not have understood the political implications anyway, so in truth that bit did not matter. A wedding was a wedding and a chance to drink at someone else's expense. The King's, as it happens. I know Father was not that pleased at how much it all cost but he had to put on a show and that was part of it.

After the feasting and the dancing and the singing and the drinking, which went on for some days, the couple departed for Ludlow Castle. I envied my brother, not his going to Ludlow, for it was far away from the excitement that was London, but his new bride and his new life.

Had I known he had but a few months of life left, I would not have envied him his new bride and his new life. But none of us are given to see into the future with that clarity. If we were, would we stand to live through each day which took us to that moment? Of course not. Such events are shielded from our human minds. All I knew that November was that my brother and his new wife had left for Ludlow and I was head of the small household that constituted my sisters and myself. I had my own desires; few knew what they were. If they had known, I dread to think what would have happened in the months ahead.

I sensed a lightness about my parents at that time. They must have believed all was settled, a good treaty made with Spain, a good marriage, a chance of heirs for the throne, eventually, a perfect royal family.

We held Christmas in great style and it was good. There was much feasting, jousting, dancing and gift giving. January, February and March were – just dull winter months when life carried on as best it could.

In April our world collapsed.

Katherine asked me to say what I remember. This is what I remember. It is an image that will never leave me. The words are said; I conjure up the image. It is this.

We were at Richmond at that time, one of our favourite homes. We had been enjoying the sunshine, the gardens, the first flowers and the first fresh produce from the kitchen garden. We were happy that the treaty with Spain had been consummated at last, well, the marriage ceremony had taken place anyway, if nothing else had happened. We had to assume they were living as man and wife, if you get my meaning. I say 'we' were at Richmond, I meant all of us. Father was there at that time, by a miracle nothing had taken him away from the family for a little while.

Into the brightness of that spring day came three men, tired, dirty, laden with sorrow.

I remember I was returning from a game in the gardens when they arrived. Messengers who wore faces of grief and distress, so we knew the news was bad before they opened their mouths.

They demanded to speak to Father immediately. Someone, a page, a messenger, I don't know who, ran to find Father. I heard a door flung open and he came out, a long black cloak swirling around him for, despite the sunshine, the house was cold. His face was grey before he heard their words, as if divining the content before it was expressed. The men fell to their knees in front of him. The rest of us stood back, waiting, anticipating, apprehensive. This is not an exaggeration; the air was thick with it.

"You come from Ludlow." A statement, cold, dire in its meaning.

They were dumbstruck, kneeling, bowed heads nodding like wooden dolls. Three men, dusty, travel stained, sagging with weariness. Outside, hooves clattered as their horses were led away for fodder and water and grooming.

Mother must have heard the commotion for she came into the hall, her fluttering women around her. She said nothing, just looked at the men, hand to her mouth, eyes wide in shock. She too knew without it being said.

I ask myself now, after all these years, how we knew it was not Katherine who had died, but Arthur?

How did we divine that from three silent men, kneeling solemnly and servilely before their king, men who had surely had to volunteer to make the arduous endless journey to bring the news?

"It was yesterday, sire." One lone voice, quiet words, ones which were laden with many, many emotions.

"My son." Father said it as a statement, as he had said the words previously. They nodded again, unable to look at his grief-stricken face.

There were shrieks, there were sobs, there were tears freely shed by many who were there at that moment. Father put a hand out to Mother, she went to him, tears streaming down her face and they walked away, lost in their joint grief.

The Seneschal took over smoothly, masking his feelings, ordering food and wine for the men, arranging somewhere for them to wash, somewhere for them to rest. The group which had gathered became fragmented, each person going to speak to another, or going to the chapel to offer prayers, whichever way they were inclined.

I had been ignored.

It was no more than I expected at that moment. The implications of my brother's death had to sink in, to be considered from all angles, before my father could make decisions about my future. I stood in the hall and thought three things in rapid progression – this I do remember so very clearly.

    1 There would be a big funeral.

    2 I was next in line for the throne.

    3 Katherine of Aragon was free to remarry.

Was it consumption, or the dreaded sweating sickness that carried my brother away? I know not. I never did discover the truth. All that mattered to me at that time was, five months away from London and his marriage, my brother was dead and his widow was free to remarry. The Princess I wanted was available. Whether I would get the chance to marry her, as I dreamed of doing even at that young age, was another matter entirely. That was in Father's hands and I had to wait until he chose to speak to me about my future. I could not approach him, not at this awful time.

I remember going to my room, collapsing onto my prie deu and offering heartfelt prayers for my brother's soul. I remember the tears coming then, secretive, burning, almost shameful tears, as if I should not cry but had to cry. Arthur was gone. I had, in many ways, looked up to him as my older brother, as the one who would be my king and I would be his loyal servant and devoted deputy as duke of York. Suddenly, with the arrival of three weary men with stark faces lined with grief, that person had gone. I would not look at his face again.

I wondered how Mother and Father felt, how much the grief was tearing them apart. I wondered if I could go to them and tell them my feelings but the arrival of Mr Skelton at my door stopped that.

"My Lord, I have heard the news and come to console you."

It was as if the dam broke then, if the tears had been secretive and burning before that moment, his coming released me to cry and cry and I did.

It would be many years before I did that again.

Chapter Six - Prince of Wales

We all went around as if in a daze, trying to cope with the aftershock of my brother's death. I remember Father being distracted, I remember Mother becoming pregnant again and everyone treating her like a precious pearl that needed guarding and protecting. I had no complaints with that; she was a special person, even if she was a distant mother. She was – well, she was Elizabeth of York, daughter of a king, niece of a king, wife to a king, sister to a king and in the fullness of time, she would be mother to a king. As with my brother, though, none of us knew her days were numbered. If we had, what we were then enduring would have been impossible to live through.

Katherine remained at Ludlow and I went to see her there. I asked permission, of course, but it was granted with such a lack of interest I might have asked if I could walk in the garden. The opportunity was taken to send a fact-finding committee to Ludlow, counsellors and clerks from Father's service were to go too. So the journey was planned, they got my armed escort together, my servants and squires as well and we rode to Ludlow. I recall it being a fair day when we set out and raining by the time we took shelter for the night but for me, it was good to be out of London for a while, seeing something else.

I knew one thing: England was beautiful.

We rode across downland and through villages of clustered thatched roofs, cottage gardens bright with flowers and vegetables and I saw well-tended fields. I saw animals roaming the grassland, really saw them for the first time, cows, sheep, horses, the occasional bull in his field, saw geese around village ponds, saw horse and cart transport, old and tired and muddy and *used*, not like ours, cleaned and polished and garnished for the aristocracy to ride in. I saw huge trees where people gathered with small tables to drink and eat, saw housewives selling wares outside their homes. Saw dogs which barked and tried to attack us as we rode on. Saw the uncovered heads and tugged forelocks when the people realised Someone Important was riding past, even if they did not recognise me. It was enough that half the counsellors and important people from Father's close circle were riding with me, for they had business with the Princess of Wales, too.

I wanted time to talk with her, to try and gauge her attitude to me. They wanted time to find out how she felt about staying in England, or so I was told, and what could be done about that. It was a fraught time for her and for us. We all rode there with our own agendas and no one knew what mine was at that moment.

Ludlow was a strikingly handsome and well-protected castle. I envied my brother his time there for it was a fine place, a goodly home, rich with furnishings and hangings, bustling with life and sense of business and efficiency. Katherine welcomed us and bid us to rest and she would arrange food and drink. I sat with her for a time and we talked. I realised she did not seem to resent me at all, which was good. She was in deep mourning for my brother: despite the short marriage, she seemed to have been genuinely fond of him even though they were comparative strangers. Or did she cling to his memory as the only sure thing in an uncertain world?

One thing was clear; she believed her parents were content for her to stay in England.

The other thing which became clear was that there were few funds for her household and the poor girl lived in poverty for many years. But that was something I found out later, when the whole mess that was her marriage was finally concluded.

Before then we had a funeral to arrange. Messengers raced from Ludlow to London to Worcester to many other places, arranging for the ceremony, the burial, the money for the whole thing, all the while ignoring Katherine, who was quietly grieving in her rooms in Ludlow Castle. I tried to talk with her, to get her to walk in the grounds, to find out how she really felt but I got the closed look, the quiet words that told me nothing. Katherine was walking a fine line, she did not know if she would be able to remain in England, it was not clear if she would welcome a return to Aragon or not, she must have felt very isolated. If she had not had her Spanish attendants with her, I would have feared for her state of mind.

In the end Arthur was buried, with great ceremony, in Worcester Cathedral. Father did not attend, nor did Mother, who was very ill at this time, partly through grief, partly through a difficult pregnancy. Whether Father stayed away because of grief, politics or concern for Mother, I do not know and never will know. I thought it strange but was well used to strangeness on Father's part. He was not a fit man and he seemed to be ageing fast, in my eyes anyway.

Another set of dreary months crept by, with messengers going back and forth to Spain, attempting to resolve 'the problem' of a widow without a child. For that became very clear very quickly, there was no heir from my brother and his wife. I either eavesdropped or took part in some of the discussions, because there were plans afoot to make me her next husband when I was old enough, of course. How did I feel about that? I was elated but kept a calm face to the world, so they did not know that I had harboured just that desire from – well, before she arrived in England, bringing that hint of exotic Spain with her.

Dispensation had to be granted but there seemed no problem with that. Rome was compliant and amenable; to do anything else would have been churlish. The poor girl had been widowed in such a short time after such a promising union, Spain and England combined in that dramatic way.

By September of that year, six months or so after she became a widow, Katherine of Aragon was my betrothed. What she felt about it I do not know, she never said not then, nor later, when we were man and wife. Not once did she indicate to me that she resented being remarried to the next in line, not once did she indicate that by then she missed my brother or that she preferred me to him or him to me. Politically she was astute and did that which she thought was right for her country and the treaty they had signed with her as the barter; emotionally, in some ways, she was sealed off, something I had plenty of time to think about in the years that were ahead of me.

Now, do I continue write this book as if I do not know of Katherine's abilities, or the fact that the Katherine that was wishes to come and tell her story at some time, or do I write it as if none of that exists and only my story will come out? Decisions, decisions! So difficult to decide!

I will write as if only my story is to come out, then if the Katherine that was decides she does want to tell her story, we will see how much it matches with my own thoughts and knowledge. Will that do for now? I see a nod; I see acquiescence to my perfect solution for the dilemma…

My thoughts, then, on my beloved Katherine. She came to England as a young woman, having left behind her the entire family, sunshine, people and the country she knew and loved. She came from sun to rain; she came from a deeply cultured, deeply religious family to one who for the most part paid lip service to religion. Few of us – I include myself here at the beginning – were truly devout, truly pious. Mostly it was expedient to show yourself in chapel several times a day but whether the heart was really in it was another matter, one that was between God and the individual. I knew, from conversations both held and overheard, that for most it was a duty, not a need, something they did to keep on the right side of the church rather than commit themselves, their souls, their lives, to God.

Katherine made a most interesting slip and quickly rectified it. She wrote, 'their lies.' We have talked of lies, have we not? Lies in other people's mouths, lies in other places. I spent my life surrounded by people who lied, because they told me what they thought I wanted to hear, rather than having the guts and determination to tell me the truth. Later I will talk of Charles Brandon, my friend, my favourite, but he lied, often, to get what he wanted. My Fool, Will Somers, supposedly committed to the truth, supposedly there to keep his Master on the straight and narrow path of not too much ego, he lied. Everyone did. Father did regularly, promising this to one and that to another with no intention of carrying it through unless he had to, especially when it came to the giving of money, but it bought him time and favours and that he needed. Lies. I lived with them throughout my life. The one person who does not lie to me on your side of life is this Katherine, she tells me – and her other spirit companions – what we need, not what we think we need, to know.

I divert, yet again! Let me pull my thoughts back to the Katherine I knew then. I was saying how I thought she felt. She was in a strange land, with a strange language, with people who did not always follow their faith as they should, as she did, with commitment and total piety – for me that came later, when I fully understood what it was all about – married to a man she did not know, sent to a place she did not know, only to become a widow. Then she found herself argued over, her dowry re-negotiated, with all the time that took. What she went through I cannot begin to say. She said so little of it when she was married to me. What happened was, she became one with my life rather than my venturing to become part of hers. Her homesickness must have been all-consuming. Her heartache must have been intense. The person she had been betrothed to all her life had died after just five months of marriage. They had not even begun to get to know one another. The shock must have been tremendous. To my shame I only realise this now. At the time I was consumed with my own problems, coping with Father and the vagaries of his wishes and whims and holding on to the one golden light I had at the time, my betrothal to someone I admired.

I only see all of that now, from the distance of hundreds of years, rather than at the time, when I was only too happy to have her as my Queen and thought no more of how she felt or what she had endured. Selfish in the extreme but at the time, there was so much else to occupy my mind. (Or at least that is my excuse which I will retain – until such time as I decide to change it…)

For me she was the golden haired, dark eyed, exotic, quiet, calm tempered, agreeable person who was my brother's widow and the subject of much political to-ing and fro-ing, for she was a desirable widow in every sense of the word. There were questions about her virginity which I ignored, having no need for such matters to bother me. There were dispensations to be sought; I left Father to arrange that. He had messengers and envoys to spare and they were despatched to Rome to secure the right papers and the right words and seals so the marriage could eventually go ahead. However it was agreed, though, by September of that year a draft treaty came into being, which said I would marry Katherine of Aragon. It was my great delight in the prospect and having so much to look forward to that enabled me to put my grief and thoughts of my brother to the back of my mind and allowed me to get on with the business of growing up. There was a lot of it to do.

Christmas came around once more, but this time it had a distinct pall hanging over it. Mother was very unwell. She kept to her chamber most of the time whilst Father was trying to cope with his own ill health and the usual problems in the country. Most of this I let pass me by, for I was young enough and at times carefree enough to take pleasure from the gifts and the feasting, the dancing, the mummers, the minstrels and singers, the Lord of Misrule and the jesting. We tried to carry on as best we could, despite the illness and general apathy of my parents. I wrote 'apathy' – or rather, Katherine did – I got her to delete it and then put it back, for truthfully that is the way it was. The pregnancy was not going well at all, Mother was ill and Father appeared to veer from sympathy to impatience with every passing hour. His hope was for another heir, in case – admitting this is difficult – in case I died too and he was left with only daughters. Was it said to me? No. Was it said in my hearing? Of course. Again courtiers and others forgot I had the sharpest of hearing and nothing got past me.

The Katherine who is writing this book for me sits at her desk surrounded by papers and books, by information of all kinds and the information fights with itself. One book says my sister was born in January and lived for some months, the other book says she was born in February and died the same day. This is one of my biggest complaints, one I will no doubt return to again in this book: the perfidy of historians. Katherine stopped writing, went and checked the meaning of that word (treachery or deceit) and waited for me to confirm I wish to use it. I do. How can historians take a simple fact, that of life and death – in this case on the same day – and translate it wrongly? Is it so difficult to get the facts right? Is it so very hard … but need I go on? You should know by now I dislike historians generally, as a breed I have strong feelings about whether they should be allowed to continue to practice their nefarious arts, that of deceiving the populace.

So I said to Katherine, leave the papers and books, this is what happened.

Chapter Seven - A Court In Mourning

Right after the Twelve Days of Christmas, my mother took to her chamber to prepare for the birth. She had endured the revelries out of courtesy, knowing her ladies would want to take part in the celebrations as much as they could, even if she herself had hardly shown her face during that time. After the prayers and the rituals of birthing, she shut herself away. I knew she was ill, I had never seen anyone so white, so drawn, so obviously suffering intense and agonising pain. She walked with the stance of someone so aged they could scarcely support their skeleton. The bulge that was the new child hung low, too low some said, her face was lined and underscored with suffering. I saw little to no support from Father and have to assume if any were given, it was in private and out of my – and everyone else's – sight. And we waited for the happening.

My sister Katherine Tudor was born at the beginning of February, in the early hours of the morning. Before the noon sun struck through the clouds, and it did, as if lighting her way to Heaven, she died. She had not cried once, not opened her mouth to take milk, nor uttered a sigh or a sound.

No one was surprised at the news, for the pregnancy had been unbelievably bad from the start. But the sadness was there, for the hope had been that there would be a living child, perhaps, with God's help. Prayers had been offered for this eventuality many times over, even though those who did the praying knew there was little to no hope of this materialising. Father went around with a face even more grim than usual and that is saying a good deal for a man of his granite looks. He looked at me with contempt, as if resenting the fact I was alive, well and thriving, as if I was not nearly as tall as he and capable of winning a wrestling match four times out of five with skill and strength. Did he think of my dead brother at this time? Did he see the 'replacement' as someone he could not accept? I ask myself this because of what happened later in our lives.

I was allowed to see my mother on a few occasions following the birth. I am not sure if she asked to see me or whether those who tended her thought it would be a good idea for her to see her living son. What I saw will remain with me forever. Her beauty had become even more refined; the flesh had fallen away, the delicate bone structure of her face stood out in stark relief. Her eyes were darkly shadowed and her sadness was emblazoned over everything. She was polite but so lacking in any kind of spark of life I wondered each time if my visit would be the last one.

On Mother's thirty seventh birthday, February 11th, the complications following the difficult birth proved too much and she went to join her tiny baby.

The court plunged into full mourning and grief.

The odd thing is; she was a distant mother, ever caught up in the politics and drama of being a Yorkist queen married to a Tudor king and yet I missed her terribly. It was a blackness that sat in my heart and would not let go. I looked for her at banquets, especially the one held to celebrate my being officially created Prince of Wales. I felt she should be there to see her second son take on the title and mantle of heir to the throne. I listened for her name when people were speaking. I told no one at the time, it didn't seem manly and I needed to seem manly, for I had the role of first son to fulfil and to show the world I was ready to assume kingship when it happened. Not that I wished Father to be gone from life, you understand. It is a mental thing; you know you are going to be king one day by the natural order of life and you prepare yourself for the moment when the crown is placed on your head and the governing of the land is placed in your care. I was glad at that moment; I have to admit, that Father had not gone ahead with his plans to place me in the church.

I have seen some reports in Katherine's books that Father displayed grief on her death. I think he did, a little, but I also think he almost sighed with relief that a political marriage which, despite its relative fecundity, had become something of a millstone to him – again I overheard and again I cite no sources, believe me when I say I heard these things from his Gentlemen of the Bedchamber - because of the one thing he did which shocked me. I am not easily shocked, but this did shock me – he suggested that he should marry Katherine of Aragon instead of me.

Did he cast covetous eyes on the young, pretty, exotic princess cooped up in a big castle in Wales and think, she will do well for me? Did his aged libido kick in at that time? What possessed him to make such an outrageous statement I cannot begin to imagine for I do not and did not understand the mind of my father. Diplomat in some ways, complete idiot in others, lost without the guiding hand of his mother who ruled his life, who put him at Bosworth complete with enough knights to ensure victory, who no doubt had a very big part to play in his politically correct marriage, my father came out with that suggestion.

The outburst from her parents stopped that dead in its muddied tracks, I am happy to say. He was old by then, old and ill, showing great religious devotion and every evidence of bad eyesight to go with his infirmities. He was not a suitable husband for a young woman like Katherine. I say this with as much dispassion as I can, knowing that I wanted her and was actually betrothed to her. If he had gone ahead, though, there would have been nothing I could have done about it.

In June of that year the final treaty was signed, the final dowry arranged and the marriage – between Katherine and myself - was set to go ahead.

But then, oh yes, Katherine asks me, what happened next. She asks, she says, 'I need you to talk to me about this.' The report is there that in 1505 I demanded that the treaty be made null and void.

Rightly I know what she is thinking, after all my protestations of love and desire, I wanted to turn my back on Katherine of Aragon? In part, she had become a distant figure, someone removed from my court and my life and there were delectable females around who flaunted and fluttered, who tricked and tried and who sighed and simpered and I thought perhaps I would find a better one among them. So you see, my obsession with women was always there. I didn't think it was unhealthy … not at the time, anyway! Now I see that I should have kept myself away from those inviting warm waiting places all my life. No one suggested I should, though. Why should they? Every person I cast an eye over was a potential wife for the Prince of Wales and later, a potential queen for a king.

I also confess Father had a hand in this. More than a hand, actually, most of him was involved in this. He still harboured a desire for the beautiful widow and although he knew he could not have her, it didn't stop him making political capital out of it. The dowry was re-negotiated, concessions were sought, Katherine suffered the results. If things went well, she had affection and money, if things did not go well with her father, King Ferdinand, she had no affection and little money. How can anyone retain a sense of well-being in the face of such turbulence? I knew little of this at the time, I only knew I was a growing person and had growing desires.

It was then that my determination to be taken seriously, to be better than the next and the next, better than the 'experts', even, paid off for I was tall and strong and capable of controlling the wildest of stallions, hitting the smallest of targets, of winning every game of tennis anyone was foolish enough to participate in with me, to attend council meetings and absorb the minutiae of council life and policy and so people took me very seriously indeed, consulting with me on many decisions. None, though, spoke of Katherine's dowry problems in terms of 'what would you do about it, Lord Henry?' Father retained his iron grip on that, determined, I later believed, to drag the most pesetas out of the Spanish family that he possibly could.

Finally King Ferdinand tried to break off the negotiations and asked for his daughter to be returned to Spain. Father refused. Now, the question is, was she being held hostage here in England? Did Father really want to be rid of her, to leave himself free to find himself another suitable bride, to find me a more suitable – in his eyes – future queen? Or was this a genuine desire on Father's part to arrange something really worthwhile out of what had become something of a fiasco, taken all round?

The one thing I cannot do is give you, my reader, a straight answer to that. Father had become – strange, I knew him not from day to day. From rages through silences, from outbursts to single words, the king of England became a cipher to his son and to those around him.

It was at that time my life was stood on its head.

One day Father's men came with orders to secure me, a few possessions and a few clothes, in a room adjoining his. No reason was given, no argument would sway them for they did the King's work, not mine. I never did discover why he made this particular decision but I found myself locked away, on his orders, confined to a room. I was allowed out for exercise only under supervision and that with his permission. I could not speak to anyone outside those who attended me without his permission. My friends were excluded completely from my life. I had few books, mostly religious in nature, few clothes but where would I go, apart from those short periods of exercise, what would I do with my time? I knew then, without being told, that Father was afraid both of me and many of those around him. I had heard that he was paranoid over plots being hatched to remove him. His claim to the throne had ever been tenuous, he lived with that for years and it slowly ate into his mind, or so I believe. He knew he was unpopular with the people. He had made many mistakes over Katherine's dowry and negotiations, he knew she was rightfully betrothed to me but he did not wish it to go ahead. That had, in turn, upset the landowners of the country and damaged the relationship with Spain.

You need to consider this: I was then seventeen years old, verging on the prime of my life. I was tall, well built, strong, handsome – not my words, but those of others – and ready for life. I was capable of taking on the government of England, even if my political experience did not match Father's. I sensed a fear in him that if he was not careful, he might be deposed and I be placed on the throne in his stead. He did not say this outright but oh Katherine, how he hinted at it, in this phrase or another, in sentences half said and the remainder left to my imagination!

You will ask, rightly, why I was seemingly in awe of him, to the point when I did not speak to anyone without reference to him.

The answer is obvious, to me, anyway. He may well have been my father, but he was also my King. At that time in 'history', people were subservient to their monarchs no matter what they did or thought, whether they were demented or sane, ill-advised or sensible.

How did I feel about that time, Katherine is asking.

I was bored senseless. And angry. I was in a room next to his bedchamber, ignored – but that was something I had become well used to – and fed a diet of religious instruction and prayer, endless prayer. Yes, I became devout through this, I prayed on my own outside of the set prayers, but the rest of the experience left me with a hatred of confined spaces and a determination never to allow anyone to imprison me again. I was allowed to bathe, be shaved, barbered, dressed by silent servants, brought food and ale by equally silent servants. Clerics arrived; they were permitted to speak with me and me with them. Tutors came to talk with me on points of law and philosophy. I had no outlet for my mental abilities apart from study. If I dared ask any of them why I was being held like that, a prisoner without having been tried, they would pick up their books and leave. I learned quickly not to do this, for their conversation was the only diversion I had.

During this time, my memories of Katherine of Aragon grew larger in my mind. I envisioned her, wondered what she was doing, whether she knew of my captivity, whether she would care if she knew. Did our betrothal mean anything to her outside of a way to stay in England? My mind tore the situation into shreds a hundred times over but there was no one to ask for advice, no one to help me settle the incessant arguments I had with myself over it. I could not count the days, that would have driven me mad. I knew of the changing of the seasons only from my periods of exercise. Anniversaries came and went, my birthday passed without being acknowledged. I was held without trial in a prison where the warder, the gaoler, if you like, was my own father.

Did he hate me? I don't know with absolute surety but I think so. We fought; we fought man to man in blazing arguments that were won sometimes by Father, sometimes by me. Those I won, when my logic outpaced his and out-manoeuvred his, resulted in the coldest bleakest looks I ever endured from any man, then or later. And believe me, I endured some looks from those around me!

I believe, as I said, that he feared me. We knew, as you do, of usurper kings. Father had many enemies, made by his over-taxing those who did not wish to pay such high taxes, and those who resented the fines for the smallest infringement of his rules. Any one of those men could have arranged for him to be deposed and place me instead as head of the country, with the promise of lower taxation and greater say in the affairs of England.

I know full well that there was not an ounce of affection between us. I had more love and affection from those who served me than from those who were responsible for my being alive. His true emotions died with Arthur, although you would not have known it from his disposition outside our confined space, where we argued. It was there the truth was revealed, in shouting matches which it is surprising no one overheard, or if they did, they did not record it. Words were thrown which were hurtful in the extreme at times.

"You are not your brother, you never will be your brother! He was meant to be king, not you!" was the most constant of the themes of his ranting rages. It was not my fault my brother took sick and died, but you would have thought well that it was, if you knew how many times it was said to me. Fortunately, Ludlow was a long way away; he could not take the next step and accuse me of arranging my brother's early demise.

It is my belief that grief and paranoia twisted and distorted his mind. It is my certain knowledge that I was no substitute and that he dreaded the thought of my taking his place.

I know, from the books Katherine has looked at that people view me as a sexual predator or a tyrant or both. Few have sought to find out why I needed women, as in needed, not just lusted after them. Few thought to find out why I had favourites. In your time you would call them close friends, not favourites. It sounds wrong, as if I needed the men around me for a different reason than friendship. I have to say that was not my inclination. I leave that kind of love to those who appreciate it. No, I needed men for their manliness, their ability to drink, eat, hunt, fornicate with women, fight, challenge me at the tourney or to a race on thoroughbred horses: the delights of male company. I know Katherine understands this full well. Ever did she smile at me when she was my wife, when I went off to do 'male' things, like hunt and dice and gamble and drink. And eat. Let us not forget the eating!

My parents were not true parents. I sought affection, approbation, friendship even from others, because my mother was distant and my father disliked me. This was not a good comforting childhood, such as Katherine had and enjoyed. I had responsibility thrust at me from a very early age, with the imposition of so many titles and honours when I was scarce able to stand, let alone understand them, through to the entertaining of visitors and escorting Katherine to her marriage at a very young age. I was taught everything I needed to become a perfect diplomat and courtier, but I was taught nothing about kingship. I hoped that being shut away with Father would have rectified that omission. Instead we spent the time fighting. It taught me much more than kingship, it taught me survival.

This state of 'imprisonment', for that is how I viewed it, lasted somewhere about a year, I believe.

I do not recall the date it started.

I do recall the date it ended.

It ended when Father died.

Chapter Eight - King At Last

There is a strangeness for me in the way historians seem to write about my life.

Father died.

A KING died.

Someone who, revered or detested, feared or admired, held sway over England for many years. He taxed people, judged people, brought in laws, made decisions that rebound through the law books to this day and yet writers of both kinds, the historian and the fiction ones, dismiss his passing and leap to my marrying Katherine and assuming Father's role in the country.

No one seems to stop and ask the question: did Henry mourn his father's passing?

I did. The one obstacle to my marriage, my freedom, my pastimes, my friends, had suddenly been removed by the Grim Reaper himself. Oddly, instead of rejoicing, I felt lost. I had no one to stop me doing things and I had become used to someone stopping me doing things. Freedom is good, if there are boundaries. The boundaries had been removed. Does this make sense? It does to me.

When they came to tell me, the men with long sad faces who stood in the doorway of my prison and called me Your Grace and bowed to me, I felt as if a huge weight had gone from my shoulders and my mind. I was light headed for a while. I was officially king at the age of eighteen.

As I sat contemplating this, free at last from Father's tyranny, free to leave the prison I had been confined to and able to use my own suite of rooms again, free to wear what I wanted and do what I wanted, the thought burst into my overcrowded mind that my grandfather became king at eighteen, too. The difference was he had fought battles to get the crown, as in physical battles, as in riding destriers and swinging a battle-axe at men and killing them. But then I thought, I had fought battles too, battles of the mind, battles against a man who detested me and had done for eighteen years. Battles against being ignored, overlooked, deprived of that which I craved. I know the one thing Katherine seeks to do at all times in her work is find the motives. So many care to think it is just the person's personality. Maybe it is, in part, but all that lies within a man – or woman – is put there by others. You suffer something, endure something, live through something and it changes you. It changes your outlook. I had thought myself a Prince of royal blood, able to do more or less what I wanted, within reason, within that which Father had decreed for me. As in his intention at one time to commit me to the church for a career. I believed I had some say in my life, but then Father imprisoned me - there is no other word for it. When I was freed, by his taking the biggest step of all, that into the Afterlife, I made up my mind there and then that Things Would Change.

I decided there would be no more of that kind of life ever again.

Simply put, King Henry VIII had arrived and was about to make his mark on the world in the best way possible. King Henry VIII would start by stamping his authority on the country and doing what he wanted. Starting by marrying Katherine of Aragon as soon as possible.

I do not know if any of the many books that appear to have been written about me say what I did next. I don't much care if they do or not, this is my life and my way of telling it. It's just that I am aware so many leave so much out. Maybe it was not documented, if so, you really are getting the truth, the whole truth and nothing but the truth.

During my first day of freedom, I called all my friends to me, James Worsley, Charles Brandon and others, those who had been long without my company and who told me how desolate they had been - and I believed them - called drinking companions to me and we all got wildly drunk together. I spent the entire day drinking fine wine, not the cheap wines my father had arranged for me. There were, I knew, many things to be attended to, not least my father's funeral, but that was, for me, a day of celebration, freedom from imprisonment, freedom from my father's tyranny, freedom from all the impositions placed on me by his rule. I was free. I was king. I could exactly what I wanted – and I did.

The very next day, despite a sore head and aching stomach, I got myself organised, got a load of secretaries and messengers together and sent messages out: to European heads of state to tell them of Father's death, to the Pope to tell him I was going ahead with my marriage to Katherine of Aragon, to the court in Spain with the same message, to Ludlow to tell Katherine I was coming to see her. I asked for arrangements to be made for Father's state funeral, running through an essential list of who needed to be notified and who needed to be invited, authorised monies to pay for the whole long drawn out procedure of lying in state and then internment. I arranged for my father's possessions to be removed from his rooms and for my few possessions to be taken back to my original room and for the one in which I had spent the best part of a year to be locked, bolted and barred so no one, especially me, ever set foot in it again whilst I was alive. I did not want to take over Father's rooms. I had my own and I preferred them to all the others.

There was one other Large Decision hanging over me which I needed to settle – and soon. I had given the whole question of marriage to the Spanish princess much consideration during my long term of quiet contemplation. I had asked the Lord God to guide me and show me what to do.

The day after our wild drinking session – which I felt I had earned after so long a period of abstinence from everything but my Father's company – I said I wanted to eat. Everyone went rushing around to make sure that the meal was fit for a king, a real king, as I thought myself.

It is possibly coincidence, but who can say, that meal, the first I had as King, was laid on a table with a centrepiece of fruit. Someone had procured a pomegranate and it was atop the display. Pomegranates were rare; an exotic fruit which no doubt had come from the Spanish Ambassador. All manner of gifts had arrived for the new king, in order to curry favour from the start. I looked at the pomegranate, read it as a message from the Lord God and within a few minutes of that message arriving in my conscious thought - Spain = Katherine – I made up my mind to ride to Ludlow and see her.

Doing all this thinking and giving orders and making plans lifted the sore head. Good food settled the aching stomach. I quickly got used to people deferring to me as they did to Father and realised I was enjoying the feeling very much.

There was a stack of state papers to go through, documents left unsigned, others left unread but I knew that in the aftermath of a king dying, some things could be left and so I left them. I had other matters on my mind. The funeral needed to be got out of the way, if I can put it so bluntly. That was done, Father's mortal remains laid to rest, but not his memory, unfortunately. That lingered for a long time, his papers, his signature, his seal, his influence, all hung over the court and the country like the funeral pall it had been. I was anxious to dispel it but needed to follow the requisite period of mourning to appease all the diplomats who had attended and who would report back to their Lords and Masters precisely what happened and when and who said what to whom. I knew how these things went, having lived through them several times.

As soon as it could be arranged, I went to Ludlow to visit Katherine and asked her to marry me.

The journey to Ludlow was completely different from the one I had made as a much younger person. For a start there was the fact I was older and more able to appreciate the country I rode through but the big difference was, of course, I went as king. My escort was bigger, showier, the pennants were bolder, brighter and everyone knew Someone Important was out and about. I was greeted everywhere I went with deference and great enthusiasm. I knew, of course, that everyone loves a new king, they look for change, they look for great things and they hope for a bright new future. I wanted to promise all that but did not dare promise anything to anyone anywhere at that time. I had accounts to look over, decisions to make, laws to consider, all before I could make any changes to anyone's standard of taxation and of life. I needed time but fortunately they understood that and merely wished me well in my new life.

Ludlow seemed quieter than I remembered but recalled in time, before I said anything foolish, that only Katherine lived there, not a Queen or a King. No doubt the staff had been reduced accordingly. What I did not expect to find was the increased level of poverty.

Katherine came out to greet me with a look of pure happiness which quickly changed to embarrassment. I dismounted, took her hands as she curtseyed to me and asked what was wrong. She didn't answer immediately, just took me into the Great Hall where the fire was out and meagre furs and blankets were thrown onto the settles. She told me then that she had no money. She had not paid her ladies in an age, she owed money to the local trades people and wages to the servants, she had nothing to offer me when I rode in with my entourage, which was the reason for her look of pure happiness at my arrival being immediately smothered by her look of total embarrassment at the conditions in which she was living.

I asked for a bag of gold to be taken from my baggage, which I then threw at her steward, telling him to arrange to buy what was needed to give us a feast and set a fire raging in the hearth. I asked for a rendering of all accounts outstanding, all remuneration unpaid, everything that needed to be attended to. I asked for a complete rundown of the stables and condition of the horses kept there. I asked for her seamstress to come the next day with different types of cloth and arranged for new gowns, warm cloaks and undergarments for my bride-to-be and all her ladies – you do not need me to go on. I have realised I used the word asked and yes, I did ask. It was later, when kingship became a way of life that I demanded rather than asked.

I arranged to settle everything and everyone went around smiling and calling me a saviour of their sanity, their health and their livelihood. It pleased me very much. Back in London my tailor was working at rebuilding my wardrobe, much depleted during my time of imprisonment at my father's demented hands. I wanted fine clothes and I wanted my Queen-to-be to have fine clothes, too. It would not do for her to be shabbily dressed. That went for her ladies, too, for they were part of her entourage and her persona to be shown to the world. It had to be right. It had to be impressive.

Katherine was as shy, as delicate and as beautiful as I remembered. Whilst the steward bustled away, there is no other word for it, he was a fussy little man who took his position very seriously, I walked in the castle grounds with Katherine and asked her to marry me. I cannot tell you how her face lit up with happiness as she accepted, with great dignity and obvious joy. I cannot tell you how my heart leapt with happiness too at her acceptance. I believed I could not have found a finer queen to share my reign and my life.

Once the question of finance was out of the way and Katherine had accepted my marriage proposal, as if she had any choice in the matter anyway but it was courtesy to ask and for her to answer, after all, we were about to spend a lot of years together, there was genuine happiness in her smile which reached her eyes. That, for me, was something wonderful. Too many around me were devious in the extreme, their smiles did not reach their eyes. As I have commented before, I watched for it and marked it when it did not happen. I was very aware when it did. That person became special to me. With Charles, my beloved friend, it happened every single time. I have to say the same thing about James, too. They were devoted friends who stood by me no matter what I did or said or didn't do or say. It worked both ways. It happened with a few others whom I later regretted losing but that is for the future. At that moment I was in Ludlow with Katherine who was shining with happiness at being formally committed to being my Queen. I regretted leaving her but I had to return to London to make arrangements for everything that had to be done, the wedding, her suite of rooms, her many servants and maids, places for all her ladies, rewards for the servants at Ludlow who had taken good care of her as best they could with limited resources, all these thoughts flashed through my mind and I found myself dictating lists of Things To Be Done on my return to the greatest city of all. There was work ahead, a lot of it. I delighted in the thought that Katherine would be there with me, to sit at the table, to help me through the tedium of the formal banquets and suchlike, to be my companion in day to day things. I had little idea of the joys to come, how much I would rely on her wisdom and clear thinking.

Katherine and I didn't have a big wedding, none of the pomp and ceremony of her marriage to my brother. In the first place the court was still officially in mourning for Father, of course, and in the second place, she had the big wedding ceremony when she married before. It didn't seem right to do it all over again with me, although part of me hankered for the public display. I wanted England to know I had captured my Spanish beauty. But she did not want it, she just wanted a quiet ceremony and that I granted her. She had been through so much under my father's reign I could do nothing else. I will just say that in June 1509 we were married and after the ceremony I brought Katherine of Aragon, my new Queen, to Greenwich.

Katherine has said nothing, so why do I see a huge question mark hanging over her head? Is she waiting for the answer to THE question? And, how do I know what the question is anyway? Forgive me, I need to think about this.

(Having sat for a few minutes awaiting my answer, Katherine, without a word, left her desk. She returned the book, Rubaiyat of Omar Khayyam, to the bookcase, she rubbed menthol on her aching head, she took pills and still she has not looked at me or said a word. I have the distinct impression that the book will not progress unless I answer this very personal question. Personal, yes, critical, even more so, considering the impact it had on what became known as the King's Great Matter in years to come.)

The question?

Katherine wishes to know whether she/my first wife was a virgin or not.

My answer is the truth: I do not know, because – I was virgin when I laid with her and was so entranced by the sheer sensuality of what we did that wedding night that I cannot say for a moment if anything was broken. If that sounds foolish, well, so be it. I was about to experiment with sex when my father locked me away for that year. Before then I had turned down many chances to bed someone, in part through an embarrassment of not being sure I would perform well, in part from being afeared of contracting something. My squires and others had talked of someone catching this disease or that and boasting about it.

Katherine has realised, in a flash, how this cleanliness/disease phobia, for it was little short of that, affected my whole life. I did not know then it was a phobia, that is a modern term but one I understand well and identify with it strongly. I hated dirt inasmuch as I could not stand body odour. The good clean dirt of being a boy roaming the castles and palaces was one thing, that was easily washed off with a cloth before attending a meal or going to my bed. Body odour meant that a person had not washed for some time. That displeased me and bothered me. I would wonder what else the person harboured on their body. I hated illness for it was as if the body was unclean, hence my leaving London the moment the word 'plague' was mentioned, even, as happened later in my life, leaving my pregnant Queen to her own devices to escape from the dreaded disease. I kept her at arm's length, well, to be truthful, many miles' length, if illness was mentioned. I loathed and detested the ulcers which afflicted me, as they were very definitely unclean. Yes, my fear of illness and disease prevented me from 'experimenting' with women in my formative years and then I was locked away. So, I went to my new bride as a virgin.

Katherine asks the very personal question, was there blood?

My answer, there was but I do not wish to go into anatomical details. I only wish to say there was blood from both of us and it mingled and it could have been from – well, to say anywhere is wrong but you know full well what I mean. I cannot say it was virginal blood. I cannot say with honesty what tore within Katherine whilst knowing well what my damage was, in a manner of speaking. I can say she was not experienced in the arts of love. I can say she was not even a novice at it. She simply had no idea what to do.

Did I? I am surprised Katherine should ask such things! I will say this: I knew what to do as I had been told but doing it was something else.

Enough! This is embarrassing me! That was a knowing smile. I tell you the truth, I am embarrassed! Yes, the king who bedded his several wives and other women too, when they were all but thrust into my bed or contrived to make their way into my chamber and into my bed, I say that speaking of such things with you is embarrassing!

Why? Because I see this one even now as my pure Katherine and whilst we talked of many things, of religion and history and geography and politics, we spoke little of the act of love. Now, with permission, we will move on!

Ah, before we do that, Katherine has just – with a shock to her system – told me the truth of that night and of her marriage to my brother. No, I am not revealing it here. Katherine of Aragon will write her own story one day and then the truth will be told. But this Katherine has had a flashback to her past life in that time and has told me what happened. The shock was that she should recall it so vividly. She has not had to use her portal in her 'other realm' to look into the past and see what happened. The past life has presented its own answer to her.

Now you are intrigued and want to know the answer. I bid you wait. There will be time enough for my beloved Queen to write her side of the story, the sad life she led with me, the awful way I treated her. My time with this Katherine is an effort to compensate for the way I treated her then. So far, she said, you are doing a good job…

Fortunately for me, Katherine fell in love with Greenwich. I loved the palace, always had done and it is gratifying when someone you love feels the same way about a place as you do. It brings that person closer to you.

We had been granted little time to get to know one another as people. We came together as virtual strangers with nothing between us but mutual admiration and a developing affection. I was anticipating talking with her about her home country, she in turn was anticipating talking with me about my home country and even more than that, of knowing something about English parliaments, government officials, law making and the like. I was surprised at the depth of her interest and gratified that she did not intend to spend her days sewing and chattering with her ladies. Father had not allowed Mother any access to his meetings, his papers, his consultations and I would be surprised if he had allowed her access to even his thoughts. My parents were my only real experience of a married couple, albeit a royal married couple, I assumed my marriage would be the same. It was good to find out that it would not be like that. Katherine spent a good deal of time in prayer, attending services and the like but that suited me well as I had emerged from my year long sentence with an increased piety and knowledge of God, so I was able to go with her and participate fully where I would not otherwise have done so. Out of every bad thing comes something good. Katherine would have known if my piety had been forced, half-hearted, indifferent. Instead she welcomed me into her love and her life because my piety matched hers and my learning of the Scriptures and philosophical matters arising therefrom was extensive, as the world was to discover later on.

Chapter Nine - Husband and King

The books will tell you I was happy with my wife. The books only have half the story but we have found that is about right for historians generally. I did not simply adore my wife; I was totally in love with her. Everything about her, from her golden hair to her accented voice enchanted me. Her body enchanted me, for it was plump in the right places and curved in the right places and she moved gracefully and elegantly through court. She was pious, as I have said, and I was happy to attend services with her. My Spanish improved and her English improved and together we set many things in motion, building work, new court fashions and rituals and, of course, plans for the coronation. Well, give the people something to do, I thought. The court had been in mourning for Father but it had to end some time and the sooner the better. I needed to stamp my authority on the country and how better to do it than with a big showy ceremony like that?

Katherine is following a book, it is easier for her to ensure we stay in the time line of my reign but – what is this reference I see to the Tower being a place of bad memories for me? I read this over her shoulder and I have to say I disagree most heartily with that author. For a start, my mother may have died there but to me that made no difference to the place. The children, who would have been my uncles had they grown to adulthood, were last seen there. Now the implication is clear in this book that it was widely reputed my Great Uncle King Richard III had them murdered there. This I deny emphatically. Is that clear to the readers? Nothing was 'widely reputed' at that time. It was a rumour that went about and then disappeared for a long time, until revived by those who wished to blacken his reputation. You may find references to them here and there but in truth, the country had enough to think about with taxes and impositions, with plagues and sweating sickness and poor harvests and too much rain or too much sun to wonder about the whereabouts of two young boys who did not make it to adulthood and thus had not become yet more land owners and aristocrats.   Oh yes, for a short time one was a King but he had no real reign to speak of.

Does this sound callous? Remember my brothers and sisters who, for one reason or another, did not make it to adulthood, remember the one brother who did and who died of some unknown sickness or disease or fever, a death that left me free to become king and marry my Katherine. Children die. It is a fact of life, then and now. Not all of us are guaranteed a long and healthy life. Some are destined to have short lives, some are destined to have no life at all, like the last child my mother birthed and which took her life in the coming and the going.

Death stalks us all. None of us know when our time is through; none of us knows when he comes, scythe in hand, skull face grinning, to take us. The boys, the Princes, were conveniently dragged into the play by Shakespeare to add to the villain he was creating and since that time you have seen it as a 'mystery.' I will cast no light on it for I cannot; I know nothing of what happened to the boys. My father never mentioned them in my hearing. It was as if they never existed. But I have to say this; my father did many things of which I was much ashamed. His pre-dating his reign to the 21st August 1485 was a very big mistake. His greed in snatching estates and wealth cast a very big shadow over his early years as king of this country, a time when he should have been healing wounds, not creating them. His efforts to denigrate my Great Uncle Richard were shameful. His suppression of the Titulus Regis was shameful.

Katherine has just asked me to find a chair and sit next to her. I was pacing the floor of her office and probably radiating too much anger and emotion for her. I have heeded her words; I am sitting in a large chair next to her now. I am watching the words appear on her screen.

What else, she is asking me, what else is bothering me about that time, that battle, that transferring of the crown from one king to another? I confess it is like a boil which needs to be lanced, for this is something I have held inside me for all those many, many years. Father never knew that I hated everything he did, I dared not tell him. We had enough fights as it was without my throwing that in his face.

My thoughts then. My father should have come to England and fought an honest battle had he sought the crown that much. He should have come with sufficient men and boldly challenged King Richard III to fight. He should not have relied on the treachery of nobles to help him win. And, having won, he should not have allowed a King's body to be mutilated. He should have granted his slain opponent a decent burial. If he knew aught of the children's whereabouts, he should have said what he knew, produced them if they were alive, given news of their whereabouts if they were dead of whatever condition had taken them. I thought often of my mother's feelings and my grandmother's feelings at the disappearance of two young boys. But I know nothing of their demise or their resting places. I do know the so-called impostors were not they. What I do know is this:

I stand ashamed in my father's shadow.

I feel – relieved. It has been good to say these things. I thank you, Katherine, for pushing me to say them.

Enough philosophising! If we do not move on, this book will be a lifetime in the telling, the many authors queuing impatiently to tell their stories will become even more impatient and my name will be mud in the spirit world!

Where were we? Ah, yes, the Tower of London.

I liked the Tower. I liked the rambling rooms, corridors, different buildings, different styles of decoration and the odd gardens and courtyards. I liked the sense of history it had, knowing that my father and grandfather had arranged for this to be done and that and, going further back, buildings which were ordered by Richard II, by other Henrys, even William Rufus had a hand in some of it. The Tower was engaging in its complexity, its history and its quirkiness. Katherine loved exploring it every bit as much as I did. We would wander about, with our inevitable escorts, of course, and find ourselves in some overlooked room or corner where we might discover a chest containing goodness knows what. We were like children let loose in some wonderland.

And there we stayed the night before our Coronation.

If Katherine was excited about the major ceremony and celebrations she did not display it openly to me, rather she seemed to share my joy and happiness at the prospect. I loved ceremonial anyway, when it concerned something as wonderful as my Coronation. It almost destroyed my appetite, but it didn't quite succeed.

Katherine and I shared the same deep faith and we spent the night together in St Stephen's Chapel lost in our prayers and thoughts. It was cold in there, so we wore heavy cloaks and had our feet on cushions. I admit I dozed a few times, found my head on Katherine's shoulder when I woke with a start, but then who would not, confronted with hours of prayer and no stimulation of choir and sermon, of no service to follow and respond to? I have admitted this to no one up to this time but now it doesn't matter, I can admit it and none can reprove me for it. Oh I prayed too, endlessly, my rosary was fair worn out that night as I went through the prayers, for the task ahead of me was huge. I had to reverse the unfairness of all that Father brought in and yet remain constant to the needs of the treasury to have sufficient money at all times for that which was needed. I required the support of the gentry and their money but fairly, there were laws I wished to look at, statutes that needed amendment, diplomats I needed to speak with to settle England's relationships with countries in Europe. All this went through my mind and I asked for God's help to do it, to give me the strength to get through each day, to give me the wisdom to be a kingly diplomat myself, not just a courtier, to give me the power to rule this land I loved and make the people love me in return. I prayed for Katherine to be fertile and give the country the heir it needed, if not more than one, to guard against sickness and death.

And in the darkness of the night the spectre of the Grim Reaper came to haunt me again, as it would so many times during my life.

I confess again the fact that I feared death. I feared it from the time when my sister died and even more when my brother Arthur died. Somehow I believed he would live forever. The spectre would come in my darkest moments, the bony hand reaching out and I would wake sometimes with a scream locked in my throat. It was part of my being determined to live my life to the full, to cheat death, to say 'when you come for me, I will have lived every day to its fullest, I will have sampled all the joys, all the temptations, all the foods, all the wines and all the experiences that life can give me!' and then I could laugh when the hand touched me. Or so I believed, but considering how many times the nightmare bothered me I was inclined to think that belief was misplaced. By day I could laugh at my fears, by night they came to haunt me.

We had a magnificent coronation. Purple robes, gold jewellery, beautiful clothes for my Queen, a ceremony fit for a true king of this wonderful country. I loved every moment of it; I remember every moment of it still with tremendous pleasure. It sealed my standing, it was the public declaration of I Am Here, I Am King. How much of my pleasure in the day relates to that fact is anyone's guess. Oh, I was already king and knew it and so did those around me, for sure! But this was different, this was – what was it, the presentation of the king to his people?

Onward! Our night's vigil ended when the servants came to collect us in the very early hours, before dawn. I thanked God they found me kneeling and praying, not sleeping with my head on Katherine's should which would have looked bad and would surely have ended up in someone's report somewhere. Those diplomats who doubled as spies would have had a game with that. Instead I was alert, upright, praying when they arrived. They stood back until I indicated the prayers were done, then they escorted us to our rooms. Our clothes had been laid out; well, mine were so I assume Katherine's were as well. A bath, then dressed in gold and purple, highly fitting, I thought. Jewels adorned everything. New hat, new large signet ring too, fit for a king, a massive emerald. Breakfast was brought to me and I ate and drank just enough to see me through the ceremony. Then it was time to go downstairs to the Great Hall and await my Queen and my wife.

She looked amazing. She had on a dress of cloth of silver with black and gold lace adorning the hem, the sleeves, the neckline, and it was arranged in a pattern down the front, too. Her cloak was black velvet with a silver trim. She had on silver shoes adorned with jet buckles set with diamonds. She wore a choker of black pearls, my Coronation gift to her, and they looked wonderful. She looked up at me from under her long eyelashes and her eyes were full of love and unshed tears. I could have swept her into my arms and hugged her there and then in front of everyone but I dared not disrupt the gown and her composure. Instead I took her hand and led her out into the courtyard. There was a specially made carriage waiting for us, with a gold canopy to shield us and matched greys to pull it. We sat there, regally I have to say, and were taken out into the streets of London.

I was taken aback at the decorations. Huge tapestries hung from windows, there were arches across the road with our names in flowers, there were great 'portraits' of us in silk and wool displayed at various strategic points along the way. People threw flowers in our path and onto us. Katherine waved and smiled and I could see people melting under her influence, in a manner of speaking, you understand. She had the right touch with the subjects. She was perfect at it. There were musicians along the route, people were shouting: "Long Live Your Grace!" "Good King Hal!" "Long Live the Queen!" and other such loyal expressions which were music to my ears more than the music itself. Add to this the noise of the carriage, the horses and the ever-present London birds, screeching and wheeling overhead, everything from seagulls to crows and sparrows, and the whole made a cacophony that was almost deafening. I loved it. Every part of it.

From the cheering crowds to solemnity, to the regal thrones, to the serious prayers, the anointing, the solemn music, the psalms we chanted, the oath I took, was a big step. It was like going from sunshine to shadow instantly. The moment we stepped through the doors into the magnificent building it was secular giving way to religion. It was an additional cloak dropped onto my shoulders, a heavy one. I could be king in my own court, but here I had to prove I was king before God

Himself. And so I followed instructions, I prayed my sincere prayers and in the moments of silence, few as they were, I contemplated my thoughts. The Coronation is the sealing of the monarch's oath to the people he has to govern, it says 'I am your king, I will do my best for you.' When it goes wrong, as it does repeatedly, then the person, that soul, has to answer for that when he confronts his God when that life ends. There will be those who will say that the spectre of death is my reign coming back to haunt me but no, it was there long before I became king, or even thought I would become king. But yes, there were many things which came back to haunt me when I reviewed my life from this side. Many, many things. With hand on heart I tell this Katherine that she was - and is - the biggest one of all.

Then we walked back, hand in hand, from the shadow into the sunshine, to the cheering crowds, to the celebrations, to the drunkenness already present but they deserved it. They had endured a long and difficult reign under my father. That was ended, once and for all ended.

It was time to celebrate.

The celebrations, the jousting (at which I consistently won, of course) the feasting, the free-flowing wine, all was being enjoyed when Grandmother Beaufort inconveniently died. Yes, I know I have said we do not know when the Grim Reaper is coming but I found it very spiteful of him to interrupt my celebrations. I had just come of age, I had been crowned, I had a new wife, I had a court full of people tripping over each other in their efforts to please me and a stop had to be put on it all because an old lady departed this life. It was another tie with the past that had been cut; I found myself both saddened and relieved in equal measures. To please her soul I had the bells rung for six days until I thought my head would burst if I heard another bell ringing. Eventually even that ended, we had a great funeral and it was done.

Katherine has just asked me what I thought of John Fisher, Bishop of Rochester, someone Grandmother had appointed to be my mentor. For her sake I said yes, he could come and be in my court, but for my sake I went around ignoring everything he said and did and pointed out to me. For once I was determined not to do as a family member wanted. I would choose who I wanted to counsel me and it was not John Fisher. His piety seemed to me to be overdone, his scourging himself and starving himself seemed to me to be the result of some kind of extreme disorder of the mind. You did not need to do that to prove yourself to be a man of God. Such a man would not understand my need to fill every moment of every day with activity of all kinds. I was probably a source of great despair to him, but there was little I could do about that. He was not in accord with my thinking or I with his.

I did fill my life, didn't I? I wore out hunters and men alike. Off one exhausted horse onto another and onward, ever onward. None could stand the pace I set. We hunted daily when the weather permitted. I rode to hunt in most weather, I played tennis with skill, I danced most evenings; I was a fit and healthy and handsome man capable of taking on the world.

Vain? Of course I was. Would you not be, in my position? Would you not flaunt a shapely leg, a muscled arm, display a strength that was outstanding? I could throw a javelin further than anyone, I could outride them all at the tourney. There was none to match me with musical composition, singing, playing of lutes and other instruments. A virtual paragon among men, I swear I was! I wish Katherine could remember more of that life, remember how she applauded and adored everything I did. Well, not exactly everything, she was not that enamoured, as I recall, with having the dripping carcasses of deer brought to her at the Coronation hunt. Oh, she did her best to disguise it but the abhorrence was there! Poor Katherine - and poor ladies, too. I am sure, on reflection, that none of them cared to see so much blood but we had to show how good we were and what better way than the traditional act of bringing meat to our women?

Chapter Ten - A Cruel Man?

I am aware that there are many who find the hunt cruel. I am aware that there are those who see me, a hunting fanatic, as a cruel man anyway and add that to my list of supposed sins. I need to talk on this question of my being a cruel man, if only to put my side of the story, which is what this is all about, of course. Why else would I waste Katherine's time?

The word 'cruelty' is often used in connection with my history, my reign, my time of absolute power. Be aware, you who read this book, medieval kings had absolute power over all persons and that meant the power of life and death. 'Cruel' to me means someone who delights or even revels in their cruelty. I did not. Those I condemned were executed for a variety of reasons, not my whim. I knew better than to alienate people by doing that!

Katherine's books lay at my feet the first deaths, those of Richard Empson and Edmund Dudley, indicating that it was the start of my reign of terror. It is said they were loyal servants of my father, that all they did was his commands, that I rigged their trial and had them executed as a way of ridding myself of men I did not like.

Not so. They were schemers and stirrers. They were devoted to my father and not to me. They had plans afoot to curb my powers, using statutes that Father had drafted and wanted in place. I distrusted them and knew full well there was treason in their hearts and minds. It wasn't fictitious, believe me. These men had to go and I had to rid myself of them.

Father had been working on statutes to limit the power of the monarch. I think he was doing it under pressure from the great land owning magnates, those to whom he owed his position and a lot of his money, in truth. I say 'I think' for I was not privy to his private discussions but … like all sensible people, I had my spies at work and they brought me details, trivial and large, of this intent. Empsom and Dudley were devoted servants of my father, they were determined to make me their servant if they could, by limiting my powers and taking my influence from me. There were others also at the same game, same goal, it was a widespread conspiracy. But remove the head and the creature dies.

The word of a king is supreme at all times. I watched and waited and pounced, served execution orders and had them both hanged in a very short space of time. They had a chance to protest their innocence – which I ignored, knowing better than to believe that – and to be shriven and that was it.

It sent a warning shot across the bows of any who thought the new king would be easy to manipulate, to make pliant in their hands. I wanted the touch of fear in all who were with me, around me, serving me. I wanted to be sure of their loyalty and what better way than first to buy it with positions and wealth and second to coat it with a veneer of fear that I would turn on them as I did on Empson and Dudley and remove them from the living world.

It worked.

It worked for some time.

My first executions but as you well know, not my last. How did it feel is the question I see hanging there. The top part of my mind, as it were, said: 'this is good, this is power, this is what it is all about, why I wear a crown, why I am the supreme ruler of this country. The lower part of my mind, where the insecurities lived – and there were many of them, did you know that? – said: 'are you sure you're doing the right thing? Could they not be useful to you in other ways? Would you play God and take someone's life? Is that not tantamount to murder which is forbidden by God? Through a long dark night I fought the insecurities because of the need to make the statement, I Am King. I will not stand treachery in any way, shape or form, no matter who you are. I fought the insecurities and I won. They were executed. I felt a sharp pang of remorse and then put it from me. There is no place in a king's life for such feelings.

I would ask you not to make judgements by what you read of me, which is twisted through the minds of those who wrote – then and now – but by what I did in light of the time in which I lived. Remember that there was much that was never revealed, never recorded, not even known by many. And, above all, no one – no one – knew what was in my mind.

You have the sweet facility of hindsight. You have the ultimate 'gift' of being able to review the whole of my reign in one fell swoop. My entire life is contained in one book. But for me ... I lived it day by day, hour by hour, minute by minute. I lived with the paranoia, the double dealing, with treachery and stark ambition writ large in the eyes, the words and the movements of those who were around me, those professing to be my loyal and devoted friends.

Katherine asks, did you not trust anyone completely?

No. There were levels of trust, as in:

You are trusted to see to my clothes, polish my boots, provide me with food.

You are trusted to write my letters, attend any meetings I have and go on missions as my envoy.

You are trusted to share my more personal life, to advise me on spiritual and religious matters, on whether a woman can be trusted or not. (Yes, all right, I sense the disapproval! But these were different times, very different times from yours, where women demand equal rights whether they are entitled to them or not. Yes, I remain chauvinistic, would you have me change?)

You are trusted to drink with me, party with me, hunt with me – and believe me, that was a dangerous time!

Levels of trust. Those were the levels at which I accorded trust. Share my innermost thoughts, worries, cares and fancies? No one. As my first wife, Katherine came close, very close.

In this time, the 21st century, I have told her things which have not appeared in this book and she has kept them close in her heart. I have told her things which no living person has ever known. But in that time, in the 16th century, no, although I trusted her, there was much she did not know.

It had to be so. I had to keep so much locked in my heart and mind, things I knew, overheard, intercepted. My spies were at work day and night, each bringing a tiny piece of information which I matched with another piece and so on until I alone held the total picture. From that I decided what move I would make. It is this which bothered so many, for they had no idea how much I knew and how much I deduced and how much I could make from three quarters of a picture – it did not take much thought to complete it.

She was clever, thoughtful and intellectual enough to have been able to help me with the deductions but I did not want her involved. It was simply a question of my being the supreme head of the country, controller of the Treasury, the laws and the people, by myself. I had seen Father's will damaged by those who argued persuasively against this policy or that; sometimes they were policies that would have been good for the people and bad for the aristocracy. I wished my judgement to remain my own, that way nothing would ever reflect on her if it all went wrong.

There were others, favourites, friends, associates I trusted and spent some hours with but life was full and sometimes I felt I did not have enough time for my friends. Poor Charles Brandon, James and all the others who were devoted to me hardly saw me some days. Then I would make a determined effort to put aside the affairs of the country and go hunting, hawking, drinking and cavorting generally, as only a king can when he has limitless power and seemingly limitless money. I turned a blind ear to those who said money needed to be generated before I could spend it. I thought of Father's niggardly reign and determined mine would not be seen that way.

Ah, how blind I was! Of course they were right and it took desperate measures later in my life to rectify what I did earlier in my life. But again, hindsight. I lived for the moment.

Chapter Eleven - Living Like A King

It looks very much as if we are discussing lifestyle rather than policy. For the 'average' reader - dear reader, I do not wish for a moment to denigrate your level of intelligence but I hope for a great many people to read my book which will mean a great many levels of intelligence – lifestyle is surely preferable to policy. After all, the books are there, lots of them, seemingly endless books on my life, which contain details of the politics of the time. I could go into it, but if I did, Katherine would tell me this book will be far too long, my liege lord, and the publisher will not be interested. I have already discovered, to my astonishment, that you are all more concerned with my wives than with my policies. So be it. If that is the direction your interest goes, then that is the direction I will take with the book. I will be content to leave policy behind, it was a pain and a bore and a burden at the best of times and most of my reign was not the best of times. It was hard work dissecting everyone's motives before working out what political statements could be made, so as not to upset this apple cart or that nation's rulers. In my eyes they were often one and the same…

On a day to day basis, there were courts to encourage, households to control – and a good deal of the day to day administration often came via my hands in one way or another despite men being hired to take care of it for me. There was glorious decoration to be imported, installed and displayed. Decoration designed to show my wealth, my power, my vast interests in all things beautiful. There were buildings to be built, paintings to be acquired and a wife to take care of. For she, my beloved Katherine, needed time to learn to be my Queen, to take part in all that was needed to be taken part in, from tournaments to plays, from feasts to ceremonials when European visitors arrived. The biggest part of her 'tuition' though was advising her, as best I could, that court was a hotbed of paranoia and discontent, with every courtier wanting more than he could have and bringing with him more hangers-on than the court could accommodate. Between us we created the rules that swept many of such hangers-on from the court, as far as we could.

Katherine also needed time for her devotions. Having such a devout wife made a difference to the court, those who were not so inclined had to make themselves go, to be part of what was going on. For some, I know, it was a salutary exercise and they benefited from it, others found it a bore and a chore. That was their problem, not mine.

I was thrilled to find my new Queen fertile; she became pregnant almost immediately following the wedding and Coronation. I was happy and it showed, my court was full of musicians and singers, together with many of my dogs, which I adored, and we jousted and partied and hunted and got up to all manner of things. Katherine looked well. Pregnancy suited her, she blossomed is the best way I can describe it. I tried not to cast an evil spell on the forthcoming child. I refused to speak of 'my son' but in my heart I said it and in my prayers I said it. I asked God, that great and all seeing spirit who had given me so much, the crown of England for a start, a beautiful fertile wife for a second, a court full of people whose one desire seemed to be – please note the word seemed for none could be truly trusted – to please me.

So imagine my shock, my horror, my hurt and my torment when the child, a girl, was stillborn.

We had held Christmas in great style, I had showered my Queen with expensive luxuries and jewels and thought of more I could buy her if she would but give me a son. Every king wants a son; every king needs a son. It is difficult for us, in our time, to impress upon those in your time, you who have had the great Victoria and the even greater Queen Elizabeth II for so many years, to understand that a male heir was everything. But it was.

I felt guilt that my shock and horror had kept me from Katherine's chamber until I came to terms with the disappointment, for she too had been torn apart, not only by the birth, which had been troublesome, but by giving birth to a dead child. Ah, the words are harsh, are they not! Stillborn looks better than dead, but it is semantics. The child was dead. It breathed not. It moved not. It was nothing. We did not even name it. Where and when it was disposed of, I did not enquire nor did I want to know. I paid the midwife, for it was not her fault, the child had been dead in the womb, not dead from some mishap or incompetence on her part. Katherine told me later that the child had long stopped moving, she had felt no heartbeat but had been afraid to speak of it.

She became pregnant again that year. April is a good time, for the sap has risen, the earth is moving after its winter sleep, everything is creative and bountiful and good.

I entertained myself, outside of parliamentary work and many, many visitors and diplomatic discussions, by setting building work in place, new palaces, new chapels, all sorts of changes and designs, all needing intense discussions, plans, thoughts. I loved it. I also loved spending time studying the stars, the movement of the planets, the whole universe. Never has the work of the great God been so magnificently displayed for us humans to see.

Another great Christmas to spend in style and luxury, another birth to anticipate. I paced the floor, which apparently every expectant father does but did any do so as anxiously as I did at that time? I waited and I demanded news and it was brought to me, every contraction, every cry, every utterance from my Queen, as if that made any difference to the outcome. This time, the longed for son!

I recall the sheer joy which flooded me at that time. I grew even taller and bigger than I was, it seemed, I could not stop beaming, could not stop shouting my joy to the world. I was a father with a son, at last.

How happy we were, how the church bells rang all across London and across the country, I am told. Me, who did not want to hear a church bell again after Grandmother Beaufort died was glad to hear them. I heard how everyone shouted the news from the pulpits and platforms across the land. My Queen was radiant and glowed in the great love surrounding her from all of us. She soon left her bed and began to regain her strength and her figure. In due time she was back in court, at my side again. I felt wise and comfortable, if that makes sense. I felt I could take anything on with this security, this fulfilment of my dream.

My son Henry, duke of Cornwall, arrived in this life in great style and with much – so much – anticipation and affection and every conceivable requirement made for his comfort and his wellbeing.

My son Henry, duke of Cornwall, departed this life some fifty-two days later. Count them. Fifty-two days of my being so happy I had a son, looking forward to more children, looking forward to a nursery full so that when I visited, I would be greeted by the joyful shouts of children at play.

Those triumphant church bells were replaced by the single tolling death bell. None knew of the savage pain it caused me. Of course they knew I was in grief, who would not be? Of course they considered my loss, why not? But none, not even my Katherine, knew how deep the knife had gone in my heart at the death of my much-wanted son.

Here I need to confess that for a long time I did not think of the heartbreak Katherine suffered too. Am I that selfish a person? Was I that selfish a person? I was not used to sharing, even then. I shared a bed, yes, of course, how else did she get pregnant? I shared some thoughts, I shared some insights, but over and above all that I kept my thoughts, my impressions and a lot of my emotions to myself.

Look now at my portraits. Look hard at them and ask yourself, does that face portray anything to you? Not the portrait in this book, but the portraits which are on display in galleries and the like, the ones chosen to illustrate the many, many books on my life and times. You will see nothing but a blank stone face. I would like to digress here for a moment, it is the perfect opportunity to say this: one of the better biographies written about me, one which attempted to bring me, Henry, the person, to life has the most appalling last line. The author refers to my cruel piggy eyes. For this I condemn him forever! Cruel I was not. Piggy; any person who becomes grossly overweight as I did through diet, lack of exercise and age, finds their face puffing up and in so doing, the eyes become deep set in the flesh. Piggy is a cruel word. The sentence itself is cruel. And the author refers to me as cruel! Methinks not. Does Katherine agree with me?

The smile says she does. But then, she would, wouldn't she? We were married, after all…

It might be a long, long time in human terms but I remember my marriage to Katherine as if it were last year. I will be honest and not say last week, as most modern people say, because I had a few wives after her … just a few. And you all make such a big thing out of it! You constantly surprise me, you modern people. A wife is a wife is a wife – six times over in my case, but consider this: I stayed married to my Katherine for longer than any of the others. One Queen I did not even take to my bed! No, that's a lie, I took her to bed but I left her as virgin as when she arrived.

I do divert, do I not? It is a bad habit and one I should try and control but Katherine says all thoughts are good, that the reader will be interested in every thought process of mine regarding matters appertaining to my time and my reign. I trust she is right.

And so, we are moving on with the book, we are moving on with my heart shattered by the loss of my son and Katherine shattered by the loss of her living child and neither of us telling the other how we felt. How stupid we were!

Chapter Twelve - Holy War

I wish to continue with this story, being aware that there is a date by which we must be done. Apart from any other consideration, though, my dear one, the entire story is firmly in my head insofar as I know what I wish to talk about and what I don't.

In 1512 I launched a Holy War. At twenty-one I was mature enough to rule a country so I counted myself mature enough to launch a war. It has been said I had my head filled with stories of Agincourt and the like, maybe that was so but not consciously so, I have to say. I did not leave my books and ride out to war with battle cries on my lips, but it seemed to me, taking all things into consideration, France needed to be taught a lesson. When has it not…

France was busy trying to consolidate land holdings in Northern Italy. This was a step too far for the papacy and so a Holy League was directed against France. Ferdinand, ever the wise fox, had long been troubled by the French land-grabbing and wanted a chance to fight back. So, with two allies, we were able to launch a war.

Ten thousand archers went to France – ten thousand of the finest archers this world has known went to France on ships which were commissioned and built. That ten thousand held down the French at Bayonne whilst Ferdinand, against all the agreements, got his troops into Navarre and ended the conflict that way. Months of planning, of preparation, of rushing hither and thither, of messengers fair worn out and clerics and clerks writing quills down to mere stubs – for what? It didn't work. You have to agree that at times the best plans in the known world do not go according to your desires. That one did not. The fact is I wanted to look good. I didn't.

Ferdinand reneged on his agreement. He left the English soldiers with no food, bad wine and bad tempers. Some didn't come back. Many didn't come back, truthfully, not because they deserted but because they died. Fever, dysentery, fights … played havoc with my army. Ferdinand bold face lied and said it was us deserting him. I had to keep my temper, I was after all married to his daughter but I was Not Pleased.

The archers came back. They came back and they continued their practice and I told them, wait on, wait on, we will go back and next time I will go back with you and we will flatten the damn French and show the Spanish king how to fight. No king likes to be humiliated, especially this one. There may have been other kings in other places who could stand that level of humiliation and go home and never set foot outside their country again. Tudors with Plantagenet blood cannot and do not do either of those things.

So in 1513 I went to France where, with negotiation, tactical manoeuvres and a bit of luck, we won a resounding victory. So the history books say, anyway and who am I to argue with them when for once they take a small situation and make it a large one, to give me the benefit of this particular turn of events?

Doesn't that sound simple –'we went to France.' Yes we did. A flotilla of ships, carts, horses, weapons, men, women, all transported across the Channel and set on French soil, there to start the march to Bayonne, camping out along the way, each time erecting my pavilion, made of double and even triple layers of silk draped over many supports, with a door that could be fastened to keep out the unwanted. Gold encrusted, of course. Within it there were benches, seats, a bed, quilts and comforters, a small brazier for my mulled wine and foods and blankets for those who slept at my feet to ensure my safety at all times. The person who slept in the doorway had two blankets. (I was nothing if not kind.) There were rugs; I could not walk on an earthen floor. Who said being a king was easy … no, sorry, I meant, serving a king was easy. Or did I?

Everything had been arranged; Maximilian was part of the plan for this war, he joined in against the French. Ferdinand was to cross the Pyrenees to take Guienne …

And in April 1513 it became clear that Ferdinand again was double-dealing. He arranged a yearlong truce with France.

And there I was, ready to fight …

By June of that year we were all in France and we did fight a bit and I did charge up and down in full armour and make a show of being leader of all and somehow I impressed enough people to make me look good in the eyes of Europeans and if you can think of a better reason to parade your wealth, strength and influence in France, I would like to hear it.

Of greater importance to me was the fact that while I headed the army in France – and believe me I did – Katherine was acting as regent of England and carrying our third child.

My queen seemed to take longer this time to become pregnant following the death of our son. I wondered briefly if there was a physical reason for this but was assured by those who counselled her that grief did strange things to some women. This I could understand, but for me the driving, overwhelming, all-encompassing need, was for an heir. I saw others with families, with heirs to their titles, their estates and fortunes and I had none. I labour this point for a very good reason; you need to know what was at the very root of my future decisions when it came to my wives.

Ah, you will say, but surely love – for which read lust, in many instances – had a large part to play in this too?

Katherine will not forgive me if I end this evening's writing session with a lie. Katherine will not forgive me if I lie to you anyway as by lying to you, my reader, I lie to her too. So this is the truth. Lust played a part in it, of course it did. No man can admire a woman without a hint of lust – all right, a very large chunk of lust – entering into it. But that is for later.

So, we had this situation then. I was in France and you cannot begin to believe the arrangements that needed to be made to get me and everyone else there, to keep us there, to keep us moving, to keep us fed and watered and healthy and ready to fight when necessary, whilst back at home Katherine was overseeing the battle of Flodden.

Don't ask me to go into it! I was in turn annoyed (a mere woman taking on the role of head of the army) infuriated (I wasn't there to do it myself) pride (that she did the job and did it well) frustrated (stuck in France without the chance to hold her and tell her how proud I was of her, truly I was) and outright pleased that the task was well done, another glory to add to the Tudor crown, if tinged with regret that it wasn't I at the head of the army and taking all the credit. Not that it bothered me overly, you understand …

If only France had fallen to me in the same way but that is another story, one well covered by those who choose to write of me. Heaven alone knows why.

On the other hand, looking at the reverse side of the coin as I now can, France gave me a greater crown than that of the prospect of ruling a troublesome land full of troublesome people.

It gave me Thomas Wolsey.

In any court are men of ability and men of outstanding ability and men who you think you cannot manage without. The trick is to find the one you think you cannot manage without but never let him know that. I observed Wolsey for some time, watched how he acted around people, tested him with a secret or two, set my spies to investigate his background. He came up blameless. I thought I would take a chance and promote him. What I saw was a man of outstanding ability to handle the minutiae of my life. Oh there would be jealousy, there always was. It mattered not who I chose, the others resented it. I could not promote them all, there were not enough 'close to the king' places to do that and in any event, some of them would not be so promoted if I lived to be a hundred and had a thousand places to offer them. But try telling that to the ambitious, the greedy, the thrusting newcomer to court who thinks he can walk in and take over. I knew whatever I did there would be 'something' awry, no matter what and where. Repercussions, the domino effect, call it what you will. You promote a family by putting responsibility on the head of one of its members and that family thinks it owns England by proxy. You can believe me, that is the way it worked. Probably still does, if truth be told.

Truth is, the man was outstanding. He handled everything I did not wish to, in France and in England. One of the books Katherine has by her side here on her desk says I wanted only to hunt, feast, joust and dance. Yes, I did. I ask you, given the chance to be king of England at that time, when everyone looked up to you and revered you and wanted to please you – in return for honours, of course, let us not for a moment forget that part of the deal – and what you disliked doing was writing letters, signing letters, dealing with diplomats and contrary ambassadors who sent back biased reports to their masters if their accommodation did not meet with their approval and generally being a busybody clerk, what would you do?

Precisely. Call in the one person who can handle all that for you and say "deal with that for me." And he did.

He made me feel slender. Not that I was growing at that time, I had enough hawking and jousting, playing charades and dancing, hunting and archery to keep the fat from piling on. No, at that time I was fit and slender and elegant and very, very handsome. Ask Katherine if she did not get the better brother at the time…

Wolsey was big in every way, body, head and intellect. His knowledge was as wide and as far ranging as mine was. We talked for ages on every topic. I delighted in having him with me.

Then in the November of that year, which should have been glorious and in many ways was, Katherine gave birth to our second son, also called Henry. He didn't live as long as the first one. He didn't even live for a whole day.

In the privacy of my room, I berated God for not giving me a living child. I called Him to account, asking why He was refusing me a living child, asking where I had gone wrong, what I could do to rectify the matter, what I had to do to please Him and so allow me to have that which I so desperately sought. Right at that point even a daughter would do. Yes, that sounds cruel and heartless, yes it was cruel and heartless but – let me remind you, for fear of your forgetting in the few pages since I mentioned it, I wanted and needed and longed for a nursery full of children. Nowhere in that statement did I say only boys or only anything. I said children, I meant children.

You need to remember that I grew up with brothers and sisters. I knew the joy of being with siblings, with having others to share with or fight with or study with. I also knew that my father was not the kind of father to delight in having children to play with or have them run to him but I wanted it, because I did not have it? One of your clever psychiatrists would no doubt have much to say on the subject were they able to discuss it with me but I will avoid them as I would the bubonic plague. I have had sufficient time to think on these things and these are my conclusions.

Katherine accepted this without so much as a glance at me for me to read her expression. I have to ask Katherine if it makes sense to her or whether I am blundering around in the darkness of my own thoughts.

It seems she agrees with me. For that I am most grateful. I have long thought this.

I am there, in my elegant, expensively furnished room, hung with rich tapestries, with thick rugs on the floor and thick coverings on the bed. I have gold dishes from which to eat and jewelled goblets from which to drink. I had only to tip a finger in the direction of a squire, page, messenger or courtier and I could have my wish, for music, poetry, talk, paper, quill, food, wine, anything I chose.

I could not tip a finger in the direction of my queen and produce a living child.

Yes, I know I would have to do more than tip a finger at her! And before she asks, to lie with my wife was a supreme pleasure for me. I loved her intensely still, she captivated me in every way. Her voice, her face, her body, her thoughts, her piety and her willingness to please me, nothing could have been better in my Queen.

She sought much in the way of advice from herbalists and medical men of all kinds.

She became pregnant again.

In December a year later she gave birth to a stillborn daughter.

Each birth tore the heart from her. Each birth was difficult and draining and to know the child was dead before its arrival in this world was doubly heartbreaking. I know this now. I know now from considering Katherine's part in all this that she had a terrible troubled time. Ever did she seek to please me, to be my Queen consort, to work with me and guide me and help me, prayed with me, walked with me when we went anywhere. And inside she was being torn apart by her inability to give me a living child.

It was one thing we found we did not speak of, not once during the whole of our marriage.

She came willingly to my bed, to my arms, to my body. It was not for lack of love or lack of trying. Later events proved that I was fertile, so it was not my body failing me. Not then, anyway.

Katherine is looking at notes made and stored in the folder she keeps, the one with my name on it. Katherine knows she must venture a question to me about dalliances. She is asking if there were any.

I hesitated to avoid the question so Katherine walked off, as she does, to attend to bodily functions, get a glass of water, do anything but sit in front of the screen waiting for my response. I understand that, it would be like waiting with a quill dripping ink on a sheet of blank vellum and no words coming. I am also aware that I am doing my best to avoid the question.

Honesty, she tells me, honesty. All right, I concede her victory – again. I did dally with other women.

Ha! was Katherine's immediate reaction, coming straight from the 16th century into now. *I knew it!*

Consider this. A good looking (other people's opinion as well as my own) man with a healthy virile body and a healthy virile interest in women. Add to the equation very pretty if not outright beautiful women of all ages, from young to middle aged, for many retained their looks and figures without resorting to too much artifice well into what I would call later life. Add a further ingredient – I am madly mixing metaphors here, yes I am, I admit it – that there are many good looking ambitious courtiers and favourites around me, all looking for their chance too. Your imagination is capable of supplying the answer to the question, a chance at what?

Faced then with a choice of dukes, earls, knights of all kinds and the king himself, who would you flaunt yourself at in the hope of some reward, some favour, some permanent change for the better in your life? And if limbs are white and limber and bodies are warm and welcoming and the king needs a diversion from the diversions which divert him from matters of state…

Am I not my grandfather's descendant? Doubt it not. The Soldier King, Edward IV, who strode through the Wars of the Roses like a conquering hero, strode through a good many bedrooms too. He had ten legitimate children (which I envied, I have to say) and about an equal number of illegitimate children too.

It did not for a moment mean I did not love my Queen any the less. Sometimes the dalliances made me love her more, for her quietness, her determination and her whole persona became more dear to me after being in the presence of another.

For some reason best known to herself and who can truly fathom the mind of a woman? Katherine chose that moment to end the evening's writing session. Today we resume …

I understand from Katherine's memories that although she knew, as in being told by her women who gossiped far too much, in my opinion, that I was bedding this one and that, she never heard it from my lips – until now. So she chose to disbelieve it – until now. It is fortunate for me that the 21st century Katherine is more forgiving even than the 16th century one and I swear by all that is holy my Queen had much to forgive! My obsession with hunting, with hawking, with tennis, with all manner of sports, with music making and song writing, with being busy ignoring the despatches Wolsey sent me, I rather neglected my poor wife at times. I also spent a lot of time eating, bathing, choosing magnificent clothes –

what a lifestyle, I can almost hear you saying. Ah yes, a lifestyle indeed. I also kept a whole – what do you call a collection of spies? What was the word we used earlier today when we talked of my spies?

Network. That was it! I had a network of spies. This I am sure I mentioned earlier in my book. I will ask Katherine to go and check.

"That, together with a network of spies and informers, guaranteed few things got past this Tudor."

Thank you. That is it, precisely it. Whilst I did all those things and had a wonderful time doing them all, I freely admit that, I had my ears, eyes and mind attuned to all those around me and all those not around me whose information was fed back by my spies.

And so, when Wolsey thought he had a wonderful scheme going that would revolutionise this or that but which was deeply flawed – as it often was, unfortunately – he would find the scheme cut off in its prime and its flaws exposed for all to see. He soon learned not to – no, that's a lie, he took some time to learn not to try and pass something off on me that had not been thought through properly from every angle that he could think of and then a few he hadn't.

And I lived the life of a king.

Chapter Thirteen - Scandals

Life was good. I was doing all I hoped to do when I became king, have a good life, have the women I wanted, but I hadn't taken into account the seemingly endless details of government and day to day running of my homes. Always someone wanting something. Wolsey was good, I admit that, he had the touch and the foresight to stop most things getting to me but not all of it. There was still much to do.

And making time for the women. We are back to women again. But then, I could not really leave the subject, could I? Women were there; women were more than there. Women found every excuse to get close and even closer if they could. Women schemed and planned and got under my skin.

The problem was, I was king and I wanted everything my way. That meant controlling the lives of those around me. Oh, interesting, Katherine's fingers made that controlling the lies of those around me. Would that I could have done that, I would have spread better rumours than were actually doing the rounds at that time.

Right now I need to talk of another woman, my sister, Mary. She was very important to me, I adored her and wanted only the best for her. As any brother who was king would, you can't blame me for that.

I thought … wrongly, that when my sister was widowed I could arrange something equally wonderful for her and make some unbreakable tie with some European family that would benefit England in every way. I had overlooked my best friend, Charles
Brandon. Viscount Lisle, Master of the Horse, twice married to great ladies. He had the effrontery, the sheer gall, the impudence, to marry Mary, then dowager Queen of France, without my permission! I was furious, in part because I had managed to underestimate the

affection between them - I hated to be caught out in that kind of error of judgement - and in part because I really did want another dynastic marriage for her. Truthfully, I thought she could do better. That is no slur on my favourite friend, by the way! It is a fact of dynastic life that you have a widow of her standing, you seek another high ranking marriage for her. I was in the process of searching out an appropriate husband when the news came of the surreptitious marriage which, having been concluded, was irrevocably sealed as far as I was concerned.

But what do you do when it is your favourite sister and your best friend? Say 'every happiness to you both and here's a huge estate, go play at keeping house.' Which is what I did, with great magnanimity and a lot of biting of tongue and internal raging. And which they did, in great style, not realising the anguish they put me through. The real problem lay in their glowing happiness. I knew my sister had been in love with Charles long before they went off to their respective impressively high-ranking marriages. It was a relationship of deep love and I could not fault that, no matter how much I wished to. So they had the royal blessing and got on with their lives.

And I went on loving my Queen. Truly, I did … truly I did.

But I cannot ignore Bessie Blount if I am discussing women, even though this was a little way into the future. Might as well talk of her now as then. Bessie was buxom, pretty, enticing, interesting in a different way than my beloved Queen. The question which is often asked is, was the child mine? Would that we had your clever technology to find out! It is easy to say. My view was and still is, if she welcomed me, who else did she welcome… I made no real claims on the child, but I presumed enough to say he might be mine. I gave him a title, I gave him honours and an education and held in the back of my mind the thought that he might be my heir, if Katherine proved incapable, as I was beginning to think she was. But I had no real proof. The fact the child looked like me was good enough at the time and I was sure people would accept him.

Mary Boleyn's child? If we are talking of children, that one I am not sure of and I did not ever claim that one to be mine. It might have been, but I repeat, if I was welcomed, who else was? My court was full of opportunist people looking for a quick fumble, if I might use that expression, in the hope of securing favours from me via those I cared about. My tumbled women. As if I would take notice of their pleas for honours for this one and that! Deluded people thought they could get to me that way. Deluded people had their fun and no honours. Honours came the hard way, through service and devotion to me, not to my women.

I have a problem. It is a simple one, it is a large one; it is what to leave out and what to put in. The politics of the time are well represented in every book Katherine has and there are many she does not have. The double-dealing by Ferdinand and Maximilian, the thrusts and counter thrusts, the plans, the schemes, the plots – what is it you really want from me, is my question. So what does Katherine think the readers really want? Sex and scandal or politics and power play?

Katherine whispered to me 'sex and scandal.' I knew it well before I asked the question, actually, it was just a test to see if she and I thought the same.

So, we will leave European politics and power play to the politicians and the historians. Katherine is a historian, her 'time' is the 15th century, but even there she is more concerned with people than with politics. She rightly says it is people who make events, not events that make people. Although it is important to know who and why and where – events such as my magnificent achievement of bringing together all the heads of various countries or their representatives in St Paul's – my St Paul's, not the one you have now, all round and elegant – for the Universal and Eternal Christian Alliance for International Peace, for example. I remember kneeling before Wolsey and thinking this was good, this was better than bloodshed and terror, whilst admitting bloodshed and terror had its place. I believe we are, we as in Mankind, addicted to bloodshed and terror, why else would such savagery take place on your streets and in your football grounds and other stadiums, why would people delight in truly awful horror films and films expressing nothing but violence? These are questions which the greatest minds have turned themselves toward and come up with nothing. There are few places where aggression can be worked out, there are no tournaments as such where men can ride at one another in anger, if need be, and decide by skill who is the finer man. Knights no longer ride to battle, they are ceremonial. Princes are ceremonial, more's the pity.

I divert, yet again.

Let me move on with good news.

Katherine gave birth to our daughter Mary in Greenwich, February 1516. And, thanks be to God, the child lived. She not only lived, she thrived. She grew. She cried and vomited and did all the things babies do and I held her and admired her and handed her back to her nurse and waited for the day she had brothers and sisters to join her in the nursery for their devoted father to visit bringing sweetmeats and comfits for their pleasure. I thanked God for His great gift to me and asked for another child, please, to go with this one.

I found comfort in Bessie's arms because Katherine had been weakened by this last birth and I was considerate of her physical condition. I did not impose myself on her. I was happy to have a living child, a loving wife and an outwardly affectionate lover. I hate the word 'mistress'. It has connotations I dislike. It makes me seem subservient to her rather than her subservient to her liege lord. So, for all historians who describe her – and others – as my mistresses, forget it. Call them lovers or loose women. I took advantage of them because they were there and willing to be taken advantage of. They were not my mistresses. Any of them. Oh, I know that in my correspondence at the time to Anne, that which has survived, I refer to her as mistress but that is a courtesy title to someone I planned to marry. That, in turn, is for later. Katherine, we are getting diverted! She has smiled and said nothing. She knows full well it is I who divert and not her.

Queen Katherine welcomed me back to her bed. The result was another stillborn child. I would not allow myself to put her through that again. We decided it was best to end our marital relationship in that way. I had no wish to damage my Queen, to ruin her health forever. I know she was sad, I was, too. I had a living child. It was not a son but a living child, after so many stillbirths and unexplained and unexpected deaths, was a matter for rejoicing. Life should have been quiet, should have been peaceful. Instead, to my everlasting regret, I came into greater contact with the Boleyns.

Chapter Fourteen - Extravaganza

But before we venture into that fraught territory, Katherine mentioned the Field of the Cloth of Gold event, occasion, what would you call it? A huge vastly expensive show, I think, is the only way to describe it. At the time I thought it was magnificent. Since then I have wondered why we did it, but that is another matter, one for my conscience when I wonder how I got through so much money in so short a time.

What was it? A show. A spectacle.

Let me, for a moment; revert to the spectacle of the tournament held by Earl Rivers, when he was Lord Scales, for my grandfather and grandmother, Edward IV and his Queen, Elizabeth Woodville. This was a two day affair in the City, with representatives of great high ranking families and most of the dignitaries of London, if not all of them, there to see two men do 'battle'. I am told, by the Earl himself, that the entire thing cost him about half a million pounds. Then. 15th century. Go calculate it in your currency today and gasp at the wealth which was displayed.

As an aside, I wish I had been able to see it, I wish that the modern technology, the wonders of your age, could have captured the whole thing so it could be viewed over and over. For I do so love the joust and a fair fight between two well matched noble knights. Another comment on this, if I may, if you wish to know more about this, ask Katherine. She has researched this for the Earl's book and can talk about it at length. She often does...

What then did my 'spectacle' cost? Shiploads of people, animals, supplies, you name it we had it, going to France. We, my Queen and I, had 5000 followers to attend to us. We had every fancy outfit you can think of and then some. The figures in Katherine's book seem about right to me, 6000 workmen building a city of tents and pavilions, 2000 workmen transforming Guisnes castle and making a summer palace. The cost is incalculable. The cost was astronomical, on both sides of the water. My feeling now is we must have been mad, possessed, insane, to spend that kind of money but my feeling at the time was – I had it so let me spend it and do it in style.

I need to talk on this great occasion, forgive me. I loved it, you see, being on display to so many people as I was, oh sorry, as we were. Wolsey's connivance brought together two heads of state very cleverly. There was a newly elected Emperor Charles of Spain was heading through the Channel and Wolsey asked if I would like to meet him if he could get the Emperor to divert for a meeting. It seemed like a good idea, so with much ceremony, arrangement and a lot of money, it happened. This was in the middle of the arrangements for the great Field of the Cloth of Gold event, but it didn't matter, we had a fine series of meetings in Dover Castle, guaranteed to impress any Emperor, no matter how much wealth he had. I could put on a show to equal or outdo anyone's, when I chose, and of course I chose to do it at this time.

Then we sailed for France and the Big Event.

We had some 'moments', didn't we? I mean, there we were, all ships and arms and enmity, there was France, directed by Francis, all ships and arms and enmity, confronting each other in the Channel. One false move and we would have been at war and what a disaster that would have been for England! But we were kind, we were diplomatic, we landed, we made a ceremonial meeting at a point indicated by a spear in the ground, I hugged the king of France – much as it caused me inner turmoil to do it – got off my horse and we did it again, just to add to my inner turmoil. I swear I saw Katherine laughing behind her fan when I returned to her side. She knew how I felt about the King of France.

We had two weeks, not two days, of jousting and wrestling. Mostly jousting, which we all loved. One day the wind was too high for a joust so a wrestling match was set up. Francis said he knew of my prowess as a wrestler and wanted to test my ability. So we did. Oh but it was good! He threw me once and I immediately got my revenge, to great applause. I saw Katherine standing up and applauding me. Clever woman, she knew well what I liked best, adulation first foremost and always.

Two weeks of dancing, singing, jousting, riding, eating strange food, eating English food and pressing it on the French so they would admit we too could cook. They did admit it but how much of that was real and how much was 'let's keep the English happy' is anyone's guess. I could not read them, they had closed faces for the most part, Francis most of all. He was almost impossible to deal with; he was so closed in his mind and his words. I was used to 'reading' people and there I could not. It irked me.

We rode, we ate, we sang, we danced and at the end of it a massive reconciliation and a promise of lifelong friendship and love. I loved it, every last moment of it, every part of the ceremonial, the jousts, the music and the dancing, the discussions, the drinking and the eating. I loved it. I relive it many times in my mind for it was the most splendid of occasions and one never to be seen again. Oh, the spectacular set pieces of your Olympics' opening and closing ceremonies, yes, they are expensively extreme and wonderful to behold but they are done with modern technology. The Field of the Cloth of Gold had no technology but the skill and the hard work of the partisans who were commissioned to arrange it and build it and take part it in and serve us whilst we were there. And then the sailors who brought us all back home again. It was an event like no other and never will be again.

It was two years before we were at war with one another again.

Was it worth it, you ask me? Yes, at the time it was, for the peace was needed and the display of English power and wealth was needed for me to be able to walk the European stage of politics and make my presence known.

I grant that the Field of the Cloth of Gold was a masterpiece of coordination on Wolsey's part, he must have had endless sleepless nights working out every last detail, including the gold trapped mule he rode and his 400 crimson clad escort and the massed choirs which sang at the closing of the great ceremony and the bonhomie we generated at that time. But surely, forgive me if I am wrong here, that is the job of someone who is employed, rather than the employer himself? I asked him – and we all know a royal 'ask' is the equivalent of an order – to arrange the ceremonial and he did. It was good and I am glad I can say this.

And that is the last you will hear of politics for a while.

Apart from my receiving the Defender of the Faith title, that is. That made me feel rather good and crushed Wolsey for a while. He thought he deserved it. Poor man. Poor deluded man. I did not ask him to write a book defending the faith, to labour long over texts and philosophical discussions and put it together, did I? No, I did that. Henry himself. Author of a bestselling piece of theological discussion. I earned that title.

Wolsey was working hard, but in the wrong direction, to raise money to replace that which I was spending. The problem was, I needed money for the palaces, the lifestyle, the hangers-on in the court, the army, the navy … you name it I needed money for it. But demanding was not the way, as Wolsey found out, because it provoked resistance and that meant rebellion. He tried all sorts of ways to get money, some of which Parliament rejected, some of which I rejected.

Fact: Wolsey constantly wanted money to replace what I was spending, but Parliament fought back, granting him very little. Eventually a compromise was sought whereby he asked for a levy of four shillings in the pound, Parliament agreed to half of this and arranged for it to be spread out over the years to come, to ease the burden.

Wolsey ignored this, which was a bit – stupid? He sent out commissioners to raise the levy from all men of property. So what did they do? Rebel. Wouldn't you have done the same? It had not been ratified by Parliament. I could see Trouble brewing, knew Wolsey had overstepped the line quite a bit, so I made my move. I publicly said I knew nothing of this Act, which was partly true. I rescinded it, pardoned all who refused to pay, put Wolsey in a position where no one believed a word he said. He should have learned long, long before you Do Not Mess With Henry when it comes to his people.

But that was not the downfall of the great cardinal. That came later.

Did I grow tired of Katherine? That is the question so many ask. I think 'grow tired' is the wrong phrase. You know how it is, marriages founder after a certain period of time because of familiarity, of a lessening of ardour between the two people bound in the partnership. There's a sense of boredom, almost. I am being truthful, Katherine, as it appears to me. Others may see it differently. That I cannot say, cannot comment on. You asked me how I felt – this is how I felt. Katherine had not changed with the fashions of the court; she wore her Spanish dress, her Spanish head-dress and began to show her age. I know now, on reflection, that it was the endless pregnancies which aged her for each had taken its toll of her physically and the loss of the children had taken their toll of her emotionally which added to her 'ageing' process. I saw other, younger, prettier women around the court, all flirting with fans and sleeves, with bodies that summoned and eyes that promised, mouths that invited and – need I go on? I almost added the obvious but decided against it. You know full well, my reader, what my next words would have been.

Above and beyond all that inviting flesh, I still longed for that nursery full of children.

Somehow, somewhere in the dark hours, I began to think of putting Katherine aside. For me it was a terrifying and terrible thought at first, for I had not been brought up to think of marriage as being impermanent. I knew my parents were a political marriage but they stayed together. There was I, alone, lonely, thinking thoughts which no monarch should think. But they persisted and I began to be swayed by my own arguments, as in, I needed an heir, I needed a consort who would look the part, I needed – dare I admit it to myself even then – a change. No, that is a lie, I wanted a change. I did not need it for Katherine could have remained my queen to the end of her or my life without any problems at all. Outside of those which plagued us, lack of living children, my desire to save her further agonies of childbirth, her knowing I was not the same toward her as I had been, Katherine, this hurts to write so I know it is something I needed to say. I am glad we took time to begin this second revision, for the reader's information, this was added as went through the book for the second time, for it took me that long to find the courage to say these things. They needed to be said, for nowhere in the books does it explain why I began the thought. You see, all you historians and others out there who think they know me, I began thinking about this long before Anne Boleyn walked into my life. I knew there were other women, more appealing, possibly more fertile, definitely more interesting to me at that time, I could elevate to the status of my queen. So, don't be carried away with the thought I needed freedom just because of the Boleyn pressure. It was there before that. Nothing happens overnight. No situation erupts overnight. Everything has its roots in the past, near, or not so near. You can always trace the thought process to a much earlier time.

So when did the religious aspect come in?

Somewhere in the sleepless nights, when I contemplated my future which was childless apart from Mary who was growing fast, I have to say and becoming a lovely princess. And in the endless nights, I thought on the Biblical exhortation that you do not lie with your brother's wife. Yes, I knew well it meant not in an adulterous way but it was a thought which grew and grew until it became an obsession. Katherine could not carry more than one child to the end of the pregnancy and have that child live. All the others died or did not live. Was that God's Will being imposed on mine? Did He disapprove of the union? Was it just nature that denied me my children or the wrath of God? None could tell me, they argued this way and that and they argued with one eye on pleasing me whilst maintaining their stance. Everything anyone did or said was coloured by the need to please me. Few would stand against me.

Lost in this maelstrom of righteous thought, upset and unfulfilled lust – Katherine asked me to be honest! - Mary Boleyn crossed my path, my life, my bed.

To this day I am not entirely sure if it was manoeuvred or whether it was accidental. I tend toward the former, as the Boleyns were a conniving striving cunning bunch – and I don't say that lightly, for most of the court was a conniving striving cunning bunch, it is the nature of the beast. I fell for her in a sort of lustful way and we were lovers for some time.

One relationship was ending. I arranged for the delicious Bessie Blount to be removed to the country, out of sight, out of mind. She had a son to bring up and I did not want him brought up in court where names were mentioned and gossips abounded and evil could come to those who were least expecting it. Mary Boleyn filled the gap, as it were. A beautiful young lady, full of vitality and promise. She was everything poor Katherine was no longer, if you see what I mean.

My Queen was ageing and not moving forward with her wardrobe of clothes. Mary Boleyn was young, energetic, up to date with her fashion sense and very willing. How much was an act and how much was real affection for me is anyone's guess even now. I learned early on that pleasing me came first, genuine feelings came second. I had a good time…

There was avarice in the eyes of the Boleyn family as they fawned around me at that time. Avarice and pure unadulterated hunger for power. But I ignored that for the affection I thought I saw and the warmth I know I felt – you cannot fake that! – and the comfort I thought I received. Maybe I did, who can say after all this time? The fact she became pregnant was a bonus. I had begun to think there was something wrong with me. Her pregnancy proved it was not my fault but unfortunately that pushed me even further from Katherine. I could - and did - blame her for the failed pregnancies and that did not help.

So there we were. Mary Boleyn was lording it over my court, taking my fancy, indulging in my favours, and me in hers, I hasten to add, with the Boleyns all but rubbing their hands together in great glee.

Then Anne arrived from France, to find Mary the court favourite, everyone's friend, as everyone is when they are in favour with the King.

Then Anne arrived and my world was thrown into total confusion.

In truth, I fell in lust instantly.

Chapter Fifteen - Anne Boleyn

What is it that imbues a person to the point when imperfections of facial bones or the occasional beauty spot or perhaps too long a neck or whatever can be overlooked and the whole become something utterly desirable and beautiful in the eye of the beholder? Is it an innate sexuality, is it a sense of radiance, is it – does anyone really know? Throughout the ages there have been women who have captivated men and if we men were to dissect their looks, their bodies, we would wonder what we saw in them. But taken overall, with their mannerisms, their demeanour, everything, they become perfection and are much sought after. I knew Anne Boleyn was sought after, outside of myself, that is. I saw it with the courtiers and hangers-on who were still there, despite my efforts to remove them. I saw how they followed her around, how they hung on her every word, her every gesture, ran to do her every bidding in a way that they never did with her sister Mary.

Was she beautiful? To me she was and to others too, from what I overheard and was told, but I think it was as much the aura of her as her looks.

Did she have six fingers on one hand? No.

Was she magical in bed? We will get to that in due course.

Did she practice witchcraft? No. She was foolish, unfaithful, greedy, demanding and ever enchanting to the very last.

Did I believe the stories of her adultery? Of course. Do you think me that much of a tyrant I would put someone to death without good cause? Maybe you do. Those of you who consider me a despot will say I tired of her and concocted the charges. Not true. I did not tire of her, but she of me. She sought escape from me in other's arms. The fact she did not present me with a son but another daughter is neither here nor there. By that time I was becoming used to the idea that there may not be a son to inherit.

From the moment Anne arrived Mary Boleyn did not exist for me. Pregnant or not, she was not the person I wanted in my life. She paled into insignificance alongside the startlingly exotic – and erotic – Anne. She had the aura of the French court about her; she was desirable in a way no woman had been to me for years. If anyone had told me that I would make a fool of myself over some chit of a girl fresh in from France when I was enamoured of poor Mary who has since been labelled – unfairly – 'the other Boleyn girl', I would not have believed them. I would have laughed in their faces and denied them a place at court had they persisted in the notion. Courtiers who pandered to me talked of Anne's beauty and desirability. Those who wanted the Boleyns out of court tried to say she was not all she appeared to be but I ignored them. Love/lust is blind when the object of desire is there, in front of you, able to dance with you, feast with you, walk with you in the gardens, delight with their smile, their perfume, their dress, their aura, their very being. Mary had her turn in the limelight; it was Anne's turn. The Boleyns, the men who contrived all this, cared not for the feelings of the women, one or the other, either way they had my attention and strove for honours for themselves at cost of the women's feelings and – eventually – their lives.

Outside of that, I told Anne I wanted her for my lover. I even used the word mistress, I do believe. She was clear in her response; she would not allow me to bed her unless it was within the sanctity of marriage. She had the nerve, the unbelievable cheek, to say not all Boleyns were the same, some had higher aspirations than others and she was not prepared to be just another on my list of paramours.

We argued, I could say we fought, even. I told her I loved her, she said if I did I would find a way to marry her. I demanded to know if she loved me in return. She said she did but that was not a good reason to leap into my bed. We walked and talked as if lovers for the world to see, but within our chambers we fought for she would not give way to me and my desire was overwhelming. It was ever present, ever painful, if you understand my meaning. I sought solace with others, I had to! Others benefited from that which she would not have, would not receive. It was hard to understand. I had a wife, a Queen, I had paramours, everyone expected that and it was something I enjoyed, why did Anne hold out for a position above that which she was entitled to – unless the Boleyn men were at the back of it? I was then slim, handsome, healthy – no bad legs then – strong enough to hunt all day and joust all day and eat and drink and fornicate all evening without feeling a bit tired. There, is that honest enough for your readers, Katherine, do you think? I went ahead and said it, didn't I? But not, I have to say, as often as some people like to make out. This business of my having a different woman every night to the detriment of the love life of my wives, is just nonsense. Plenty of women, yes, one every night, no. I know I have said it before, I have to repeat it. When it is flaunted in front of you, openly, coyly, surreptitiously, blatantly, every way you can think of and still be decorous – just – do you expect a red blooded male to turn away and ignore what is offered on the plate of silk sheets, as it were? As king it was there for me, as king I was not going to turn it down. But there were nights I went to my bed alone because that is what I wanted, to be alone, to toss and turn and use the whole bed as I wanted, to stretch out, to roll around if I so desired, to thump pillows if I so desired without bothering someone. And at times I did not sleep but laid awake and stared at the ceiling or the hangings and thought my thoughts and planned my plans and schemed my schemes and then none, no one, knew of my thoughts and my plans and my schemes so that when they were sprung everyone was taken by surprise. I loved doing that.

Katherine has asked me about my Fool, Will Somers. She has been scrolling back and forth through these chapters to find the right place in which to talk of that crazy man who became a most loyal and most outrageous and most difficult of friends I ever had. He came at a time when I was in the process of losing Mary and gaining Anne, a time when court was divided, some following the Mary declining star, those who could not see the writing on the wall, others who were following the Anne rising star, who could read their monarch correctly and see the writing not so much on the wall as writ clear across the firmament. Will came as a poor creature with the sharpest of wits and the most delicious sense of humour imaginable. Mischievous does not really describe it; he was a Fool to his bones, although I have told this Katherine I could have been a better Fool than he, were it possible. I did act as Lord of Misrule one Christmas and loved every moment of it. But then again, thinking on it, I knew the people around me better than he did and could puncture their pomposity with a word or two where he had to work at it. Charles loved him, James was not so sure. Others eyed him with great suspicion for he had an ability to see through their posing and go to the heart of the matter with a few well-chosen comments or a bawdy song if they were engaged in a new affair. It was as if he was not there and then he was there and completely at home in the court. I paid for new clothes for him, gave him a small allowance, granted him a high place at table, all for the love of a crazy young man who later became my most devoted servant. How much of that did I see in him all those years earlier? I do not know now, I just knew I had to have him with me. He comforted me when Anne left for then I needed comforting.

You see, Anne left court. She removed herself to Hever Castle, some distance away, some long travelling time away. She did not write or send me any messages. I wrote endless letters, yes, me! Katherine has read some of them in the book she found. Letters expressing undying love and heartache that she was not with me. She would not capitulate. She did not want to be my lover. She wanted to be my wife. I raged and stormed and demanded and knew all the time that she would win. I wanted her and there was no cost too costly to pay for her, as it were. The fact was simple. She wanted to be Queen.

How Katherine must have suffered at that time! I was told she paced the floor of her chamber, her ladies in attendance, patient, understanding ladies, with her declaiming – demanding more like: "why does he want her and not me?" and in every step she took was suffering, deep painful heart-breaking suffering. For the answer was clear to her then as it would be were I to do the same thing in this time: Anne was young, beautiful, erotic and desirable. She had grown older, aged through pregnancy and the passing of years and clung still to her Spanish roots. She knew I had grown weary of Katherine, she in turn knew the truth, that the marriage was to all intents and purposes ended, but she clung on with the great love she had for me, the one which was bigger than I ever conceived or realised.

And how much there was for her to mourn! There I was, besotted with a slip of a girl, of younger years but greater cunning than she ever possessed. I was busy with plans to promote my love-child by Bessie Blount to the role of heir to the throne, giving him titles and status. She knew it, she agreed to it, reluctantly for it set aside the child we had together but oh, he was so like me! In looks, in stature, in nature, he would have been a perfect

Henry IX. What games does Fate play with our lives that it did not happen!

I confess now, with sadness, I never gave her feelings a passing thought. I was busy with diplomacy, with politics, with longings and with plans. She was kind enough to agree to the promotion of my son but she must have fumed and burned inside with anger and sadness for our daughter Mary. Our one living child being put to one side in favour of a love-child. Why did I not see this at the time? Did the minx cast that much of a spell on me? Was I so jaded already with life that I could not see further than the face, the figure, the sensuality and the liveliness of Anne Boleyn? Even now, these hundreds of years on, I find it hard to sort out my feelings.

I have heard Katherine say to people that everyone has one great love in their life, one burning, all consuming, all powerful and blinding love. It ends as quickly as it comes but whilst it is there, no sense, no reason, no understanding can get through. I know she has endured this herself. I believe that to be what happened when I first saw Anne Boleyn. All reason went out of the window. All sense fled. I had to have her and if it had to be on her terms, so be it. The feelings I had were as Katherine described, a burning, blinding, all-consuming love that knew no sense, no reason. It came like a bolt from the blue, a lightning flash, a thunderbolt. I was with Mary, I thought I loved Mary, she was lively, pretty, willing and obedient. I thought I was happy. Then Anne walked in and everything I had turned to dust in the light of her flaming personality and – let me be honest – challenge.

I do not think she realised it at first. She was herself, she was Anne, the magnet, the beautiful dragonfly that flitted hither and thither and everyone followed, besotted. Courtiers swore they would die rather than allow her to go to another person, they vied with one another for the wildest compliments, the most outrageous demands, all of which she blithely ignored. For when she looked at me, it was as if no one else existed.

But – I was deluded, so very deluded. I took the look as one of love. It was one of avarice, ambition and power hungry – I run out of words. I have no more words. I know what I thought was love was not so. It was on my part; it was not on hers.

And so, in that time, we had the following situation:

I was married and did not wish to be.

Anne was eluding my bed and seeking Katherine's crown.

Wolsey was trying to cover all my requirements and stay on the right side of me, for therein lay his wealth and his power – again Katherine's slip of the fingers actually created a truth which she rectified. She typed 'and his poser' and she was right. Wolsey posed as a great statesman but Wolsey was, deep down, only interested in Wolsey and he forgot one thing: you do not make yourself greater than your king. It was only a matter of time before the Boleyns contrived to bring him down. Part of it was his own fault, his arrogance, his belief that he was all but impregnable in his position as my chief counsellor. This proved to be wrong and in his disbelief he was furious as he was cast down from his own pedestal. And, to complete the scenario, the Boleyns were busy with their own power hungry schemes.

I sought to create a legitimate male heir for the throne. I cast Princess Mary aside, much as I had come to care for my one living legitimate child; I could not see her as monarch.

And so I sought to have a change of wife, the only way I could see to get Anne into my bed and into my life. And so the great wheels were set in motion.

All those secret midnight dark hour thoughts returned full blown, worked on in the deepest recesses of my mind, awaiting only the spark to revive them. Anne provided the spark.

I revived, to my shame now, the theological arguments of lying with a brother's wife. I drew up many papers; I set many to work on the question of annulment. I worked at it ceaselessly and still Anne taunted and teased and held me at a distance until I was quite beside myself with rage, impotence and desire. Rage that she should keep me dancing like that, impotence that I was not free to do anything about it without involving the Vatican and all that entailed and desire because -

It has been said by many people that I remained celibate for the six years it took to free myself of Katherine and the Holy Roman Church and marry Anne. I say, if they want to think that, then let them go ahead and think it. Of course I wasn't celibate! Would you think that someone who had his pick of the women of the land, who had been tumbled and rumbled and rumpled and held and loved by beautiful women, including Anne's own sister, could decide that 'one on one' and that one wearing a crown, would do? There are ways and there are means and I used all of them to find the women and the time and the solitude and have my way with them and go back to my bed satisfied and content that I could go on with my fight for what I perceived as freedom.

And now back to the main narrative.

Wolsey thought he owned me. I need to say this because it is true. He thought he could confuse and distract me by getting me to sign papers without reading the words so he could carry out his own plans. I used to but then I stopped doing it. I know the world believes that he was cast down because Anne and the Boleyns wanted him out of the power base that was court. I know they despised him because he ended up breaking the marriage proposed between Anne and Percy. I know that was the man she loved more than anyone in this life. I also knew that the Boleyns were power hungry and desperate and would put any of their women in my path and my bed if they thought it would promote their fortunes. I realise now that it was their ploy to make Anne hold out for a crown, rather than settle for a tumble and a precarious position as my lover rather than my wife. I was too blind with lust at the time to see it, I have to admit.

How much did Anne want the crown? That's the question I often asked myself. To be Queen is the ultimate accolade for any woman, it means she has captured the heart and mind of the king. The King is all-powerful in the land. The Queen is the second most powerful person in the land. Did she want it at the cost of her marriage to Percy? It would seem so. Did she want it so much that she was prepared to risk her happiness and her health to get it? It looked very much that way.

But the equation – as far as Wolsey was concerned - looked like this.

The Boleyns wanted power.

Anne wanted Percy.

Wolsey stopped it.

Reasons are vague, motives are vague, emotions were running wild at the time. I never got the truth from Wolsey about this, he disseminated, he flustered, he mumbled. I put it down to a long running feud between the Boleyns and Wolsey. I know he resented their influence in court, I know too he did not want me to marry her no matter what. Does he think I didn't know he sought to use her to distract me, help me get the divorce and then divert me into a dynastic marriage with some European princess? I heard rumours of being tied to the sister-in-law of Francis I. Wolsey played a lot of double dealing games. This was just one of them. Like many of the other games he played, it failed. He under estimated my total obsession with the chit of a girl who ran rings around everyone in court.

The odd thing is, and I do find this odd, if Anne had married Percy, she could not have become Queen and the Boleyns were set on the highest goal of all, the crown. So, Wolsey stopping her marriage to Percy would surely have suited the Boleyns. Am I not right? So why then did they so take against him and conspire to bring him down? Did they just want part of his riches and his position? Possibly. As for Anne, she wanted retribution, dire revenge; when we were together she spoke often of his influence, his shortcomings, his inability to arrange that which I needed, an annulment. I saw past the rant to the unbridled need to shift him from power and for the family to have its own way. Gaining her wish to become queen would mean she could exact her retribution in the perfect way, one that cast no aspersions on her.

Anne believed that her influence made me begin to sideline Wolsey. In part she was right but there is also the small point that I had my own reasons for wanting to limit Wolsey's power in my court, in my affairs and in my life. I was, after a very long time, ready to take all affairs into my own hands. I had the distinct feeling that I was not going to win the battle with the Pope over the annulment, that I would have to do something drastic to get my way and I was determined to get my way. That meant, literally, dropping everyone out of my sphere of influence and taking my own decisions, at least for a while. As I said, Wolsey had not taken my relationship with Anne anywhere near seriously enough for my liking. Was he so incapable of seeing the difference between a mere dalliance and a possible marriage? Did he think I was exploring the theological problems for the sake of my health? Did he not see the intensity of my feelings for her? Was the man so blinkered that he could not see undiluted desire and love? If my Katherine in this time is right, and I do believe she is when she speaks of the One Great Love we all have, then it must have radiated from me. I believe it did, for the amount of letters which passed from me to Anne outdid the ones which passed from Anne to me. Ever did she keep me dangling, hanging, attached to her by a silken rope and held it just tight enough that I did not feel trapped, but merely caught. For me it was a convenient thing that she wished to remove Wolsey as it accorded with my own wishes. How few historians have seen that, how few historians – if any - have seen further than the fact I appeared to dance to the tune the Boleyns played!

It is easier to sideline a great man than many think. Wolsey had enjoyed immediate and instant access to me at all times. That stopped. I allowed him to come at a time that suited me or Anne or both of us. It shook him quite a bit and I had to contend with a lot of bluster and protestations and promises of this and that. I'm good at letting that bounce off me, even though I wasn't that big in the body then. I was big in strength and personality and little got through to me that I didn't want to get through to me. Outside of the Boleyns, of course, accursed family!

I wonder if your medical people know the meaning of the word 'pandemic'? I mean, the true meaning of the word. Seems to me, from my perspective, they do panic over the merest sniffle and chill. I would advise them, no, more than that, give a royal order to them, to read their history books and consider the plague. Now if that was raging through your towns and cities, they would have reason to mention the word and stockpile coffins and the like. Instead they tend to dramatise the smallest thing and make it horrific. I am bemused by this whilst wondering if they have an ulterior motive, such as selling their dreadful drugs and holding down their highly-paid positions. I am being cynical, I know.

I understand from Katherine and the books she reads that in your time you have no idea what the sweating sickness was – medically that is. It seemed to come from nowhere, sweeping through towns, villages and cities alike. It was devastating and no respecter of rank or station in life. From sickness to death in a few hours is a dramatic illness and it seemed to spread like a fire through tinder dry thatched cottages. Was it in the air, in the water, transferred by touch? No one knew. Each time it arrived, like a gale sweeping through England, I was constantly assessed for feeling apprehensive, for shivers, for giddiness and pains anywhere, especially head and shoulders, and exhaustion. Then, apparently, the sweating would start and a great need for sleep. If you fell asleep you did not wake.

The great God knows I had read enough about the Black Death to fear that coming anywhere near me. Despite it not being in England for some time, I checked myself often for the bulbous growths that signalled its onset. With the Black Death, I could have called a doctor and been treated – for a while. I knew that was a terminal one, like it or not and I feared it so much.

With this illness there was no escape and no cure. No time even to consult a doctor and make plans for the future. I had visions, nightmares, of being in one of my palaces with the shivers and the sweating and no doctor to be found. Foolish, I know, for my physicians travelled with me everywhere. My orders. I was afraid of illness and even more afraid of death. I make no secret of that – now. Then I just said I feared the illness for England needed her head of state and I had much living to do. When the reports came in that another epidemic had struck, I panicked. A king can control most things, his country – to a certain extent anyway –

his parliament, same applies – but his health is beyond his control, if it is something outside the skills and knowledge of the practitioners. This was proved by the ulcerated leg I suffered later in life. None of them had a cure for it, not a one. The Lord God knows I tried enough cures and none of them worked. Some made me ill, some made the sores worse. What good are doctors, I ask you…

So, when the sickness came yet again, I left London. I did this anyway, fearing the epidemic every summer, but this time Anne was ill and I ran. Literally. Gathered everything and everyone up that I needed and I escaped London and went into the country as fast as I could. I wrote regularly to Anne but I stayed away, a long, long way away.

Does that prove I did not love her? When you love some with heart and soul, body and mind, surely you do not run from them, no matter who you are. You stay with them for comfort and consolation. You do not leave as fast as it can be arranged. But I did. It speaks volumes about my feelings, does it not?

Should I talk about my panic? The Masses I heard daily, the confession I attended often, the potions I endured? Some of them made me sick and caused a greater panic for I was sure the sickness had begun. The letters I wrote to Anne to assure her of my love but asking her to keep away until she was well showed that panic, if you look closely at the words … looking back I am ashamed at some of my actions but ask you to see them for what they were, the panicking of a king who could not be taken ill to the point of death with so much left undone! In particular, as I mentioned earlier, why did I think going to Mass more often would ward off the sickness? Foolish thought! Foolish person! As if God would put a protective cloak around only me and save me from the illness if He wanted me to go home to Him! Actually, if you think about it…

If He had, the course of history from my reign onward would have been vastly different. You would have had Henry IX and where would that have taken English history…

But this fear of illness, of something unclean invading my body, goes back a long way, as I said earlier. This panic on my part was no more than a manifestation of that long held dread and disgust of all things unclean. That also tells me, apart from the fact I did not love Anne as deeply as I thought I did, that the phobia was very deeply entrenched and there was no way I would overcome it. All is so clear when you look back at your life, isn't it? The clues are there, the pointers are there, it just needed someone to highlight them and all is revealed.

And, again I admit to shame, I never gave Queen Katherine a thought. I was too busy being besotted with a chit of a girl and her power hungry family. I wish I had been able to see then with the clear vision that I have now.

Taking that then as read, the fact I disregarded her completely, left her to her own devices and unhappiness, Wolsey and I awaited the decision of the Vatican and the arrival of the Pope's delegate to sort out the problem.

Poor Henry, battling his fears of Death, the survival of his people, the dissolution of his marriage, watching the slow decline of his chief counsellor, waiting on the slow wheels of justice in the Vatican, and they do turn exceedingly slow, meant I was distracted to the point of near insanity. My temper grew ferocious and many were afraid of me.

For me the annulment was everything. I wished to put my queen aside with the minimum of fuss and inconvenience to my reign, to leave me clear to marry Anne Boleyn, clear as in legally and as regards my conscience. I have to admit here that it troubled me a good deal at times, wondering if I really was doing the right thing.

Needless to say, like anything to do with Rome at that time – dare I be controversial here and say nothing has changed? – there were delays, procrastination and downright stupidity. All right, I am being controversial. I would suggest anyone who doesn't like it goes ahead and issues a writ against me. I will accept it provided it is delivered in person.

Let me encapsulate the proposal made to end the problem of my marriage to Katherine. It was suggested she become a nun. We all argued with her about it and I do mean all of us. I saw it as a way out. She countered with the most stunning argument imaginable. She would agree to become a nun if I agreed to become – and remain – a monk. Needless to say it did not work. And could I add, it would not work. Imagine me as a monk … me, who needed women the way some people need ale, food and wine…

I had another problem to contend with, Katherine's popularity with the people and Anne's lack of it. Everyone wanted the beloved Queen Katherine. No one wanted Nan Bullen as Queen, outside of her family and me. It did make life a little difficult.

I'm going to cut a few corners here, just as I cut off a few heads; I'm saying it before you do, reader! I know well the comments made about my tendency to remove people from this life in that way. The truth is, the story of my long drawn out battle against – literally – the Vatican is well known in every quarter. You do not need it recited. You have it there in every book on my life and goodness knows why there are so many. So we will cut the talk of politics and go to why I wanted the divorce, annulment, separation, settlement of the King's Secret Matter which became the King's Great Matter, whichever way you want to label it.

The fanciest of labels does not cover up the fact I wanted two things:

(1) to be free of Katherine, who had become an encumbrance to my life and (2) to bed Anne, whose tempting bosoms and flashing eyes were tormenting me to a degree I did not think possible. Did she love me? I doubt it. Did she do it because she wanted to be Queen? Very likely. Did all this happen because that father of hers put first Mary in my path, my life and my bed and then when Anne returned from France and he knew she had captured my heart and my attentions, pushed her forward? What do you think? I am still undecided how much was one and how much was the other and then I ask myself, in the name of Heaven, does it matter? Truth is, she was there, I wanted her, she wouldn't let me have her without a ring so I stopped England in its tracks, changed direction, assumed the role of Supreme Head of the church, threw the Vatican's considerations out of the palace window and went ahead and married her anyway. I had to. She was carrying my child – she actually capitulated when she knew the crown was hers.

And I found that after all that, her body, her sex, her lips and her arms were not so different from all the others I had bedded before, during and after our wedding. I found that I could have called her any name from Bessie to Mary and it would have made little difference to the love-making.

Was I disappointed? Of course. Did it matter? Not at first. She was attractive and light hearted, a natural flirt, entertaining in many ways, sharp of wit, sharp of mind and very sensual. For a while the novelty kept me distracted.

And I was distracted – for a while.

Chapter Sixteen - Problems

But before we were married … before all that nonsense, I mean, why didn't the damn woman just jump into bed with me when she could … I had a few problems to resolve. Wolsey was one of them. Fighting the Vatican was another. Being injured in sport was another. Becoming somewhat overweight was another. But the legs, oh the thrice-damned legs, were the biggest problem of all. Pain, suppurating sores, more pain and no thrice-damned physician able to do anything about it – there was the true problem. All else I could handle.

It wasn't all pain and suffering and agonising over decisions, though. I was still fit enough to play tennis, at which I won consistently, by the way, despite my friends' best efforts to beat me. They didn't have my tactical skills. I won consistently at bowls too, but there I do believe some of them 'let' me win, especially when things were not good and my temper grew a little – hot?

Bowls. Bowling. Whatever you want to call it. The game is played with several balls. Each person has five. Mine were beautifully crafted from the finest woods with a Tudor rose carved into them. Not that anyone needed to know which was mine, it was those which reached and knocked down the pile of balanced balls at the end. The first ball is thrown as far as possible along the main course of the bowling alley which is very long, by the way. If it doesn't reach the collection of balanced balls at the end and knocks them over, you relinquish your turn to the next person who also tries, but they have to get their ball past yours. Hence they need to either throw it over yours, not very easy, or send it up the side so that it will come down in front of your ball. If they do that, they get a second chance to throw. The ultimate score is the one who knocks down the pile of balls, but failing that, the person who gets the closest to the pile, by whatever means that is achieved, and believe me, with sloping sides to a bowling alley and a bit of expertise with directional throwing, you can use some highly devious methods to get your ball in front of everyone else's. There were intermediate rules and points, pushing another ball out of the way, rolling yours so it touched the other person's ball without moving it, and so on. The one thing you need to know is that as in tennis, the rules were I was not 'allowed' to win, I had to do that myself. Only in the hunt or a wild race, did I become aware that they were holding back to let me be first. In other games I had to win by sheer strength or ability or both. I was proud of my wins and would go to Katherine to boast of the successes. I recall even now her great pleasure in them. Sometimes she came to watch the games, for she delighted in seeing the bowling. Charles was the only person who could really challenge me at the game. The others were good but not as good as he was. He had that additional skill but even so, he didn't beat me. I never caught him actually pulling a throw so as to ensure I won, so I think I won because I was better than he was. I like to think so, anyway.

But the joust was my true love. There I truly excelled.

We learned, all of us, from an early age to wear armour as if it was nothing more than a set of clothes. It wasn't, of course, it was very heavy and very hot. Can I say something here … I am sure I can. The exhibitions to commemorate the 500th anniversary of my Coronation showed some of my armour. Someone measured a suit and said I had a 54" chest, obviously, because of the size of the armour. It was not made clear whether that measurement excluded or included the several inches of padding I wore under the breastplate. Did it? That could make a considerable difference. My tailor swears I never got bigger than 50" chest and he should know, he made enough of my clothes for me. Well, all of them, actually, he was the only one I trusted to make what I wanted and get it right every time.

So, first the linen shirt, then the thick padding for protection, then the amour. Then, with a series of clanking noises and a walk something resembling a duck (no one can be elegant in armour) you make your way to the stalls at the side of the tiltyard and there use a block to mount a horse. You also use a couple of squires who are strong enough to give you a lift. The horse has no say in the matter, it has a solid weight of a man plus armour – a lot of it – on its back. I had a stable of fine horses especially for the joust. I had others, those with more endurance, for the hunt. (Even then I exhausted several horses during a day's hunting. Believe me, no one at the time I lived had as much strength as I did and as much energy as I did. You can dismiss that 'overweight old man' you see in the thrice-damned Holbein portrait. Look at the real me for a change!) Someone hands you the lance, you drop your visor down, peer through the slit and wait for the call. At the other end of the field another knight is doing the same thing, peering at you through the slit in his visor. You can just about see a shape, the man you are riding at, you can't see much of his lance or what his horse is doing. You trust to luck, your own skill and the power of the horse you are riding. You know by the colours who your contestant is. He knows who he is riding against – his king. Imagine the pressure that puts on a knight! He wants to win but at risk to his liege lord. Does he go all out to unseat his opponent? I demanded that they did, I always wanted the joust to be fair and equal.

The call goes out: *'lesses alers'*! You kick your horse with your heels, it starts off at a tremendous speed, launching itself into a gallop and you can just about hear the cheering above the sound of the thundering hooves and the clank of all that metal on the move. You are racing down the side of a high barrier, lance ready, waiting for the right moment to try and knock the other person clear off their horse. If your lance connects, if the other person hasn't skilfully moved aside and missed your thrust, the shock goes down your arm and into your shoulder. It takes a fine horseman to remain seated when that happens. Sometimes it's a glancing blow, you score points rather than a victory, sometimes you miss and he gets you. When it happens, when that lance hits, it's like being hit in the chest by a charging bull. One moment you're racing down the field, the next you're flying through the air and then hitting the ground, hard. All the breath goes out of you, you are weighed down with armour so you land twice as hard as you would do otherwise. You lie there gasping and wondering what it is you missed this time. Your horse has stopped, turned around and is waiting patiently, wondering if you are going to get up and start over again or whether it will go back to its stables and some food. At least, that's how I interpreted the look in the eye of the horses I have managed to lose in mid gallop. It didn't happen very often. When it did, I was not in the best of moods.

Between the moments of charging down the lists and the moment of hitting the other person or the ground there is no time at all. It does not exist. Watching it I see that there is a time when the person flies through the air and you wonder what they are thinking or feeling. In reality you have no time to think anything. You are there, you are on the ground. It's all part of the thrill of jousting.

We knew how to have fun, didn't we? That's when I wasn't dancing, singing, composing, playing musical instruments and eating. And drinking. And...

I got rid of Wolsey in the end, well; he just got in the way, didn't he? We talked much; I admired and cared for the man but in the end ... no. Not even for this book will I disclose that which Wolsey and I discussed at length, or my real reasons for 'disposing' of a problem. I know, I know very well the first thing which will be said is that this is not a true channelled book from the King himself, or he would say what and why. My rejoinder to that is, no, I am not bound to do or say anything I do not wish to. Let me remind you, this is MY book and I will tell it my way. I said earlier, did I not, that politics and power play were to be thrown out of the window and that sex and scandal were to remain? That is where we are going. Well, as far as I can. Damned politics keep creeping back in, though, rather like those women in my bed. I can toss out the women but the politics tend to remain. Not that I did much tossing, you understand…

Wolsey was political.

Riding, hunting, jousting, bedding, these were the sex and scandal activities.

My being injured was my own foolish bravado in the field.

The first ulcer was probably caused by my being a bit overweight but hell and damnation, I did so like my food – and my drink! And by falling in the joust. Stupidly, I allowed someone to outwit me – me who had won every joust up to that moment. I found myself in shock when the sore appeared, it was unclean. You know I had a fanatical thing about being clean. I bathed all the time, much to the horror of those around me, even more so when I insisted they too bathed regularly. As I said earlier, I could not stand body odour of any kind. Katherine knew this, so did the women who crept into my life.

Now that is an odd expression I just used. Where did that come from?

The original Katherine walked into my life as a proud beautiful Spanish princess who became, through the death of my brother, my wife. The others crept into my life, sidling up to me, flashing bits of body and teeth, dancing eyes, yes I know it is a bad expression but forgive me, I am working out something here – so yes, apart from Anne, they all crept into my life. The word was right after all. Go with gut instinct every time, Henry, why dither around with other words when the right one is in front of you all along?

Back to the narrative. The ongoing six year saga that was the dissolution of my marriage to Katherine of Aragon.

Katherine held on to a piece of damning evidence that all but demolished my case against her, the witch! But whilst I fumed and ranted and raved, I admired her tenacity, her royal stance, her dignity. I could not do otherwise.

They organised a hearing to investigate whether she was virgin after her marriage to my brother or nay. I hated the thought she had to talk on such things and was concerned at how she might react, what she might say.

On the day she swept into the room and spoke to me direct, at my feet, with all her impassioned words and heart and mind poured out to me. I was confounded and struck dumb by her eloquence. Her words, her posture, her stately departure from the room, all shocked me but did not make me change my mind. I could not, I was committed to a course of action which I could not reverse without causing problems and making enemies. Heaven knows I had enough of them already, more would have been what you call overkill. I tried to pretend it hadn't happened, that my Queen hadn't walked in and made me look like some kind of oaf in front of everyone. I tried but it didn't work and everyone knew it didn't work, either.

The crux of the matter was this; I knew full well I was doing wrong in putting Katherine aside. She had been loyal and devoted, she had come to me as an innocent and I had taken the best years of her life and made them mine. Then, because I had seemingly tired of her, I sought to put her to one side. No wonder she was a bit angry with me. She was so much a queen on that day I felt a serious pang of sympathy for her. But… I could not turn back from the course I was set on without losing a good deal of face and no king wants to do that. I was tired of her, I wanted a new queen, one who could give me sons and daughters, preferably in that order, one who could dance and sing and entertain me in bed with new tricks and generally make me feel like a new man. So I could not bring myself to reverse my decision to send her and the Princess she gave birth to away from Hampton Court and into apartments at Greenwich. It was a demotion, whichever way you looked at it and I knew she would hate it. Right then I didn't care. Her regal attitude, her ringing denouncement of me as her king and her stance that she was legally and truly mine, had almost had the opposite effect she must have hoped for. I felt affronted, hurt, shamed, a whole gamut of emotions. Underneath the robes, I was just a man. I hate to admit that, but it is true. And men get hurt very easily when their egos are damaged. She damaged that which I relied on so much, the royal 'face'.

I put Anne in the royal apartments at Hampton Court in her place. If I thought it would soften Anne to allow me into her bed, I was sadly mistaken. The whole thing was a disaster from start to finish. Katherine had her supporters, more than I had at that time. I felt disgraced by the whole thing. I felt diminished. For a man with my ego, it was awful. My favourites, my friends, my courtiers, took the worst of my temper at that time. It says much of their loyalty to me that they did not walk out.

Sometimes, alone in my room at my prayers, I wondered if it was possible for one man to make so many mistakes and still retain his position as revered monarch. I would ask myself if it was only the fact I wore a metaphorical crown all the time that let me treat people so and still retain their service.

Six years. Six long years to get a divorce. It was an endless time, a boring time, which is why I went ahead and dissolved a few monasteries, see what Anne would have staved off had she submitted? I got rid of a few people, wrote my book – now that would not have been written if I had been otherwise occupied, of a surety, so that was one good thing which came out of it – I spent time with Will, my Fool, and learned how good a friend he really was to me and I mourned the fact the One True Love was not mine.

Now the question is, would I have seen through her act and discovered her infidelities sooner if I had been with her from the start or she with me? The answer is most definitely yes. I feel that in some ways I wasted those six years but in other ways, yes, things were done which had to be done – as far as I was concerned, anyway. Had I been playing 'happy husband' maybe they would have been delayed a few years. Truth to tell, though, I would have dissolved the monasteries at some point, regardless of marital difficulties and best-selling books.

Back to politics, even though I said I wouldn't, unfortunately I have to, because I need to mention the man who played such a large part in my life, Thomas More.

Thomas More was political but oh, he became a very big part of my life. I loved the man. Complete unconditional love. Never had I met anyone like him. Calm, quiet, sensible, learned, unruffled, how many words can you use to describe someone like him and how many words can you use to explain why an idiot, a pathetic drooling stupid idiot like me had him put to death in the end? No, let me not consider it yet. There is much ground to cover and things I need to say before then. But that is there because I want the readers to know that despite my refusing to discuss my conversations and decisions with Wolsey for all to know and pick over and snigger at and talk about behind my back, I am prepared to admit my shortcomings, few though they are. Thomas More's execution was one enormous mistake on my part. Having committed myself to the order, it would have meant too much loss of face to draw back. To rescind a royal decision would show weakness. I had no intention of doing that. I lost enough face going to Rome when ordered. I decided then, never again. Never. Ever. Again.

Wolsey had gone. All who were seconded to help him were headless chickens, sorry, bad metaphor. I did not ask Thomas More to take on the task of freeing me from my Queen; it was against his conscience. I knew it and I respected it.

So I did what I should have done from the start. Took control myself. That was when, in a burst of blinding clarity, caused by one night's stargazing – you did know I was an astronomer, didn't you, dear reader? If you didn't, let me assure you it was yet another of my passions, of which I had plenty – that I should simply rid myself of the yoke of the Roman Church and take over the church myself. An English church, beholden to none but the Supreme Head, me. I wondered, even as I reeled with the shock of that sudden explosive idea, why the hell I had not thought of it earlier, like six years earlier. I could have avoided all that back and forth with Campeggio, that doddering old fool who tried every delaying tactic in the book to get me to change my mind. I could have avoided all the arguments, the travelling, the humiliation of being summoned to Rome and lectured, I could have wedded and bedded Anne long before that time and found out sooner that it was not what I thought or hoped it would be.

What in the name of Heaven did I think it would be? All women are built the same. And a man joins with them in the same way. What did I think would be different?

I thought she might know some new erotic tricks. I thought she might have some magic for someone becoming a little jaded, for I admit I was by then. I thought she would be more courtesan than wife. If she was, it was not with me. And therein lay the seeds of her downfall. For I saw in her demeanour a flirt, a taunting dancing flirt. I thought, believed, entrusted my reign to the illusion that I would have a queen who would make me feel like a new man.

There comes a point when I need to decide how many bedroom secrets to reveal to the world. How much sex and scandal can you put into a book? How much should a proud monarch reveal? No question marks there, for they are statements, not questions.

For the moment let me talk about The Defence of the Seven Sacraments. The best-selling book of the 16th century. How many editions did it go to? Twenty or more? I spent hours, days, weeks, months, writing that out.

I did it for two reasons.

The first is that I wished to disprove the Lutherian heresy. Despite my break with Rome, I remained a Catholic in all but name. I despised the heresy being broadcast and the inept way some clerics were dealing with it. I felt their theology was at fault.

Now who was I to tell a cleric their theology was a fault? I have to say I could, for I studied theology at length when my father decided I was destined for the church, before my brother Arthur died so unfortunately. I studied long and hard during my year of imprisonment, heaven knows there was little else to do when confined to one room. I continued my studies, my discussions, my deep conversations, with many people, including Wolsey. I knew a good deal. But still it meant time going through books and papers to present the facts to the world. And the world, as I knew it then, was enraptured with the work. It was all the compensation I needed for the time spent working on it. As with wealth, gold, jewels, anything that added to my standing, my persona, compliments, accolades, even arguments over what I had written were good, were welcome, were absorbed and I grew a few inches taller as much as I grew a few inches wider.

The Pope endorsed it. The Pope awarded me the title 'Defender of the Faith.' The thrill that went through me when the Papal document arrived giving me that title has never been capped. It was indescribable. It lasted for days. My face ached from smiling, my mind ached from considering it over and over and my eyes ached from constantly reading it. That title has stayed on the coinage of England to this day. What other monarch can say he gave such a lasting and important legacy to his country?

But then I became bored. A bored monarch seeks new thoughts. Was I that bored? Yes. And so ... I had new thoughts on the church, how to reform it, how to organise it, how to stop it breeding money and conspiracy and back-stabbing priests. I knew they were there and it was time for something radical to happen. I was that something radical. I could see it in my mind's eye and I knew it in my blood and my gut that it was my turn to do something, really do something, to – all right, partly to fight back against the recalcitrant Roman church who refused to see sense on my annulment or divorce, whatever way was the legal way to separate me from Katherine and partly because it was time the whole system was shaken up, from top to toe, from flower to root, from roof to foundations.

I sent men to check into the Vatican archives for evidence, solid written verifiable evidence, that the king of England was truly independent. I knew I was, I knew the throne of England was independent of all others, but Rome and the world needed proof. I sent them to find that proof.

Then we launched the charge of praemunire. You pay allegiance to Rome, you defy the king.

It was described as an act of darkness. It was. It had no set clauses; it was open to interpretation – mine - as if anyone else's mattered at that time. And in saying that, I realise I was beginning the slide into despotism without realising it. I took it upon myself to manipulate that Act, to make it work in my favour, because I could and because that was what I wanted. I did not see it at the time. Then it was a natural thing to do, to curb the excesses of the church.

Your history books say I wanted to be known as protector and only supreme head of the English church.

The books are right. It was my clear intention. I had decided that Rome had no authority over me or my clerics and my church. I asked myself why should that not be the way of it, after all, I was king of England and therefore rightly should be head of the church.

And we were six years into the long tussle for freedom. I was fed up, frustrated with the delay, upset with the clerics, annoyed with my advisors and generally out of sorts with the world until Thomas Cromwell appeared on the scene.

Reverting for a moment to my book, the second reason was I wished to be known for more than my hunting, jousting, tennis playing, wrestling, dancing, lyre playing, song composing… I wanted people to know that behind the jovial monarch, with his feasting, dancing, hunting (and everything else) reputation was a man of thought, belief and learning.

I did it. It was a resounding success. Just as this book will be when it reaches the shelves. Just as the people then went to buy, to study and understand my thinking, my reasoning and my theological arguments, so the people will buy this one to read about my thinking, my reasoning and my sexual activities, for I have not forgotten that is also what I am known for in your lifetime. What a reputation has come down to you over the years!

What do you immediately think of when my name is mentioned? My weight, my size, my six wives, my disinclination to suffer fools gladly or at all, my inability to produce an heir to carry on the Tudor line, my spendthrift nature, my dissolution of the monasteries, my disposing of many people in the best way possible, separating their heads from their bodies? That thrice-damned Holbein portrait? Although accurate at the time it was painted, it was not all my life, or all of me. Before the weight crept on I was slim and handsome; I was fit and capable of riding any person into the ground. It was unfortunate that I was also capable of eating and drinking anyone under the table – and did so regularly. That, combined with those thrice-damned legs of mine that later rendered me incapable of moving about very much, meant the weight soon began to gather itself to my waistline.

Which is about where we were. Had Anne succumbed to my desires six years earlier, if I had experienced that blinding moment of clarity six years earlier and thrown off the Roman shackles then, Anne would have benefited from a younger, leaner, more energetic and highly sexed (all right, admitting it, damn it!) man. Instead she inherited one that was bigger, heavier, older, one who tired a lot quicker.

Whose fault was that?

Chapter Seventeen - The Boleyn Era

Whosever fault it was (Katherine hesitated there, wanting to correct the word but it stands, it is grammatically correct, in my opinion) life had to go on.

Katherine has been what she calls revising the earlier pages of this book. I am aware I leapt around a good deal with my thoughts, bringing Anne's pregnancy in earlier than I intended, then going back, then dropping this in and that, but thoughts never progress in a straight line from here to there. We deviate from any given subject in a short time. So … it is very much a question of 'whilst this was going on' or 'where were we?' But I think you, my intelligent discerning reader, can follow this king's thoughts without too many difficulties.

In case though it has been overlooked in the narrative which I have dictated, Anne held out for six years, until the very moment she was sure she had the crown in her sticky little enticing fingers. Then she gave in. And then I realised she could have been any woman. Disappointed? Wouldn't you have been?

Let me jump a few years. I had Cromwell, who thought the way I did, who worked with me on everything that needed to be worked on: my annulment/divorce, the dissolution of monasteries and the great wealth that brought into the Treasury – and me – and the changing of the direction of the church in England. With his help, I got my annulment/divorce.   To this day I am not sure which one it was. All that matters is that I was legally a free man, a single man.

I married pregnant Anne Boleyn.

In short, I broke with Rome to marry this woman, this temptress, this deceiving dancing flirting tormenting creature and I did. The whole path of the English church was changed, diverted, so I could have a new queen. Of such small lusts are great things made. Who would have thought it? Who would have believed I could do such a thing? I did, for a start, but few others did. The Pope and his many advisors did not.

Ha! Resting my case, as it were. Katherine has turned a page in her book and there, confronting me, is the most awful portrait imaginable of William Warham, Archbishop of Canterbury, drawn by Holbein, damn his pencils and inks! I mean, if ever a man had been captured on a bad day … yes he was lugubrious, yes he looked like a churchman but not like that! So now, how much can you take as truthful those portraits of me? Or am I clutching at straws here, Katherine?

If I might divert to something that means a lot to me, just for a time, I would like to tell you about James Worsley, and about falcons and hawks and the Isle of Wight and Appuldurcombe House. I can tell you that Appuldurcombe was a magnificent home, with magnificent tapestries, great hunting, a falconer to be proud of, a kitchen to boast of and a fine stable of good horseflesh for me to ride. As if that were not enough, James was a fine host and had a cellar of good wines. Now, I ask you, could any person want more than that?

I spent many hours in the sunshine hawking with the birds James kept at his home. There is nothing to equal the sight of a bird homing in for the kill, knowing it will return to you when it is done. A truly wild creature still with the killing instinct yet tame enough to sit on a glove, albeit hooded and tethered, but it would return to you of its own free will. A bird is not like a dog, once freed of its tethers it could take off, fly anywhere it wanted, go across the water and find enough prey to live on, but it chooses to stay. That in itself is a miracle. James had fine dogs too, hunters, every one of them. I adored dogs, still do and his pack of hunting dogs were a delight and a pleasure to work with and be with. They seemed to like me, too and as I cared not about muddy paws and dog hairs, they would romp around me and try to climb onto me and I would let them, for the sheer joy of petting them.

I was well aware of the cost of hospitality for myself and my entourage. I knew well that every person I took with me, who had to be there to take care of my every wish, whim and command, needed a place to sleep, bathe, eat and drink. I knew this and took it into consideration every time I decided to go somewhere. Those I liked I visited regularly but not so regularly as to be a burden on their finances. Those I wished to penalise in some way I visited a lot. Simple, isn't it? Do you know, hardly any of them realised what I was doing? They thought they were being honoured! I also have to say that my regular Progress trips around England were as much for the benefit of my household as for the people I visited, it gave them all something to do outside of their day to day work. Was I not the most considerate of monarchs?

Katherine says nothing but gives that smile that says she sees right through my words to the very core of them – that everything I did was self-indulgent and so it should be. What other reason was there for being king, might I ask? Apart from laws and rules and fund raising and making sure we were safe from invasion, enemies and traitors alike, that is.

But returning to Appuldurcombe House for a moment, I liked visiting because apart from anything else, I could socialise with others by travelling out from James' home and I did, visiting this one and that. I did very much enjoy my visits to that blessed island and am very glad and content in my mind that my Katherine lives there; it is good for her to be in such a sublime and beautiful place. Me as some kind of tourist guide and that will not do, so I will cease immediately.

I fear I am rambling quite considerably. In attempting to leap many years it is possible I have confused the reader. For now, let it stand as a narrative and we will ask the clever person who edits my Katherine's books to say if he has lost the thread of my story at this point, in which case I will rework it to suit him and the reading public.

So, shall we return to my history? My life, my thoughts, my wives and my libido?

Briefly, I broke with Rome with the help of Cromwell, declared my marriage invalid and married Anne Boleyn. After six long years we were man and wife. I had a new Queen.

I played 'happy husband' with Anne and told myself I was indeed happy.

It was a lie.

Her pregnancy made me happy, but she did not.

Her Coronation made her happy. It cost me a fortune in bribes and actual outlay, but it did not make the people happy and it was the people of England I cared about. My subjects. They did not like this upstart Queen; they preferred Katherine with her quaint Spanish ways and quiet dignity. Maybe they saw something I didn't in both of them. Maybe I was and am at fault here. I thought they would like a dazzling beauty for a Queen, someone to admire when she went out in all her finery with her ladies and her men-at-arms to guard her. But no.

I wondered what was wrong with her that no one liked her. I felt their attitude affected me, that by association they disliked me, too. Many disliked what I was trying to do with the church, that was made clear.

But – I wanted a male heir. I wanted children! I wanted a nursery full! I wanted a male heir! The thoughts went around and around, trapped inside my head, unable to escape. Everyone knew I wanted that male heir, no one knew I wanted children, any children, just to fulfil the dream I had. I saw other people's children, they ran to me, they played with me. I could play their games, be silly with them, join in the make-believe. I loved them. I wanted my own. Anne was pregnant. Anne would surely give me the heir I craved. After all, I had given her so much, six years of my life, endless negotiations, arguments, theological discussions, money, time, Wolsey's removal, in the name of Heaven, what woman ever had so much? Not to mention the great showy Coronation and all she ever wanted in the way of ostentatious display. Was it enough to guarantee the child I wanted? Of course not. I had to pray and hope. And I did.

Chapter Eighteen - Disappointments.

Anne produced a girl. I did not pace the corridors this time; I did not spend time worrying about what was going on elsewhere, in the birthing chamber. I had every confidence that the page would come and say "Sire, you have a fine son." He didn't. He came and said "Sire, you have a fine daughter."

I know now that it is common knowledge that 'it takes a man to get a girl' and that when there are girls as offspring the man is usually more dominant than the woman. It didn't matter to me then. What mattered was the crushing disappointment at being told I had a healthy living daughter.

My first thought was – I did all that to get what I already had.

Therein lies a sense of cruelty, yes, but can you begin to appreciate or even understand the level of disappointment? My contention, the only thing I had to hold on to at that time, was that she carried to full term, produced a healthy child and that the next one could be, should be, better had be, a son.

My second thought was; I chose the wrong Boleyn after all. I should have stayed with Mary.

The baby was christened without my attendance, without bonfires, without bells and without shouts of acclamation. I wanted a son. I didn't get a son. I got another daughter. Hell and damnation, I was disappointed!

A small aside. Katherine is well used to these by now.

It is a source of great bemusement and – up to now – secret pride to me to know that the daughter I dismissed so cavalierly at that time became a revered monarch in her own right, that she reigned for many, many years, that she had great triumphs and equally great disasters, as we all do, that she surmounted them all and lived out her days as she wanted: unmarried, devoted to her queenship and her country. I wish I had known her better when she was living in my time. I wish very much I had given her more attention, more affection and more respect. It is to be acknowledged that she became a great queen without these things, greater and more respected than her half-sister, of whom I shall not speak at this time – if at all.

The Reformation brought me more problems than I ever anticipated, not even in my darkest hours. I got – trouble.

Among other problems, uprisings, protests, letters and proclamations on this that and everything else, telling me I was wrong, I was damned, I was destined for hell and all the rest of the nonsense, I got the damned Holy Maid of Kent. This nun, I doubt not she was a holy woman, was predicting a villain's death for me should I divorce Katherine and marry Anne. She had devotees around her who swore to the authenticity of some letter or other from heaven that said all this. Total rubbish of course but she was gathering people to her. We discussed her and her beliefs for a whole three days. I do not understand even now why we gave so much time to the foolish woman, but there you are, we had to be seen to be doing the right thing. Personally I wanted her executed as a traitor and heretic and eventually I got my way. Before then she was displayed as a figure of fun, stowed in prison and kept out of sight so her followers lost their impetus and drive and then – gone. Curses I did not want, dissenters I did not want.

Katherine is looking at the section of the book where it is said I wanted to implicate More in the affair, to be rid of him too. It looks from the book as if I wanted to toss everyone aside, have them executed, remove them from my life, because I did not like the way they thought.

The truth is, I did not like the way people thought because it was contravening my thoughts. They cast doubts on what I held to be right.

I believed in the divorce. They didn't.

I wanted freedom from Katherine and they thought it wrong.

I got Cromwell on my side and he rewrote the laws so I was supreme head of the country and the church and to hell with interference from outside our shores and so it was done. And so I was 'free' to marry.

There were those who did not believe I had that right. Were I a reasonable man – which Katherine says I am, now – I would have said, sir, you are entitled to your opinion but mine is the supreme authority here, as king and lord of all so forget your conscience and allow me to live the way I wish to live. I was not a reasonable man. I was in torment. I stamped, raved, ranted, cursed and swore at everyone. I felt my world collapsing around me. I felt as if everything I had done was for nothing. All those wasted years, all that wasted effort, all that politicking and research and decision making and all. I could have stayed with Katherine and ignored the whole damn mess of it, stayed with the one living child and been content.

Being far more belligerent and aggressive then than I am now – Katherine will attest to this truth – that didn't happen. Instead I blustered and flustered and ordered and commanded and people were killed. As I said, the Holy Maid of Kent went to prison, along with her cohorts. The Holy Maid of Kent ended up at Tyburn, along with her cohorts.

I sent Fisher to the Tower. He was an awe-inspiring figure, severe in clothing and lifestyle. He sought no glory but God's. He sought no riches but that given by Heaven. A true priest. A true man of God. He would not sign the papers to say I was right. He stood out against me. At that time I saw all who stood against me as traitors. It was as if I was blind to common sense and logical argument. I wanted my own way. I was king. I wanted everyone to know it.

I sent More to the Tower one day later. A man of conscience, of learning, of intellect and of great emotion. He I trusted but he 'betrayed' me by keeping to his conscience and his understanding and not accepting mine.

I intended to become a king whose word was total law and whose will was to be obeyed - no matter what. I would have it at any cost.

What changed?

There are those who date my 'reign of terror' from the executions of Empson and Dudley. They were wrong. I have said I had good reason to dispose of those two men and I maintain that to this day. I had good reason to dispose of the nun and her cohorts, too, they were festering trouble.

I had 'good' reason to dispose of John Fisher and Thomas More, they did not accord with my thinking. They refused to sign the oath acknowledging my supremacy. Whatever I privately thought, their refusal was heretical and traitorous. I had no option. Allow them to walk free and I would allow every free thinker in the land to challenge my position. I have said I respected Thomas's stance and I did. But … to allow him to continue with that stance would have damaged my autocratic rule and that I could not allow.

Finally that old fool Pope Clement died, not before giving judgement for Katherine and against me. But he never excommunicated me and he never judged me for my actions and I strode around, the proud king, supreme head of all I surveyed. But my two best men were in the Tower and depositions were being created and crafted and petitioners were working hard to ensure that they got out. I was working equally hard to ensure they stayed there until they did what I wanted them to do: agree I was supreme head of the church. As long as they refused, they stayed there - under threat of death. I was the colossus, I was the supreme being; they deferred to me or they did not live to defer to anyone.

Sometimes there is no fool like an old fool. Besotted by a smiling face and tormented by lust, I fell for an unsuitable woman, besotted by a sense of power and supremacy I fell for the blandishments of those who gave me what I wanted and ignored the steadfastness of those who did not give in. I lived to regret both impulses and did for the remainder of my life. There was a hollowness that would not be filled.

But 'saving face' was more important to me than saving lives. I replaced Wolsey with More; I would replace More with someone who would do as much for me. I hadn't realised how much the man had me by the heart.

Katherine, this hurts.

Katherine turned on me a look of pure compassion and said 'I know but you have to talk about it.'

She is, of course, right. I cannot ignore the man and his death and what it did to me. I cannot - but I want to. That is a clumsy sentence but let it stand. I am not going to rewrite it. It says what I felt, what I meant, what I still feel and what I still mean.

The Tower had become a grim place. I had my own chambers there, light, airy, decorated with tapestries and hangings of all kinds. I knew the dungeons were bleak and cold, I knew it virtually condemned someone to death to be sent there. It made no difference to my thinking. I had to be seen to be supreme.

I little thought I would send my queen there. But I did.

But before then, that fool Pope made Fisher a cardinal. Fisher had to die. That meant More had to die, too. No choice. No way out of it. My heartbreak could not and would not come into it. Saving face, maintaining my position, my stance, my authority, was everything. I knew the heartache I would bring More's wife and children and deplored it but endless sleepless nights and hours of prayer – or what seemed like hours of prayer – gave me no answer to the problem. Back down on one, I would have to back down on the other. Back down on two and what would that lead to? Uprising over the Maid of Kent's death and others, more people refusing to sign the Act, more dissenters roaming the land fomenting trouble. I was trapped by my own Act. I had to go on. There was no turning back.

Before we began work this day, Katherine asked me what I thought about my Katherine at that time. I am aware she is giving this to me as a diversionary tactic, she knows I do not want to confront the killings which came next. This I know, this I appreciate, this I have to come to terms with myself in my own way.

I also have to say Katherine's question is valid. My former queen disappeared from the narrative, did she not?

I thought of her, yes, from time to time. I wondered how she fared without her title, without her great household, wondered if she still wore the Spanish head-dress and clung to Spanish fashions. I missed her insights into political matters and wonder to this day whether Fisher and More would have died had she remained at my side. I found myself one dark endless lonely night recalling the time I rode to Ludlow to ask her to marry me, recalling the joy on her face and the love which radiated from her. I asked myself in that darkness whether I had seen that radiance of love on Anne's face and concluded that I had not. You cannot fake it to one who has clear insight. It was not there. It never had been there. Anne may have loved me in her own way; she did not love me wholeheartedly and completely as Katherine did. Whether she clung to me as a refuge in her time of sadness at losing her first husband and being alone in this strange land and her love grew from there or whether she loved me from the start is something only she can answer.

So I admit at this point of my book that I missed Katherine's quietness, her devotion and her devotions, her calm ways and her beautifully accented English. I missed her and held that missing her - misery loaded loneliness to me as a sort of shield against all that was going on outside, or rather inside, at the Tower. It didn't help. It didn't stop the thoughts coming in and following close on their heels, the heartbreak of what I had to do.

I cannot avoid the question or the topic any longer. Thomas More was a devoted friend, admirer, counsellor and someone I trusted. Not all those things necessarily go together, in him they did. I hated and loved him in turn for his defiance of me. Hated that he would dare stand against me, loved him for doing it for few men would stand and defy me when I was in full anger and vitriol. That I knew, that I depended upon to get my own way. I consider now that my behaviour then was as a child getting their own way in the nursery, creating such a tantrum, such a scene, that the nursemaid and nanny are dismissed and new ones come to take their place, ones who will grant the child's every wish in order to placate them. I conceived a violent hatred for Thomas which I knew was untrue and unfair but somehow could do nothing about it, as I could not with Wolsey.

I walked in the gardens that bleak awful day, saw nothing of their beauty and symmetry, saw nothing of those who bowed and curtseyed as I passed, saw nothing but the gardens where Thomas and his family entertained me, the children who ran to me when I took to my barge on a whim and went to visit him. Children such as I longed to run to me, always had done, always would. I longed for friends like him, too, ones with the sense to be logical and reasonable enough to go along with me even if his thoughts were in direct contradiction to mine. I thought all this and knew it was all too late. My grandfather fought battles and killed people; I did it by ordering their execution. Same difference, as it were, once dead a man cannot be revived. Then I recalled that my grandfather had ordered executions too, I recalled that some said he broke sanctuary and had men dragged from a church, tried and executed. I knew he had his own brother executed on the grounds of treason. Thomas might as well have been my brother, we were that close, and I did the same thing. Sometimes I wondered how much Plantagenet blood was still in my veins and how much of their influence was in my heart and soul.

I know something left me that day and I never got it back. The man's stubbornness infuriated me, his conscience cut me, his loss devastated me. There, Katherine, satisfied? You asked me again last night to talk of that day and I find it impossible, apart from saying that something left me that day and I never got it back. I trust that will suffice, dearest one, as I have no intention of probing that wound any further. And still the wound remains. Perhaps now it is written out, I can find easement of it. I can but pray it will be so.

I do wonder now, looking back at that time, if the poison of the Boleyns had seeped into my veins, my heart, my spirit and my being, creating feelings that resulted in my doing such a thing, thinking such a thing and even turning against my once beloved Katherine. Foolishly I celebrated her death, foolishly I made an exhibition of myself, along with my new queen, as we celebrated our 'freedom'. What freedom? To continue to make a fool of myself with a younger woman who was not producing the heirs I sought? For that I committed my Katherine to a damp and dangerous part of England where she finally succumbed to her illnesses. I heard one person say she had the cancer, others that she had pneumonia, yet more that she died of a broken heart. All I know is I might have shown outwardly that I did not care, that I celebrated her departure, that I was free at last in every way, but inside, in a very, very deep core centre of me, something broke. That something was never fixed again. It was irrevocable, it was final, it was painful. I went to Mass outwardly smiling, inside hurting and asked God to take the pain away. It abated but it never fully died. You can believe that or believe it not, it is your choice. Katherine, this Katherine, would not let me get away with anything but the truth. She sees into this spirit heart and mind and knows I cannot dissimulate before her, nor would I. This is a chance given by God and I must take it, to give you the truth.

With Katherine's death, something broke. With More's death, something was taken away. It was then I began to be less of the person I was originally. I did not like it.

But Anne was pregnant again, I had achieved that much at least and I hoped for the much wanted son and heir this time. Surely something would go right, surely my prayers would be heard eventually, would they not?

Or was God really that unforgiving?

Chapter Nineteen - Going Bad All Round

I jousted and I was knocked down. I remember the knight charging at me, remember feeling, as if it was a premonition, that I would not withstand the charge and I did not. I remember, just, flying back through the air but no more. I do not remember crashing to the ground; I do not remember the doctors fussing around me. I do not remember anyone fussing around me. They told me of this later. I remember waking in my bed and asking first what was the confusion and chaos all about, why so many in my room and then shouting: 'get out, leave me alone! I have a headache but that's all.' I did not realise how long I had been unconscious and if I had, it would have been a minor consideration against the news that my queen had miscarried. The physician checked me carefully, muttering under his breath, whilst a courtier I knew to be associated closely with my Queen hovered impatiently in the background. I sensed he had news, I also sensed it was not good news. I pushed the physician to one side and demanded the courtier give me the message he so obviously did not wish to give me. The news came as a blow every bit as hard and as nasty and as dangerous as the one which sent me flying from my horse.

I was impatient and irritated and disappointed and falling out of lust at an alarmingly fast rate. I had not realised it was possible to unlove someone so quickly – it was possible to fall in love that quickly, or in lust, as I freely admitted earlier, but the going of it was sudden. Was it the birth of another wretched girl that started the disappointment? I think not. I presumed that with one healthy child brought into the world, my queen would produce another and then another and I would have that batch of children I so longed for. It didn't happen. She miscarried. It brought back all the bad, bad memories of

Katherine's repeated heart-breaking and soul-destroying stillbirths, miscarriages and later the dead children. I ranted and raved against God who had given me women – wives - who could not bear the children I sought.

But musing now on how I fell out of love or lust, call it what you will, I think it went like this.

Anne was out of reach, untouchable without the marriage vows to validate the relationship. I lusted after her with all my physical strength and my heart and mind. I now see that it was that 'one great love' which we all have but I did not know it then and I did not know that those 'one great loves' die very quickly – not always when disillusionment sets in. They burn out because they are too intense, too incandescent in themselves, to survive. Katherine confirms this. She has been through that.

I have to say:

The reality of Anne was not the dream of Anne.

The bedding of Anne was not the magical wonderful romantic affair it had promised to be.

The companionship was not as good as I hoped it would be.

Given her relatively lowly status she had no right to be arrogant, to lord it over everyone but she did and her tongue was sharp in the extreme. I also felt the power and the presence of the Boleyns in everything she did, said, prepared, planned or anticipated. It was a crowded relationship and I did not care for it at all. I found I no longer cared about her, either. The more distant I became, the more she clung to me, pandering to my wishes, fussing around me, feeding me titbits and helping to make me fatter than ever. It didn't work. She knew she had lost me and she hated it. Whether she hated me is another matter entirely, she veiled herself well in that regard. Had I seen hatred in her face, in her eyes, she would have been dismissed much earlier. It was her clever dissimulation, if that was indeed the way it was, which made the difference between an early death and an earlier death. Either way the dark angel had marked her for his own and I saw no reason to stop his coming.

Jane Seymour walked the court like a shining angel in comparison with the dark vituperative witch who went by the nickname of Nan Bullen among my people. Once she had the temerity to call them her people, but she never did again, for I lashed out with the full force of my anger and she knew full well she had overstepped herself. Jane Seymour caught my attention and I began to court her even as I planned Anne's downfall. It was easy enough to do.

If I thought Anne was difficult before, she became impossible when she found I was flirting with the shining angel, as I thought of her. She screamed and shouted until I told her she had to cope with it. My Katherine had coped with her walking into my life, now it was her turn. That did not go down well with Queen Anne, as my readers can well imagine. She became red in the face and then white in turn whilst she fought to find the right words to hold me. She had no idea at that point that my affection, not love, I never ever called it love in my secret heart, only my conscious mind, was sliding away rapidly and that everything she did made it slide a little faster, made my determination to rid myself of her close in a little more rapidly. She had no idea that she was busy building her own coffin. This was one person I would be content to remove permanently from my life, for she had become tiresome and jaded, if not an outright jade.

Confidentially I asked Cromwell to seek grounds for divorce whilst hoping, secretly but admitting it here for the first time, that there would be more than grounds for divorce. I had heard enough whispers, caught enough of the rumours, to hope for treason. My spies had been very active, bringing me a lot of good information, if not evidence. Treason would be much easier, less complicated with nothing left behind but the vengeful family and I would deal with them.

I want to say here that at first I was prepared to divorce Anne, to put her to one side, pay her off, send her to the country, get her out of my sight and my life. I did not plan her death, but I was aware the dark angel walked around her. Is that a contradiction? Possibly. I knew more than I ever told anyone about the other side of life, the side I now walk openly and freely. I knew of the movements of the dark and light beings, I knew how to call them. I needed no alchemists to help me with that. Some would say it was my own darkness which drew them but not so. I had no more darkness in me than any man who was in my court at that time. All were seeking riches and power for themselves, that I knew. None served me because of my personality, my being, my essence. None served me out of love. I knew this as well as I knew the Boleyns played their power games with Anne as their spokesperson, their key, their talisman.

You see; Katherine was all open-ness, honesty and pure feelings. Anne was dark and sensual, playing games with tokens and handkerchiefs, with seductions and with love talk, with songs and dancing and play. The court changed, we all changed to suit her and we were all caught up in it. A miasma of eroticism seemed to fall over everything; we were all entrapped by her wiles. I was not the sole man she looked at in that way. I was not her sole bedmate. I have to say this: the lies that have been talked and written about me through the ages defy my powers of description.

The talk is I grew tired of my Queen and cast around for reasons to execute her. Did I do that, I ask myself? I asked for a divorce but at that time adultery was not grounds for a divorce. It was grounds for treason, though. There were no other grounds for divorce, nothing could be found. I was trapped in a marriage I no longer wanted or needed for no further children were forthcoming. Anne knew it was over, the look of terror in her eyes when she caught my knowing look was enough to tell me all I needed to know. If she had but come to me and said 'it was naught but fun, my lord,' there is a possibility I would have believed her. Just.

In truth, she did nothing like that and Jane Seymour continued to be fresh faced and angelic, to be the companion I sought for my wife and my life. Yes, I wanted out of the marriage, no, I did not consciously decide execution was the only way. Not then, anyway.

What I did say and I say now is that those who stand against me, those who are disloyal to me, those who betray me by bedding another, commit treason. Talk about me behind my back, yes, play sex games behind my back and expect me to pardon you? I think not. Was there incest? I know it will be asked, it has already been asked. I say this, I am not going to be the one to state it openly at this time because there are people even now who will be damaged by the accusation – and the truth - so it is best left where it belongs, in the shadows. But there is no smoke without fire, an old, old saying and a true one. Make of that what you will. I distrusted and disliked George Boleyn but that was not good enough reason to accuse him - at that time.

I will say only this: Anne committed treason. Her lovers, a musician in the name of heaven, one Mark Smeaton, Henry Norris, I trusted that man – to some degree – Francis Weston and William Brereton, gentlemen of her Bedchamber, had long since been sent to the Tower and executed by beheading, whether guilty or not in the eyes of the law. They denied it, of course they did. To say otherwise would have damaged their families and their standing. Mark Smeaton was threatened with torture and confessed. They didn't even touch him. Was there incest with her brother? Do I believe that? That is between me and my God. You know by now there are things I will not say and I go further and write here that there are things I cannot say, in part because of lack of knowledge, only rumour and who would decimate a person's character on a rumour? I know your newspapers do and I am not prepared to bring myself down to their level, even for the sake of a best seller for my Katherine, and in part because it would not be fair justice to say them. Disingenuous? Possibly. Politically cautious? Definitely. Infuriating? Katherine is smiling her knowing smile and says nothing. Her brother George Boleyn was executed anyway. An example to others. Whether he did or did not carnally know his sister, he was known to have spent time with her in her bedchamber. It was enough for me.

I would just say this – I did not lightly condemn my Queen to death. She was after all a crowned queen in her own right, one who was entitled to respect and deference. And so, her trial was the formality needed because of her status and her execution was that of a queen. I arranged for a swordsman to come rather than an axe man.

I sent her to the Tower. I knew of her screaming terror, her shrieking rage, her vituperative tongue against me and all who took her there, I knew of her agony in being shut up in the darkness for she was a shining glittering star who needed the spotlight and the sun at all times to cast her magic. I sent her there as an object lesson to those who would stand in my limelight and attempt to manipulate the star turn: me. Be warned, it said to them all, be warned, or you will be on the barge entering Traitor's Gate as well. I had no favourites when it came to what I perceived to be treason. Simply put, those who were not with me were against me and that included any who went against my will. My will was to end a marriage that had gone cold, deathly horribly cold,

with no love on either side and only one pathetic child –
or so I believed – to show for it. Where then my nursery
full of children, where then my dream of a companion, a
helpmeet, a love who looked not deep into the eyes of
other men even when I was in the same room, the same
hall, at the same table? I expected to be the only man
she looked at, listened to, danced for but it was not so.

I sent her to the Tower and to her death. I signed the
papers with no more emotion than I did when I
committed Empson and Dudley to death. Does that
sound heartless and cruel? Do I begin to warrant the
'tyrant' tag you put on me so easily, you historians? Do
you know of the hurt that I went through to get to that
point? Even when love or lust dies, there are ashes, there
are latent burns, there are feelings which do not
immediately go away. I walked and talked with Jane, I
held her and I looked into her eyes and at times I saw
glimpses of what might have been with Anne, had she
been a different person. I know well that there are those
who believe she loved me and I killed her for another
woman. I say to them, if she had been all that I wanted,
there would not have been another woman. If I am able
to make an unfair comparison, Anne was a glittering
erotic figure; Jane was all quietness and demure comfort.
Anne sparkled and danced; Jane was sunshine and soft
days of sitting quietly. Does this make sense to you,
dear reader? The contrast between them was amazing
and immense, they were from different ends of the
universe I examined every night when the stars were
visible. Is it so hard for you to believe I would not have
gone to the demure Jane had the vibrant Anne been a
different, faithful, loyal wife?

Was I not considerate to the end, did I not offer her
and arrange for her a sword and not an axeman?

I would say just this. However long she was
married to me it was too long. I should not have allowed

myself to get involved but foolishly I did. It cost me dear.

And so ended the rule of the Boleyns. They lived on; their star was dead. Their shining fortunes were diminished. They never shone again in my time. I would not have allowed it, anyway. They, incidentally, were dismissed to the country, out of my sight, every last one of them.

The day Anne died I took a barge and went to visit Jane Seymour.

Callous? Books say I was, people say I was, the woman was scarcely cold and I was courting my next possible wife and queen.

But … look at it from my viewpoint for a change. Look at my situation. Look at my state of health, my problems and my feelings. Is that so hard for you to do?

I had endured enough of Anne Boleyn, her sharp tongue, her flirtatious ways, her demands and those of her family. I had heard enough of Anne's exploits to know there was an element of truth in the charges which were not denied. I saw enough with favours being dropped, tokens given to others… Maybe the charges were not denied because she knew full well her reign was ended. Some of her supposed lovers were said to deny it to the end. Men of steel, men of strength, but I had enough of my own suspicions and hints and innuendoes to know there was likely to be an element of truth in there somewhere. That is without the snippets brought to me by spies, tattle-tale people and those who really were able to know, those who served the Queen in an intimate capacity. Every move, every action, was watched by many pairs of eyes. Most of them reported back to me. I can say this too: some nights she was – ah, I have a problem, Katherine. She said it was excitement at coming to my bed. No, I cannot say it. I would ask the readers to decide for themselves what I found some nights which made me suspect something. Modesty forbids me to go into it as well as prudery.

Katherine just said it was gracefully done. Thank you, beloved one, for that compliment. You have been surprisingly quiet throughout this period of the book.

I think we need to move on.

My position was this: My second wife had failed to provide the heir which I needed. My second wife had proved to be a disappointment in every way. I had already cast my eyes and my love on to another who would be my third wife, for my time was slipping away, my body was not as virile as it had been. Should I be a hypocrite and wear black and mope around the court, order a year of mourning and cancel all arrangements for feasts and dances and the like to honour Anne's death? I did not do that for my true queen, why do it for another? I know men thought me callous. I know women thought me heartless. I know what I thought and felt. It matched them to some degree but not entirely. But, the face I showed the world was one that said 'I care not for your thoughts and her death.' It was not entirely true. I imagined her beautiful head leaving her still attractive body and shuddered. I imagined myself holding the corpse and crying. I imagined these things in the dark hours before the watching dawn broke over my beloved country and left me red eyed and irritable. I vowed none would know and they never did. Katherine's books show that. Katherine's books say I never showed remorse. Why should I? I felt sinned against, I felt disappointed and unhappy and the one thing the Katherine in your time has realised, I was intensely lonely. I could allow no one really close to me. To know me, to know my thoughts, my feelings, my longings would be to have a hold on me which I could not allow. Who knew when a man would turn traitor on me and use those things to bring me down? Had I not studied the Plantagenet history well and knew of the treachery which brought down so many of my ancestors? Did not treachery bring down my Great Uncle Richard? Even with my own personal paranoia, I knew I could not guard against every person. Even favourites, even those who considered themselves close friends, were there on the surface only. Few, if anyone, got to know the real Henry, for guarded thoughts are safe thoughts. Terror is a good controller of men – and of women – and memories are assassins guaranteed to disturb and finally kill the dark hours supposedly left by God for us to sleep and renew ourselves. There was little of that for me at that time.

One night, for no reason – no, I lie, there was a reason. I had taken the royal barge to … Greenwich, Katherine, my apologies, I believe it was to Greenwich. Fortunately it is easy for you to rub out the words which are wrong in this narrative. No again, it was to the Tower, before it became a place of death. I recall going there with my Katherine, we were laughing in the barge as we did, sometimes her accent made me smile and she would smile back and we would laugh at and with one another and those around us had no idea of our way of communication.

Katherine has just said I am rambling. I am.

Let me control these random thoughts. One night, after I had taken the royal barge to the Tower to consult with those who were Controllers appointed to care for the place and to see the grounds, I lay awake in my own private bed and brought back a memory of my Katherine. We were in the royal barge, we were going to the Tower, this I recall well, for some ceremony or other. Katherine had made some comment which, in her adorable Spanish accent, came out oddly and I began to laugh. She threw a cushion at me, I threw one back and she got up to come and sit by me, still laughing. At that moment the barge hit some kind of eddy or current and rocked wildly. Before I knew what was happening, she had fallen over the side with a loud shriek. In a moment half a dozen courtiers were in the water, supporting her and then helping her back on board. I recalled in the darkness how she laughed, how white her teeth were, how fair her skin and how gold her hair for her head-dress had slipped in the accident and sun gleamed on her head. I recalled how the wet clothes clung to her body and how she treated the whole thing as a huge joke. I was in turn terrified at her accident and amused and delighted by her reaction.

"Nothing lost," she assured me, checking her jewellery, her pendant, a gift from me, her rings, her ever present rosary. 'Nothing lost,' not even her dignity as a Queen. Throughout the entire thing, that dripping wet lady whose condition was destroying the cushions and coverings of the royal barge never lost her dignity.

Nothing lost. I had lost everything. That night in the darkness, I knew it and that night in the darkness, I cried for the first time since my brother had died. I cried for the loss of my Queen, I cried for the loss of the beautiful second wife because by losing her, by killing her, let me be honest and say what is the truth, I had lost a degree of respect and I knew that I would never get it back.

I recalled that night as a child how I would break things and they would be replaced. I broke Anne Boleyn and replaced her with Jane Seymour. There was always another willing woman. Every man knows that. Well, when he comes wearing the crown which signifies him to be the King of England there is. Unfortunately, at times that is no consolation. At times we want that which was broken, not the replacement. In that dark night I wanted that which was broken, Katherine with her gentle accented voice and her all-knowing eyes and her quiet patience with me and the women I flaunted in front of her. I also wanted my reputation restored, for that mattered to me. My father gave little to no thought of his reputation with the people, all he cared about was his diplomatic standing in Europe whereas I could scarcely give a fig for the opinion of those in Europe and would prefer to leave them to their squabbles and their infighting and their intrigues, provided they did not affect me. For any king of England, reputation is everything and I was in danger of losing mine. Somehow I had to get it back.

I made arrangements to marry Jane Seymour within the month. No one said a word against me. I am not sure it was agreement or fear. Either way it didn't matter. I was supreme head of the church, the country and, I thought, my own destiny.

The Lord God knows that in that I was wrong.

Chapter Twenty - Jane Seymour, Queen No. 3 – and problems

Jane was a perfect wife in every way. I worshipped her, saw in her all that I did not see in my other wives, due to my own blindness, not due to their lack of good qualities, I hasten to add. She was pretty, demure, calm, determined, everything I needed in a wife and a Queen. The perfect consort. She never looked at any man but me. She never spoke with anyone without glancing in my direction for approval. She never contradicted me but somehow brought me around to her way of thinking. Somehow she brought in changes I hardly noticed until they were there and then I was glad they were there.

I also looked long at myself, considered my age and thought about the possibility there might not be a male heir, wondering what in the name of Heaven to do about it. I decided Elizabeth would not inherit. I decided that my illegitimate son by Mary Boleyn, the image of me, would do well if no child came of my marriage with Jane and so I arranged to put into law the fact I could name my successor. I would have done, if the boy had not suddenly died. That shook me more than I could tell anyone. Someone who looked like me, who had my temperament and personality, could die so young made me look again at my own mortality. It frightened me. It was as if I had died at a much younger age than even my brother did. Fright was a small word compared with the way I felt some nights. No one knew what caused his death, unless it was that sweating sickness but that was not prevalent at the time. He just – died. Maybe a congenital heart condition? I don't know, the doctors didn't know at the time, either. I did not know the boy, he had not lived at court, I just knew from others that he resembled me in every way and then he was gone.

Think on this: I had made some laws that complicated life, but I thought they were right at the time, of course. My son, illegitimate or otherwise, had gone out of this life. My daughters were bastards, made so by my laws. I had forbidden my daughter Mary to see her mother. Mary had for a long time had to give precedence to the half-sister my second Queen and I had brought into the world, but she was my child, for all that. If there were no son, she would have to take the throne. That meant I had to make my peace with her.

Peace had to be made and Jane was - if nothing else - a peacemaker. Not outright, not demanding, not contriving to get her own way but a gentle quietness that said 'we would be better as a family' and ' you cannot leave a child outside the court' and no, I could not, for the second child, Elizabeth, was being cared for in court. I felt it would also ease my mind and conscience over Katherine if I did, for I knew I did her wrong in refusing permission for her to see her only living child. It was a moment of clarity when I saw, when I realised, that fact. It was the beginning of a series of thoughts which led to my feeling so much regret over my first queen that it was untrue.

I tore the heart out of Katherine and I know it – now. Then it was just something I did and I wonder where, along the pathway of life, I left my courtesy, consideration, moral rectitude and sheer compassion for those I once cared for. It slipped away from me somehow, somewhere.

It began in the early days when I could get whatever I wanted by causing a scene if I did not get it. I invariably did. I have already commented that poor James was whipped, sometimes harshly, for me but because I never felt the pain, it did not touch me as it should have done. Maybe therein lie a fault in me, I cared for him, he was like a brother to me, like the one I was to lose, the one I didn't know that well at the time.

All right. Power corrupts. Absolute power corrupts absolutely. I had everything I wanted when I wanted it.

I wanted wealth, I took it, from monasteries, from taxes, from anyone and anywhere I could get it. I wanted ships, I had ships built. I wanted a palace, I had one built. Nonsuch, a glorious place which no longer exists, a bit like my reputation. I will speak of that in its proper place in my life story.

I wanted women; I took them. I no longer wanted women; I put them to one side. Conscience? Me? Well, yes, in the darkness and the long hours of sleeplessness, yes, conscience came stalking in boots heavy enough to keep me awake. I knew in those dark hours that I should not have put Katherine away from me and regretted it even then. She was, in retrospect, everything my other queens were not. Even taking into account the great love I felt for Jane Seymour, I have to say Katherine was the shining star of queens, if there is such a description. I knew what I had done to her, a slow lingering lonely death, and had no way of making up for it. I made my 'peace' with my daughter Mary. Although Roman Catholic to her bones, she actually signed the Oath of Supremacy. I know not what it cost her; all I knew was that once again my will had been carried out. Truthfully, I did not give a thought to what it cost her; all I wanted was her obedience. Did it not prove that I was the supreme head of everything, including my family?

I welcomed Mary back to court because it pleased my new wife and queen and because for the first time I saw the advantages of having her at court – I had a family. A sort of family, anyway, two daughters, a wife and a court. The son I so tragically lost was quietly and secretly bundled away and buried in Norfolk, that far off place that few visit and even less live in, or they did in my time anyway. I am aware that one of my Katherine's companions had extensive estates there but as I said to him when he told me this, there are better places than Norfolk. He didn't agree and I doubt that those who live there now will agree with me either. No matter, they cannot complain too much, by mentioning their county I put it on the map for them, do I not?

I welcomed my new family to the court and I welcomed the steady progress of the new policy I had instigated – the removal, the entire destruction, the tearing apart, the tearing down, of the monasteries of England. For this I know my name is held in great disrepute by many. Those who visit the beautiful ruins, and they are beautiful, this I know full well, sigh over what was and what might have been.

The facts are that whilst I was busy with entertaining and courting my wives, I also attended to matters of state. I knew well that I was over-spending, that there was little money in the state coffers. I also knew that many nobles and barons had designs on the monasteries and their grounds, that the monasteries themselves were not doing the work they were designed and supposed to do, that few actually served the community, as it were. Mostly they did what they wanted. And so, I thought, why not dissolve them, take away their wealth, allow others to claim the ground and remove a constant source of annoyance to me from the face of the land? So I did.

The sheer pleasure it gives me to write those three words! Because of my position as supreme head of everything, I could order something and it was done, even something as major as dissolving all the monasteries the length and breadth of England, scooping up their wealth, handing out the land, generally acting like a very early Santa Claus. Yes, I know of him from watching your life, Katherine…

Simply put, I could order something and it would be done.

What I could not order was the minds of the people of England. They didn't like the change, they didn't like my autocratic decision to take away something that was part of their lives, even if they didn't use it. They might have objected to my putting Katherine to one side and taking as wife someone they did not like, whether they objected to my having that 'someone' executed is anyone's guess. That was 'King' business, as it were. Taking away the monasteries and changing their religion was a different kettle of fish, it would seem. Then they objected. Really objected. Started uprisings and all that kind of disturbing nonsense.

The problem was, I had no army. In later times monarchs had standing armies ready for any riots or uprisings which arose. I did not. It was a time of peace as far as I was concerned and in peace time a king does not squander money on standing armies when it could be used to build palaces, ornament the ones the king already had, provide him with a comfortable living and his household with everything he could wish for – and more – and ensure good hunting, hawking and jousting. These things were more important than a standing army, until the rebellions began.

The first one reported to me was from somewhere in Lincolnshire, that desolate windswept place that had little to commend itself to me, apart from its monasteries which I wanted disposed of and a fair few barons and knights who owed me allegiance. The problem was - it spread. Just as the sweating sickness scoured the country looking for victims, so the resentment I had apparently aroused in people's minds began to scour the country and it found many willing victims prepared to take up arms and march against their king. It was led by someone called Robert Aske, who marched under a banner of Christ's bleeding wounds. He called it a pilgrimage. I called it an uprising and wanted to put it down fast, before it went too far and I had to do the unthinkable, backtrack. You will know by now I never do that. It's not possible for me to do that. It wasn't possible for me to do that.

Unusually for me, I decided to wait. I wanted to charge ahead, send in an army, if I could find one, and crush them. I didn't. You're asking why I didn't. Because I listened to someone with a quiet voice and gentle manner who spoke to me in the privacy of our shared bed and told me to play it a different way. For too long, she said, I had rushed at things, I had deposed people, upset people, executed people, in a rush. It had put a lot of people's noses out of joint, not to mention their severed heads, and it was time to take a new tack, to allow things to go quietly still and then pounce. I had not thought of this before, I had only seen me being clearly observed to be the head of the country, of the church, of my destiny and my life and here was this small person, for she was small and delicate and beautiful in every way, but not so small, I prayed, that she would not carry my child to the end and present me with the son I so craved. I had that in my mind, along with the whole of the country to think about and these thrice damned conspirators to outwit and finally crush. I did both, eventually.

Chapter Twenty One - Tyrannical King

Step forward the 'evil tyrant' beloved by historians and biographers alike. Oh yes, Henry went on a killing spree.

First I let them all go home, peacefully, pardoned. And I plotted. As advised, I waited. And it came right in the end; it fell right into my hands. These things always do, I discovered, if you wait long enough. It was a hard lesson for me, who wanted to rush in, bull at a gate, but one I was glad to learn.

They went home, they believed they had made their point and yes, they had, not that I took any notice, you understand.

Some half-witted person, well, he had to be to make a stand against his king, would you not agree, said that was a surrender on the part of poor Aske and began his own uprising. He and others sought, by violence, to capture Hull and some other Godforsaken northern place while others sought to capture other places. Right, I thought, and sent out the orders for the earls to move in and dispose of the troublemakers. In all some seventy people swung from trees. A goodly lesson to the rest of the populace, obey or else. A re-opened monastery was decorated with hanging monks. Yes, I mock but they were foolish in the extreme to go against me. Aske was brought back to London, condemned and sent back to the north to be executed.

Norfolk, eager and willing to crush this Pilgrimage of Grace, what a foolish name for something that ended in blood and sorrow, went on a tour of the country. Over a hundred and fifty people were executed. One woman was burned to death. I rejoiced that the rebellion was over. I almost threw a ball to celebrate but decided that was a step too far. No, I lie, I was counselled that it was a step too far and I listened.

Was this the turning point of one Henry to the other? The 'revered' historians might say so but I say it was a natural progression, a natural sliding from one to the other. I could - so I did. I wanted to show strength, so I went ahead with it when I could easily have stood back and calmed the situation down with fine words and a few written treaties that I alone would know were not worth the paper they were written on. I really had to show force because I knew full well that to placate and negotiate meant showing weakness and men would prey on that and demand more and more concessions, restoration of this, release of that, recompense for the other. No. In my reign there was only one king – me. If that king spoke, all obeyed or paid the ultimate penalty. In the light of subduing the entire country, what were those deaths? And so I justified it to myself and in council with my advisors who all nodded wisely and agreed with me. They had no choice. I fooled myself that I gave them choice and that was their decision, to agree with me. In the dark hours, I knew otherwise but could – and would – do nothing about it. What you did not do, ever, is show indecision, wavering, lack of commitment. Did I regret those deaths? No. They were sacrifices, examples, solutions to problems.

Not only do I say that you need to be in my place, to live my reign with me moment by moment to understand the decisions I made, good bad and indifferent, you also need to understand the times in which I lived. I inherited the mantle of God for the people of England. I was above everyone, not only the common folk but the aristocrats, the wealthy land owners, the barons, the abbots, the – you name them I was above them because I was king. I inherited that mantle and I wore it with pride. My shoulders were big enough, strong enough, padded enough to take that mantle and stalk the length and breadth of England wearing it. Not that I did so, you understand, I went when I wanted and where I wanted and nowhere else, but the example is there, my reputation went ahead of me. My kingship was venerated throughout this hallowed land of England. And I was big enough to take it and maintain it and ensure it never ever slipped through my fingers.

God be thanked; my daughter Elizabeth was cast from the same mould. As Queen she carried the same determination and did the same things as I. She was well taught, my daughter, well able to be her own self - as I was. Remember this: every man or woman is a product of his or her TIME as much as his or her upbringing, ancestors, teaching and personality. The time in which we lived, each of us who come to tell their story, dictates the sort of person we are.

I divert yet again. I reiterate, do not judge me without placing me in my time and allowing me the standing of being what I was and what I am, a product of my upbringing, my education and my ancestors. Once you take all that into consideration and add in the troubles and fomenting problems of my time, you will begin to understand why certain things happened and why certain people had to die.

Moving on.

The decision to build Nonsuch Palace went ahead.

I had already put in hand a load of building work in the place which was named Whitehall, that grew and grew, with work at Hampton Court, which I took over because I wanted it, much as I wanted Whitehall, as it happens. I could not have enough property, enough land, enough wealth, enough clothes, enough horses and enough time, never enough time! Would that I could have had all the labour saving devices you have, starting with the telephone and going on to computers and all they can do. I mean, as Katherine writes this for me now, she has a blue box at the bottom of the screen which says Nonsuch Palace, so she could look at what I wanted and created and never lived to see fully completed but never mind, it was my monument for a long time. Would that I had such miracles! What work would I have done!

Or would I? It would have given me more time to ride, hunt and entertain, that is a fact! And I would have had time to supervise things a lot more, instead of delegating it. I had to delegate the building of Nonsuch because of the sheer numbers involved, the need for craftsmen of all kinds to build the building and make it the most dazzling edifice ever. And yet more to create gardens such as no one had ever seen before. It was unfortunate that to build this great palace of mine an entire village and its church had to go but as with everything else in my life, what I wanted, I got. I now know I should have chosen another place, where no one lived, but –

The men brought me a map, pointed to an area in Surrey, said 'your palace could stand here, Your Majesty' and I said 'I like it, get going' or words to that effect. So they did and it is only now I stand here, beside my Katherine, watching the words appear on the screen, blurred slightly by the misty eyes (not the piggy eyes, biographer, please note!) as I think on the many whose homes were taken from them and destroyed, homes where they lived, worked, had their children, their dreams and their hopes and I know not even now what happened to them and their livestock. What then of the graves in the churchyard and the prayers and memories which were in the walls of the church which was destroyed? Fool that I am, I never gave it a thought at the time. All I saw was the beautiful palace that would out-do that country chateau at Chambord. Rivalry of a very expensive kind.

I see from Katherine's book that Chambord still stands. Nonsuch does not. It matters little in the great scheme of things, in truth because at the time it was being built it sent out the message I needed it to send: Henry Tudor is here, do not mess with him!

Is that not fair enough, Katherine? Had I not endured enough at the hands of the thrice damned French with their posturing and their double dealing and their plans to outdo me at all costs?

Meantime, to use that modern expression which covers so much, my Queen was pregnant. My young healthy beautiful Jane was pregnant. I was ecstatic. The world was mine and I owned everyone in it, the world as far as I could see, from the Cornish coastline to the border with Scotland, that far off troublesome country that gave me the night terrors to think about.

It seemed a long pregnancy and I worried about every headache, every pain she had, every time she did not want all her food. I insisted on lots of rest, on the finest physicians and midwives, on the most beautiful of beds for her to sleep in and the most beautiful of rooms to rest in. I insisted on flowers everywhere for her pleasure, composed songs to sing to her, asked Will Somers to ensure she was entertained when she wished to be, questioned her maidservants endlessly to see she was all right, that she was not keeping anything from me. Katherine's disastrous stillbirths and Anne's miscarriage bothered me still. I did not joust; I did not ride very far or very fast, even though that hurt a lot, my always wanting to be first was almost too much for me at times, anything to ensure I had no accident that would startle her into miscarrying. My sore leg dried up and I thought everything in the world was showing me that all was well.

In fact, I thought all was well to the point when I felt I could leave Jane in court and go into the country, afeared of the plague which was ever present in the land and in our minds and hearts. I was away from her when the news came of the successful birth. My son had arrived. The heir to the throne was finally here. Then I hurried back to be with her, the queen of my heart and mind. I was so full of happiness it was unbelievable.

Then I added the heavens and all of Europe to my world, in my head anyway. I could not believe the news even when I saw him, a healthy beautiful son at last! Caution tempered it fractionally, remembering my Henry who had died after just 52 days but this child seemed to thrive from the start.

Church bells rang to tell the world – my world – of the arrival of Edward, named for my grandfather and other ancestors who had carried that proud name. I loved my queen beyond all sense and reason – in the twelve days of life she had left to her before the butchery carried out by her surgeon took her to an early grave.

Katherine, I think I loved Jane more then than at any other time and she knew it. I had loved her before all this happened; she was everything I needed at that time in my life, she was the perfect partner and consort, she was calm and gentle and pretty and undemanding. She gave me a son and she gave me her life, for in giving me that son she died.

She died because they had to cut her to get the child out, she being rather small. She died because that wound became infected and none could control the fever which rampaged through her small body. She was incapable of fighting it. I had my regrets; I had been away from Court when she gave birth, afeared of the plague as I was. I could have spent more time with her but I came as soon as the news arrived, I came back to her and I stayed with her and I watched the decline. It was as if the earthly Jane faded before my eyes and an angelic one took her place. This sounds fanciful and almost sentimentally stupid from someone like me but I watched it happen and none can gainsay that. In truth, I witnessed it happen, as she faded from earth an angelic look came over her. She had done her duty by me and she knew it. She said no words to me, no comfort for me to hold in my grieving heart but then she spoke to no one that I knew of. She smiled often, a gentle sad smile but uttered not a word. Then, between one smile and the next, she slipped into that next world where I could not follow.

I learned an additional lesson that sad day. I learned that no matter how big you are, how important you are, how much money you have or how much land you own or govern, you cannot stop Death from walking in and taking that person whom you love. I feared it from my early days; I have said so in this book. I feared it more after it stole my Jane from me at such a moment, the moment of giving me the heir I wanted and needed. A cruel irony indeed.

True to form, the nightmares returned, those where the hands were reaching out to take me, too. In my grief and despair I ordered that Jane be buried in the Chapel in Windsor, an honour but why not? Look what she had given me, happiness and a son. I also ordered that I be buried with her when that creature came for me. Sentimental old fool that I am, it consoled me much in the dark lonely hours after she was buried. I mourned her silently, deeply and with great, great pain. Jane would have been a perfect consort for me. I needed her calmness, her quietness, to offset my own angers and rages, to temper that which I would otherwise say or do. I missed her daily and found myself remembering her many quiet ways. The feeling was entirely different from that I felt after Anne was executed. That great love had truly burned itself out, just as Katherine told me of the great love she had. It burned itself out and the next love was good, intense but without that burning sensation, that incandescent flame. I compared the feelings I had from my three wives and realised how different they were from each other.

Katherine's book, the one we decided to use after consulting many that were on her shelves, casts an element of doubt on the words I sent to Francis I following his congratulations on the birth of my son.

For those who do not know, I wrote:

'Divine Providence hath mingled my joy with the bitterness of the death of her who brought me this happiness.'

I would say to that historian, do not judge me without being there, without knowing my thoughts and feelings at that time. I meant every word.

Chapter Twenty Two - Problems

When Cromwell brought me the proposal that I search Europe for a princess to marry, it not being seemly for me to be without a queen, the idea appealed instantly. Apart from his thoughts that it would stop the nonsense about me being an anti-Christ king or some such rubbish, it gave me great scope for choosing a wife. Not that I was short of bed-fellows, or bed-women if you prefer – the rumours that I preferred bed-fellows is entirely untrue, I have to say - there were plenty willing to take on that role but none that I cared to make my permanent partner. I found them mostly frivolous and light headed. I craved something more. Yes, I know; history was to prove me wrong there but was I to know that at the time? Katherine turned one of her looks on me at that point. She's right, this old fool should have known better, but still… we are led astray quite easily, us males. Your history is crammed with stories of men who should have known better, right down to the last King Edward you had. Now there was a classic case of a man led astray by a woman, if ever there was one!

I see that in your time there is a certain freedom given – reluctantly – to those who prefer same gender sex. It surprises me, unless it is a remnant of the Puritan time and the overwhelming Victorian prudery time. We thought nothing of it. Why should we? Nature is as nature is, man drawn to man, woman drawn to woman, is there something wrong in that? To some of you, yes there is. I would just say it was not for me and leave the topic there.

I have had a flash of memory. Some time ago, when Katherine and I were talking about this book, I said something about wanting to write about all my women and she retorted that there was no book big enough to contain all that information. A slight exaggeration on her part, I have to say, but not entirely without truth.   During this time of searching for a suitable queen, I had many willing women. I am not ashamed of it; you would not expect me to be, would you? I have looked at the lives of other monarchs and know I was not alone in my ever-present need of having someone warm and willing in my bed. How much of this I owe to my grandfather and how much to simply being a male with an overwhelming interest in female bodies I leave to your thought processes. And yet, I admire the stance of one of Katherine's companions, Lord Rivers, who states categorically he did not stray from his marriage vows, because with a wife like his, he did not have to or want to. He too was left grieving, as I was. I do not think I could have waited the eight years he did before remarrying, but then he did not carry the burden of kingship and the loneliness that was an integral part of it. This he acknowledges to be true.

I have also to be brutally honest here and say I could not talk about all my women because I cannot now remember many of their names and faces, they are a blur of warmth and clinging arms, of tumbled curls and sweet soft lips and whispered promises that none had any intention of keeping. Therein lies the loneliness of which I spoke. It is one thing to lie with a woman for a fleeting time of release and enjoyment, another to have to believe every word that comes from honeyed lying lips. Am I being cynical? Yes, I am. I learned from bitter experience. I know that those who professed love for me were seeking to feather their own nests, as it were, to fill their purses at cost of mine, to draw on my favour to give them a place in court where they could become a person of note. You can sometimes go far by hanging on to someone's girdle, but I tried to distance myself from those people if I could. I didn't always find out who they were, but those I did were given short shrift. I had to dispose of a lot of hangers-on when I became king, the place was crammed with them. There are those who will say I got rid of a lot of other people too, but that is their considered opinion after looking at my overall reign. I will repeat myself, you who write of me did not live it minute by minute, hour by hour, day by day, week by week … need I go on? It is easy to say 'he should not have' and they are probably right. I most likely should not have, but I did and it was done in the light of that moment in time, not with five hundred years' distance to look back on it and pronounce judgement. Are you all so clever that there is nothing in your own life that you regret? No ill-chosen words, no ill-considered act? 'He who is without sin, let him cast the first stone.' I cannot think of anything wiser spoken by our Lord. You who write of me, none of you lived my life.

Katherine opens books on my life, books which say things like: no one has written of Henry VIII in this way, no one has looked at the man in this way. We look at the books and we put them to one side, for despite their boasting and their good intentions, they all end up saying the same thing: Despot, tyrant, wife killer, power hungry autocrat. I have not forgotten nor forgiven the biographer for his 'cruel piggy eyes' comment. Ill-thought out, ill-conceived comment that should not have been allowed to enter print. It is there for all to read and to believe. I have dealt with that already but as Katherine knows well, it rankles and the man should be informed that it does. If he has entered the Realms, I will ensure one of my servants seeks him out, wherever he is, and informs him of my extreme displeasure. If he is still on your side of life, I trust someone will make sure he sees my comments and is aware of my displeasure. Such comments, such insults, in truth, do not aid my cause or add to my reputation in any way other than harmful.

I have certain 'historians' in mind as I write this. Katherine knows full well who they are.

I want to say this about your work. Simply put, you – 'my' historians - were not there. I know this for a fact, for I have made a point of finding out the background of every person who has written about me. It is easily done when you have servants and spies aplenty to work for you still, those who sought me out and rejoined my court here in the Realms. None, not one of you, is a reincarnation of anyone who was in my court at that time. That is why I am here with Katherine, who was my Queen and not with any of you who write of me, for you did not know me and you do not know me. You lived in other times, with other people. You cannot, from the papers and books left by my court and my parliament and the books written by others, put together a picture of a king who held this country in his care and keeping for many years and who changed the face of that country's religion forever. You cannot begin to understand why I had people executed on the 'evidence' presented to you, how could you? Do you know of the paranoia of court life, of the activities of several thousand people responsible for your care and daily needs? Can you begin to appreciate the sheer volume of intelligence which passed by my eyes and ears daily and the amount of people I had to watch at all times, for fear of treason and treachery? And did it not prove that there were those who would have had their own way with my plans had I not been observant enough to watch for it?

Wolsey was a fine man. I have no argument with that. But Wolsey would have had things his own way had I not watched and then scotched some of his plans. He thought to rule me, I thought only to rule England. He was only one of the people I had to stop dead in their tracks from trying to lead me in their direction, rather than the one I wanted and needed to go. I knew my destiny better than they did. Ever did people try to gain power by leading me – it didn't work and it never would work.

No, you do not know me and you will not, until you have read this book and even then there are many things which Katherine and I have discussed that will not feature in this book, for they are between king and queen and no one else. So I say to you, write your books if you must, but desist from making claims that you know the heart and mind of one of England's great kings. Write of what you know, not what you think you know.

Chapter Twenty Three - Searching For Another Queen

We were at the point of my story where the counsellors I trusted were considering sending people to Europe to paint the portraits of possible wives for me. I sent men I thought I could trust.

Fool. I should have learned by then not to trust anyone. But, I thought they could manage that reasonably well. Surely that needed no overseeing by me. Go to Europe, find the ladies in question, paint their portraits, find out something about their personality, come back and show and tell me.

While they were away busy painting, I hoped they were, anyway, I got on with inspecting my fleet. I went to Portsmouth. It was a perfect day, I was on the battlements surrounded by courtiers, my friends by my side, myself dazzling as always in gold and fur and silk and more gold and feeling at peace with the world for the first time since my Jane had died. And then … disaster!

Do you really want me to write of the sinking of the *Mary Rose*, Katherine? It broke my heart. Simple as that. One moment a proud beautiful ship with pure cloth of gold sails, the next a wreck foundering with all hands. So, why didn't anyone see it was top heavy? Why did they let it go out to sea before my (cruel piggy) eyes and let it sink before those eyes? I had nightmares for weeks about the poor drowned sailors and mourned the loss of my ship endlessly to the point when those around me were no doubt sick of hearing about it.

All right, so you do want me to write about it, or at least that editor person does. So I will. Yes, Katherine, that was a sigh you heard.

It was a glorious day. The brightest sunshine imaginable. We were all dressed in our best clothes, as in silks, satins, lace trimmings, velvet inserts, fur edging, embroidered with gold and silver thread and embellished with jewels. The men at arms were in their best surcoats, their weapons gleaming in the sunshine. The women were even more spectacular, sweeping skirts, lace trimmed underskirts, jewels and gems rising and falling on blushing bosoms … I am never too carried away by my shipping, important as it is, not to spare a glance or two at the beauty being displayed for me. All right, several glances, if you must. I had no Queen to stand alongside me, so I looked at (ogled) that which was on show. As any man would, surely.

Charles was next to me, eager as a small boy. He has always loved ships, nothing has changed there. His enthusiasm was affecting me and I was anxious for the fleet to set sail. I wanted to see the might of the English navy go out to confront the thrice-damned French.

What a sight it was! Katherine, it is impossible for me to show you the whole thing as I saw it, the water glittering under the sun, the waves thrown out by the ships as they cut through the Solent, the *Mary Rose* with her gold sails, her smartly dressed crew, her guns bristling from all ports. The sails billowed, the waves lifted her, she began to come around for some reason and then, before I knew what was happening, she was tilting, sliding, the sails hit the water, the ship was going under, seamen were flailing around trying to grab something, anything to hold them up and I felt sick to my stomach. My heart tried to leave my body via my mouth, my guts tried to leave any way they could. Charles was white, as white as the tops of the waves being churned up by the sinking ship. Women screamed, men yelled, guns boomed for some reason I didn't understand and I stood rooted to the spot. Someone tugged my arm, I shrugged them off. I didn't want to move, I didn't want to think, I didn't want to do anything but turn the time back to the moment when my beautiful ship sailed out to sea in front of my eyes.

But I had to walk away, had to go back to London, had to leave the ship and her crew lying on the bottom of the sea. I had to. I had no choice. God knows it nearly killed me to do it. No one spoke to me for several hours. I have no idea what look I wore but it was enough to stop anyone coming near me all that time. Did they think I would kill them with my own hands if they did? Probably. I was mad enough and sad enough to do it.

Enough! Apart from the meaningful dedication which Katherine so kindly put at the front of this book, I do not wish to discuss my beautiful ship any more. Subject closed. Finis. Terminated.

Katherine is laughing. There has been a lack of this these past days and now I have managed to make her laugh properly, that is so good. Now we can move on with my story, or as she now perceives it, observations on my life. That is right, it is observations on a rich, full, satisfying life, as satisfying as it could be when the centre of it is watched all the time by thousands of others and they in turn have to be watched, for fear of treason, treachery and double dealing. Tautology, Katherine thought, but no, in truth each of those is slightly different.

Now, a diversion. Why not? If these are my observations, they will tend to go off in all directions quite naturally.

I have just seen in Katherine's book the line about the crown being plucked from a thorn bush on Bosworth Field.

I have one word for that, but it wouldn't be polite so I will not use it in this book. Instead I will ask Katherine to type a series of *************** and the reader can fill in their own word to suit their particular line of words-to-be-used-in-extreme-circumstances.

King Richard III wore a gold circlet on his helm. My father, may God rest his soul in peace so he does not trouble me, was handed that circlet of gold after treacherous knights helped my father's men cut down the young king in front of everyone. Let me state that clear and true. The other is a silly story which came about as many stories do: through one person passing it to another and another and then it gets taken up, written down and becomes 'truth'. There are many such 'truths,' this is part of my deviating recently in this book, when I spoke of historians.

I need to say this again. I have to repeat it because it is something consistently laid at my feet and is sullying my reputation even to this day.

It is not true that I was constantly looking over my shoulder for those who would say I had no right to the throne of England. Maybe our, that is the Tudor, claims were a little shaky but there had been many wearing the crown who had far less of a claim than the Tudors. Go back through your history, how many battles were fought and kings killed? Who assassinated William II in the New Forest – and why? Did Henry Bolingbroke have clear title to the throne? Ask yourself these things – and others - and then ask if I did not believe I held the throne of England by divine right of God and the consent of the people. That, I have to say, was good enough for me. If anyone cares to argue the point, they knew where to find me.

So I stood and watched helplessly as my ship went down. My ship. No one else's, just mine. I never got over that.

Three things then I never got over: losing Katherine to death, losing More to death by his own stubbornness, losing the *Mary Rose* either because of the idiocy of others or because of a French cannonball. The thrice-damned French get everywhere, it would seem. Whatever the reason, my ship sank. The whys and wherefores are immaterial, really, it had gone and that was all that concerned me at that time.

So there are three huge regrets that bother me to this day.

I hope by working with Katherine in this life I will lose Regret No 1, for she has welcomed me and forgiven me and held me and told me she loves me still.

Regret No. 2 I will resolve, because I know Thomas More has been to visit Katherine and spoken with her and it is only a matter of time before we seek one another out and make our conciliation permanent.

Regret No 3 will be settled when the book is published and royalties begin to flow into the coffers of the museum dedicated to my ship.

I must move on!

Where was I before I deviated that far from my story? Ah yes, portraits, paintings of possible queens, possible mothers for my children.

I wanted another son. I wanted a string of sons, well, perhaps not that many, overdo it and that in itself can cause problems, but more than one would have been welcome and would have settled my mind about the succession. We are all mortal, some more than others and I knew my lifestyle and health would not let me live to an advanced old age. Even if it did, I still had to return to the place from whence I came at some time. There was also a problem that I felt restless, unhappy and discontented most days. I felt the need for a wife, a queen, someone to share life with, someone to live with, someone to love. Was that too much to ask?

Was this the reason for a sudden increase in executions, you are asking? Katherine is not, she knows me better than that. I know it is a question readers will ask, historians will ask, those who are only interested in pinning labels on me, labels that do not fit and will not fit because I do not conveniently match anyone's expectations and cannot be put in a box marked

HENRY VIII = DESPOT/SEX MANIAC/WIFE KILLER.

I am more than that; I am more than the whole that is portrayed in your many books. So many books! I stopped Katherine buying more books and told her to rid herself of some of them, which she has done. Some are still for sale… so people are not that keen on reading the biased historians, are they? If they were, every book would have been bought already.

There were executions. I do not deny it for they are facts, not rumours or trumped up silly stories. The reasons for them were different, each case warranting its own investigation and decision. The decision was ultimately mine in all cases and they were, in my mind, all justified, too. Again, anyone wanting to argue... executions were a fact of life in those days. Goodness knows how many people my grandfather had executed and all my ancestors going back through history. Why pin the 'despot' label on me alone?

We have turned the page, Katherine and I, we are reading of the ridiculous Pole family.

Because I am a kind hearted person by nature, I took an interest in one Reginald Pole, son of Margaret, Countess of Salisbury, daughter of the duke of Clarence. That's an aside for people who believe that history stops and starts at specific moments in time. It doesn't, it rolls on and people from one 'era' actually do live into another one, thus making history one long 'story', rather than a series of epochs which start and finish on certain dates. As in, my grandmother Elizabeth's brother Edward Woodville played a part in the marriage negotiations for my beloved Katherine to be married to my brother Arthur. You see?

Reginald Pole was actually a Yorkist claimant to my throne. But do you see me worried by this? No, I paid for his education, I gave him ecclesiastical revenues, I … took care of him.

Nothing comes without a price, though. He opposed my divorce from Katherine, and although I did actually ask for advice, all he wanted was to go to Paris. So he went. Why not? It wasn't an outrageous request. Whilst he was there I asked him to get the views of the Paris University for me. They turned out to be in favour of my divorce. That didn't go down too well ... I wanted the young intellectual on my side. I make no secret of that. He was a good, thoughtful, intelligent person but he was opinionated and would not see sense, the sense that the King is always right and everyone else is wrong. He went to Rome and became a Cardinal. I still wanted him on my side but ...

It seems to be an assumption by the historian responsible for one particular book on my life that I was determined to kill off, in any way I could, every remnant of the White Rose. He is not alone in his assumption; it has been expressed by others. Let me say I didn't want to literally 'kill off' the White Rose 'threat' but bring the people, the Yorkists with their claims to the kingdom, into my sphere of influence, so – so what? So I could control them? Probably. Kill them? No. I thought there had been enough killing. My father might have looked over his shoulder all the time but I did not.

Let me explain. If I do it in words of one syllable, perhaps historians will understand and accept there were reasons for everything I did and lessons for people to learn, too.

There were many problems at the time. I was funding, arranging, organising and bullying people (yes, me, bullying people!) into setting up forts to defend our coastline. Threats of invasion and war littered the correspondence I received. It was there in the reports from my spies, too. In the middle of all this, Reginald, the man I had admired, helped, put on the right pathway, endorsed in every way I could, wrote a book in which he poured abuse on me.

Me.

I mean, for goodness sake! I really could have done without that blast from Reginald Pole!   The sheer effrontery of the man, not even a proper churchman, an impostor, a poser, a Catholic upstart - Katherine just commented, 'oh, you didn't like him then...' To quote one of her favourite sayings, 'I hide it well, don't I?' So he didn't like the way I ran the country, he didn't like my religion or my practices. Nor did many others but they did not make a point of publishing their opinion in a 'dramatic' document. I think he thought he would be on better terms with the Pope if he made a good job of it. He might have been trying to ingratiate himself with the Rich and Famous in Europe, who still didn't like me.

He made a mistake. A big one.

A Henry defiled is a Henry riled. In a fit of temper I packed the entire family off to the Tower and removed a few of their heads as a lesson to others. I was more than mad, I was incandescent with rage and none could pacify me.   I worked long and hard at gaining my Defender of the Faith title which I cherished. I still do. It was not for him, or anyone else, come to that, to write treatises condemning and criticising and commenting and slandering my work and my decisions. He was not an authority on the subject. He wanted to be. He thought he had tapped into a pool of support. He was a fool.

He should have learned three things before all else: men will agree with you but not necessarily support you. Men will say yes when they mean no. Men will say anything to stay on the right side of you and then turn against you the moment you cease to speak.

So, because he had not learned that, Reginald Pole had to learn this instead:

Lesson 1: You Do Not Insult The King.

He lost every way a man could lose, family gone, status gone, assassins after him across Europe and in the end, no result, for Europe decided to look elsewhere for someone to duel with.

Damn it, Katherine, we were going to throw politics out of the window and concentrate on sex and scandal, if I remember aright? So why did I deviate into politics?

The second lesson was for me, really.

Lesson 2: Kings Who Are Set Upon By Europe Lose The Chance Of Marrying European Princesses.

You see, Europe ganged up on me.

I mean it. The whole lot of them got together, or sent each other messages and letters and no doubt gifts (bribes) or something of that kind, made undying promises to one another about treaties, land, peace and suchlike, and declared me persona non grata, declaring that all of England could happily ignore my laws, my commands, my decrees because I was not the right and proper person to issue them.

Ha! They took their time in issuing the Papal Bull – I will, with difficulty, refrain from making the obvious comment about that – but the nerve of them to think that they, in their palaces and in ermined gowns and cloaks and 'superior' positions in life, could decide that I was not a fit Christian king and that all Christians should attack and depose me! It was laughable in the first place and stupid in the second. Whether they liked it or not – and obviously they did not like it – I had been crowned king of England by the Grace of God and the laws of the land. My land, not theirs. What I did within that land was my business, not theirs. That is what I consider laughable. The stupidity bit comes from their believing that the people of England would read that and immediately take up some kind of weapon and launch an attack on me, my court and my parliament. On second thoughts, you could reverse those two things, couldn't you, make the first one stupid and the second one laughable. Either way they wasted their time, energy, bribes and peace of mind because they were totally and completely ignored.

I also have to say it was also bad timing on their part because I had lost my queen, been left with a heart full of grief and sadness and had just my small child to dote on. Fortunately for me he was a bonny child with a good nature and a very knowing way about him. I foresaw a good future for the next Edward to take the throne of England and was content and easy in my mind, although another son to follow him would have been even more consoling and contenting, if you see what I mean. It meant that lot in Europe, that's the way I thought of them then and still do, picked a bad time to try and have a fight with me. I was not best pleased and they obviously had not learned one simple fact of life: you do not displease Henry VIII at any time, let alone when he is in the midst of grief, worry and uncertainty for the succession. Yes, I had a son but no, I did not pin all my hopes on him. Look what happened with my brother…

You will wonder what I did for solace at that time. Should I tell you? Katherine smiles knowingly, as she does. 'Part of you,' she says, 'wants to keep it a secret but a bigger part of you – and there is a lot of you to be parts of – wants to boast and show off. Why not? You are the biggest name in history, above and beyond all others, you are the towering monarch who bestrides the historical landscape, you are the archetypal medieval king.

The Lord God knows Katherine is right!

In which case, I will tell you.

There was this lady who had been in attendance on my queen throughout her time with me. Jane brought this paragon of apparent virtue to court with her and I had seen her many times but being faithful to my queen, yes truly! I did nothing about approaching her although she had caught my eye. She had flaxen hair and the most delightful pouting lips that I longed to try to kiss. She provided solace for me in my grief, for she was not Jane in any way, shape or form and did not try to be so. As with many others who I bedded, she was warm and welcoming and comforting to someone who needed arms around him and someone who needed a voice saying 'you are a big man and this is good!' even if it was a lie. Well, the 'big' part was true. As in size of body, Katherine, nothing else! Gracious, to think you would consider anything else… it is a good job sometimes that you do not recall all your life at that time… some secrets I wish to keep to myself. Size is one of them. Who knows what you might be tempted to add to my book, if you could remember it!

All the major contenders for the position of queen were removed from the running because of the 'ganging up' of the heavyweights on the continent. I was bride-less, queen-less and getting fed up with casual bedmates. Ha! There's an admission for a King to make if ever there was one!

Back to the point of the book. They came to me with a proposal, those who had been there and seen this epitome of womanhood.

The proposal was: Anne of Cleves. Beautiful, they said, as in all over beautiful. Charming, they said, perfect wife for you, they said.

Holbein painted a portrait. Now I have said, have I not, that this man drew portraits and did I not say at one time something about his thrice-damned pencils? Let me make that his thrice-damned paints, too. When it came to Anne of Cleves, I felt almost that he painted a portrait of someone whom he wished me to see, not the person who was there. That is casting aspersions on one of the finest portrait painters of our time but you see, I was disappointed. Very.

But before then I got excited. I wrote letters. I said yes and I made elaborate and expensive arrangements for the bride to come to me. All was good in my life, I had someone coming to marry me whom I would care for and cherish and who would be my partner for the rest of my natural life. I was elated and happy and it entirely offset my bad temper over the Pole family affair. I never even gave the hapless man another thought at that time. I've only done that since, wondering if I over reacted just a little...

And my bride arrived.

She came at the end of the year so I, in a fit of romantic passion, rushed to see her, disguised and carrying many gifts. Then I caught a glimpse and I have to say, it was the most bitter disappointment I have ever had and I have had a few. It would seem, if I might be kind and say this, that beauty is very much in the eye of the beholder and that some see beauty where others see plain or even ugly. I know not what I truly expected. All I can say is, she did not, poor charming lady that she was, capture any part of my mind, my heart or my desire. I could not imagine myself being her king, her consort, her companion. The simple fact is, her beauty was of a pale and retiring type which did not appeal to me at all. Her manner was quiet and retiring too. She was not outgoing or flirtatious, she was demure and housewifely. Nothing like the kind of person I wanted in my life. Cromwell's glowing descriptions did not match the reality. She was a pale imitation of what I believed. Books tend to refer to me as being out of sorts, of calling her names – I did but out loud to rid myself of someone I did not wish to be married to and I regretted having to do that – of being choosy and a hundred other things. As usual, everything I did was taken at face value, as no one attempted to explore my underlying concerns. Of which there were many.

Quietly, sensibly, let me explain. I have your attention, do I not? As I believe I do have it, let me say this:

Before I got the chance to see her body, naturally, we had to be married. But before then, I had the opportunity to see her face, sample her conversation, appraise her manner. To me, Anne of Cleves was plain. Her body – when I got to see it – was unattractive, to me. Her conversation appeared to be limited, her manner meek and mild. In many ways she was a combination of every casual bedmate I had taken during the intervening period and that was not, in any way, shape or form, the queen I wanted or needed. I spent some time wondering where Cromwell's mind had been when he chose her for me. I doubted I would let him choose my wine for me in future.

We married, because that was the arrangement. We married reluctantly, or at least, there was reluctance on my part. I cannot talk about her feelings, because at no time during her life did she ever express an opinion of what she thought when I entered the room to spend time with her. It is highly likely she took one look at a somewhat overweight, ageing man and wondered what the hell she was doing there, when there were no doubt slender handsome princes who would have been more acceptable. I didn't think on it at the time, any more than I thought about many other people at the time. Life had narrowed down to one focus: me. I had been too long king of my world and saw little else. People had quickly learned to fear the frown I turned on them if something displeased me. I had given up being the golden prince and later golden oft worshipped and adored king and had just become grouchy, demanding, autocratic. Again, I did not think on that at the time, it was the way I was and that was all there was to it. No one sees their faults, do they? Not unless someone points them out and even Will, clever Fool that he was, did not dare to tell me I was turning into a serious grouch who was bordering on despotism. He didn't dare, for all that I loved the man, I would have rid myself of him if he had displeased me and such a statement would have displeased me.

Cromwell, for all his cleverness, had displeased me with this choice. I needed and wanted and hoped for another Anne, combined with the qualities of Jane. I was asking the impossible, I knew that, but surely some princess somewhere was at least halfway toward what I wanted!

I also want to say here, poor Anne! She came to be a consort, a queen, to be with me and help me. In return I scorned her, called her plain and ugly, got into bed with her for one night, our wedding night, and left her in the morning the way I had found her, virgin. For me, it was unheard of, for her a disaster. I am so sorry it worked out like that, because later I found her to be a charming friend and complaisant companion to me and any person I later married.

We were divorced a short time later but she retained her title of Queen and lived quietly in the home I gave her. Charming good-natured old Henry, giving away homes and money to keep an ex-wife happy. You would probably call it maintenance. I called it good sense, for we remained on friendly terms. That meant a lot to me, for others had left me or been dismissed by me and I lost their friendship because of it. She had great courage and fortitude to remain in England and remain friendly with the man who rejected her.

And Cromwell ... I had him arrested. My spies informed me that he was conspiring with other heretics to damn the work I had done. As far as I was concerned, he had conspired to bring me someone I did not like. I conspired to remove him – because I could. Unlike those around me, I had the power to remove people who offended me. They had to tolerate those who offended them, unless they could get me to do it for them. That didn't happen very often, though…

They told me Cromwell was furious. Fool! He should have been scared then, I think he was later. I did say Lesson 1: Do Not Insult The King. He wasn't listening or if he was, he thought the lesson did not apply to him. First he brought me someone unsuitable, then he got busy conspiring with others to change my words.

Katherine is asking, Where did I stand on this question of changing the bible, changing the orthodoxy of English religion? Was there a good sensible reason behind it? Well, no. Quite simply, I did it to suit myself. Because I wanted to. Because it was right, in my twisted mind, for me to do so.

The religion of England would be The Church Of England, with its capital letters, of course, with me as the supreme head. Because that is how I wanted it to be. It was no longer an adjunct of Rome, with Romish potentates poking their noses into everything and ascribing all sorts to my reign. It was me and me alone. It had been going that way from the time of my divorce, but I wanted it to be clear to all who was in charge of the religion and the government of England. Henry VIII. No one else.

By this time I admit I had become something of the despot everyone describes me as being. I ask you, surrounded as I was by sycophants, idiots, soothsayers, nay-sayers, yea-sayers… what would you do? Go mad, abdicate, or turn on them and do exactly what you wanted to do because you could? Take your pick. I chose the latter pathway. God help me, that is precisely what I did.

Katherine just said 'you haven't mentioned your legs.'

Here I am in the middle of a discourse on what I stood for in the church and she mentions my legs.

Women … is there any way of charting the circuitous movements of their thoughts?

Katherine, our work session is ending. Let me tomorrow, if I may, answer your question of my legs. I had hoped to avoid the awful, painful, endlessly infuriating and – to me – disgusting saga of my legs.

But I know full well, without her reminding me, that they are and were and always will be, an integral part of the story of Henry VIII.

Katherine's computer tells me that we have completed 65 pages of this book, albeit that the page count includes her heading, dedications and so on but we have still covered a tremendous amount of pages with a tremendous amount of words. When we reached that point, the paragraph above, I called a halt to the book and we began a major revision instead, right from the opening to this point. Katherine knows full well that it was in part a diversionary tactic so that I could delay talking about my thrice-cursed legs, or should that be double-cursed, as I am in possession of only two of them? The revision had to be done, though; we had to rework the book to ensure that every section told the truth and sufficient of the truth to satisfy you, the reader. I was not allowed to skim over any part of it. Katherine would give me one of her searching looks if I tried to evade a topic as she knows me well enough to realise when that is happening. It was a challenge I actively encouraged and appreciated.

Now it is time to move on, to approach the next part of my life.

We were discussing the controversy over my changing the wording in the bible. So I did. I did it to preserve the supremacy of the monarchy. I did it to ensure that all remained aware the king was all powerful. It worked, to some degree.

I could control the church, the wording, the men around me, I could instigate a divorce or annulment from the plain but complaisant Anne of Cleves, but I could not control the ulcers on my legs.

I was aware of veins that bulged in those legs, of the calves, once shapely and muscled, deeply marked with these hideous veins that refused to stay hidden. I did not understand what they were or why it had happened and the physicians had no answers for me, outside of leeches, potions and cutting to let out the blood. That relieved some pressure for a while but nothing worked with the sores which seemed to spread, then dry up and then come back again. They hurt. They tormented me. They hurt when I walked, when I sat, when I rode to hunt or hawk. It was as if my most favourite pastimes were taken from me. When the legs were bad, when they ached, when they hurt, when I was being bled or potioned or bandaged and salved, I had nothing to do but sit around and drink and eat and dwell on what my body was doing to me. I hated it with a deadly vengeful hatred. Hated the inactivity, hated the inability of the quacks to cure the sores, aware that some of the potions did more harm than good for they hurt like hell and made the sores worse than they were to start with. I threw out some doctors and got others and found they were no better. Due to lack of exercise my body began to fail in certain areas: not to put too fine a point on it, my bowels became less active and that caused more problems. And the weight crept on.

Katherine's book, the one I chose to follow, says that Anne of Cleves had six months of marriage to an irritable and tyrannical old invalid.

I challenge that statement! I challenge it on the following grounds: Anne never complained once. We met and we talked and I learned to appreciate the wisdom behind the calm face and the meek exterior. I admired the fact she refused to go back to Cleves and marry someone else despite her brother asking her to do so. I never asked why. Maybe she did not like men, I don't know. I do know that she seemed to like me and welcomed me and talked with me often when I went there, out of curiosity or boredom or need to visit my home, for it remained one of my homes even though it was ostensibly hers. What was strong about her I admired, that stance, I am here, I am Queen, I will remain in England and be friends with this man I call brother rather than husband. It took a great deal of strength and self-confidence to take that stance and for that I honour her. I came to enjoy my time with her and to wish she had been better suited physically as my Queen for I would have taken more pleasure in having her by my side than I did.

I was not at that time a true invalid. My legs gave me problems; my digestive system gave me problems, but invalid? I was still a virile man, capable of dancing a turn or three, of flying a hawk, of holding a parliament, of discussing matters of state with those capable of holding their own with me. Old? What is old in your terms? Was I old? No. Even considering the brevity of life at that time, those who lived a natural life that is, not the ones who upset me and had an instant cure for headaches prescribed for them, that is, some lived to a great age. Katherine has computed the figures. I was 48. Sir, whoever you are who wrote that book, is that old? What age were you when you wrote of me being 'old'?

Irritable and tyrannical. Irritable, yes. I had been bitterly disappointed in the wife chosen for me. That would be enough to make any man irritable, I would have thought. I still longed for a decent companion and at that time, as different from all earlier occasions, I was not consoling myself with any bedmates. I somehow had no heart (or body) for it. Not that there was a lack of invitations. Despite my being overweight, surly at times, irascible, I would prefer to say, the invitations were there, flaunted, sidled, creeping up on me. There was a space, an obvious gap; there was no Queen of England. There were many who thought they could fill that gap perfectly. I had no time for them. I was seeking something but didn't really know what it was I sought. I thought I would know when I saw it. More fool me… but men are like that, assured of their own wisdom, their own ability to choose and arrange to be chosen by the right person. Ha! I am revealing the deviousness of some men, who contrive to make it look as if the woman chose them, by clever words, moves and airs and manners. I watched it many times in my court and many times women fell for it. I wish…

Tyrannical. Now there is a word. It sounds almost like a dinosaur, doesn't it? I wonder if that is how the writer viewed me, as a dinosaur in my time. I didn't die conveniently as many other monarchs had, through fighting or brawling or by being murdered. I continued to rule, to be a king for many years. But tyrannical? I find myself bemused by that. I was imposing my will on the church, on what people read in their bibles and other publications, does that make me a tyrant? Did I remove freewill from people that they could disagree – in the privacy of their hearts – had they so wanted? Was that a sin in itself? I continue to be bemused and hope very much that the gentleman who wrote The Life And Times of Henry VIII will read this book and contact Katherine with an explanation. It is all we can ask. Having said that, the books I have persuaded Katherine not to use are far, far worse in their condemnation of me or their misrepresentation of me and no, I am not launching into another anti-historian rant. I am sure that the other authors who are waiting to tell their story will have as much to say about historians as I have, for they have all, in some form or another, suffered at their hands.

Chapter Twenty Four - Meeting My Fifth Queen

Katherine took a few precious moments out of her working day this morning to meditate and visit her 'other realm' which she has discovered and where she walks when she wants peace. There is a guardian for this other realm and he has been calling her for some time, for she has neglected her duties in visiting this place. Today he called and she went. She has a window there, a portal through which she can view the past – today was the first time she had actually used it and the result surprised her considerably. Now she knows why she must of necessity go there often, for she sees things which no historian has ever seen.

She looked into my life at the moment of which we write.

She saw me walking with a stick.

I was, that particular day, walking with the aid of a stick. Will Somers suggested it, clever crafty Fool that he was and fashioned it for me out of blackthorn or ash, one of the two, ornamented it with a Tudor rose carved into the stock, covered the top with leather so I had something to grip and presented it to me. It worked well on the days when the legs were most troublesome; it gave me something to lean on. And no one that I know of has mentioned it anywhere at any time.

I recall the day vividly. It was bright, as clear and bright as only England's days can be at times and I was walking from my rooms in Greenwich, where I happened to be staying for a while, to the Great Hall along a long corridor. I had an attack of melancholy, my legs hurt, my head ached and I did not want to be involved in meetings, conferences or anything else, for I did not feel sharp enough to outwit those who were set to outwit me.

Sunlight slanted through the tall windows, casting bands of brightness across the floor. It was as if I was walking on sunshine. I had my stick, as Katherine saw so clearly and was content to walk a little slower than usual, not because of any pain but because I was enjoying the whole thing. My mood changed as I walked because of the beauty of the day. Courtiers and women lined the sides of the hall, bowing and curtseying in turn as I passed them. One young woman cast me a saucy smiling look before she sank down into her curtsey and I was instantly captured by her beauty and vitality. I was about to speak when I heard a peremptory voice all but bellowing "KATHERINE!" She hastily rose, murmured "do please forgive me, Your Majesty" and took off at a run toward the voice. I turned to see the bouncing curls, the slim ankles from the skirts held up to allow her to run, saw the youthfulness of the girl and turned back to Will, as ever at my side. I asked who it was and he told me, Katherine Howard, one of the Queen's ladies in waiting. My next question was, who had shouted for her, for I did not tolerate people bellowing like that in my presence without a very good reason. Charles said it was her guardian who did not want her in my presence.

I recall I walked on but I no longer registered the sunshine or the people bowing and curtseying as I passed them. I no longer saw Will at my side, or was aware of anyone dogging my slow footsteps. I saw nothing but the saucy smiling look that Katherine Howard had given me, could think of nothing but the fact that she could so lithely and easily run from my presence where others would have waited until I had passed. I saw nothing after that but that young body in its garments and imagined it without the garments.

If I ate that day I have no recollection of it. If I conducted meetings I have no memory of them. In a few words, I became infatuated as only an old fool could. Infatuated and consumed with lust to an extent I had not been for years, not since Anne walked into my life and shook it – and me - to its/my foundations. The reaction was instant, if you know what I mean. Surprised me, pleased me, shocked me. I wanted that slip of a girl. Wanted her despite all the cautionary thoughts I had myself, which I suppressed as being not of any importance. Cautionary thoughts such as: she is young, I am old. She is a Howard, I do not wish to elevate that family any more than they are. Everyone will laugh at me for being an old fool and pity her for being with an old fool like me.

There is no fool like an old fool, Katherine, but there was no one to stop me making a complete idiot of myself. I was so puffed up with my own importance and my own desires and needs and they were strong, let me tell you! that I would not have listened to the Archangel Michael himself had he arrived in front of me, all wings and glowing halo and everything and told me to leave the girl alone. I would have pushed him to one side and said 'I am king of England, let me do what I want to do!' This I know, this I admit, this I confess, for in the end it proved to be utter stupidity, totally ridiculous and shame making in some ways but … oh Katherine … that but …

I have to say this: I had months of pure happiness. It offset all I had been through, having Anne executed, losing Jane so horribly in childbirth, the bitter disappointment of the second Anne – why did I keep repeating names, I ask myself – the loss of Wolsey and More and trying to cope with the devious distracting Cromwell. It offset trying to manage with legs that hurt and which seemed to want to betray me and make me look a bigger fool than I was at times.

Charles cautioned me against the Howards, a devious, power-seeking family, he said, as you well know they ar. They are determined to succeed in court at all costs. They were already in positions of power and prestige. At times I did wonder what else some families wanted until I realised what they wanted – their relative wearing a crown. Behind every smiling face in court was that overwhelming desire, once their relative wore a Queen's crown they were in, they could have their pick of positions, honours, wealth and fame. No matter if it did not last, no matter if fame was a fleeting thing, for a time they could have it and hold it and breathe it and know it. Ah, the wisdom that comes with hindsight! Would that I could have seen so clearly back then, when the families were around me and the women were in front of me!

Of course I knew the Howards well but somehow I had overlooked the delectable delightful creature known as Katherine. Where had they kept her hidden all that time? How did I overlook her when she was one of Queen Anne's ladies? Why did her guardian refuse to have her in my presence? And having been so bidden, what was she doing there when it was known I would walk that way … and there I stopped in my thinking. She had to have defied her guardian to be in that hall at that time. How long had she waited for me to walk by? And why? Did she really want someone as old and decrepit as I was? Was she desperate for the crown? For fame, power and position? Did she really want to make a play for my attentions?

One thing was certain; I wanted to make a play for hers, no matter what it took.

Katherine asked me last night, as we spoke after we finished the work session, what I thought of my daughters at that time, or even if I thought of my daughters at that time. A tricky question but she has a habit of positing these tricky questions to make me think, to stop me in my headlong flight toward the end of my story. 'Bull at a gate' she says, racing to the end of my life without stopping to admire the roses – or if I were that bull in the field, the buttercups and daisies – on the way.

I accept the comment and appreciate I have ignored my family in my recital.

I saw my daughters from time to time. Mary I thought was over pious and attached to her clerics and prayers to a degree that was unhealthy but perhaps she was compensating for a lack of parents, says this father who never gave that a thought at the time. It was very much 'get on with it' in my time, the psychology of depriving a child of its parents was not considered. After all, aristocratic children were often sent away to be tutored by a relative or even a non-relative, without a thought for family affiliations and any heartbreak, with the proviso that they be taught the art of being an aristocrat, sent away at a young age, too. It seemed to have been much on the lines of what I know to be your boarding schools now. He may not wish me to mention this - but as I have said several times, this is my book and I dictate what goes in it (with Katherine's agreement...) – Prince Charles was sent away to a very tough boarding school in his formative years. I doubt it did him any harm but I equally doubt it did him any good. I would have hated it. I would take any bet you care to levy that he hated it, too.

All I knew at that time was Mary seemed over religious to me, she had a rosary constantly flicking through her fingers rather than hanging at her waist as most women did. Clerics seem to flock around her and she was in conference with them most of the time, seemingly when she was not at Mass. I did not find my daughter an easy person to be with. She was stiff and stilted in my presence, eyes cast down, no confidence about her. I wanted to tell her to live, to dance, to drop the clerics and take a man but it I thought it unseemly to do so. So I said nothing. I doubt at that time it would have made any difference to her anyway, her character had been set by then.

Elizabeth was more like me, bold, flirty, intelligent, full of questions about matters of state which I thought should not concern her at that time, but which obviously did. She attended services but seemed not to be so inclined to religion as her half-sister. As Mary had been removed from Katherine's influence, it was not that which inclined my first child to religion. It had to be part of her nature. Elizabeth had my colour hair, my vitality and zest for life, she loved to dance, to sing, to ride at hunt, she had her own hawks and falcons and was in every way a perfect Tudor, or so I thought, anyway. Maybe that was/is the proud father speaking, I cannot say from this time distance.

But we divert and we need to return to the story.

My life. My good, full life, sex, politics, wine, ale, food, hunting, hawking, tennis, dancing, singing, consulting, listening to spies, travelling, celebrating …

I did that for the fun of it, worked out everything my life consisted of at that time.

Now I need to list the bad things: ulcers on legs, body that refused to work properly, out of breath if I exerted myself, took longer to get drunk, took longer to get ready for love, took less time to get irritable and out of sorts generally with those around me – just ask my friend Charles, he took the brunt of most of it – took less time to decide to do away with someone. That one is for the historians who want to call me despot and tyrant and other obnoxious and unpleasant names. It isn't true, but I am feeling a bit devilish tonight, for some reason.

I should also add the hours spent in conferences with visiting diplomats, with counsellors of all kinds, with attending services, with just getting myself ready to go out and face the world. That walk when I first met Katherine Howard might have looked casual, looked easy, but it had occupied an hour or more of my day preparing myself to do just that. The legs had to be attended to, dressed, bandaged, more salve – some burned their way into my flesh and caused unbelievable agony. I needed to be bathed, I insisted on that and on those around me bathing regularly too. Some didn't like it but that was their problem. I hated body odour and still do. I hated unclean bodies and still do. That is why I hated my troublesome legs so much, they were unclean, impure, they hurt and they were obnoxious to me. I felt they were that way for everyone. Why, of all things, did I have to be inflicted with weeping ulcers? Sometimes bathing made them hurt more than the salves the doctors created for me. Sometimes I wanted to take a dagger and carve the loathsome things right out of my flesh but it would have caused more problems than I already had if I had done so. Who is to say they would not have reappeared in another place if I had? If prone to such things, removal does not necessarily mean permanent banishment for the ugly, nasty, painful and humiliating condition.

Katherine wrote a note in the depths of the night, Henry – son.

She asked about my daughters but mentioned that I did not go on to talk about my son. No, I didn't. I should have done but as she well knows, I am anxious to thrust ahead with the story and she keeps pausing to slow me down.

My son was everything to me. I did not see him often, the affairs of state kept me busy most of the time, my limited exercise kept me busy the remainder of the time but when I did, I admired his handsome face, his well-built body, his intellect and his graceful way of speaking with people, no matter who they were. For a very long time I was content to know he was my heir apparent, that England would have its king after me.

And when, Katherine asks, did you stop being content? When I developed an unwelcome premonition that he would not survive very long. I cannot say where it came from, whether a spirit person whispered it to me in the darkness one night, whether it came on a breeze or a look or – who can say where the first psychic experience comes from? I just knew, somewhere deep in my heart – and yes, Katherine, by then that heart was well buried under a substantial layer of flesh! – that my son would not live to carry England forward. I despaired of having another son to carry on, or I did until I set eyes on Katherine Howard.

That was a presumption on my part but, let's face it, as an all-powerful monarch, supreme in my land, supreme in my position, ever able to have precisely what I wanted, I knew it would happen.

What I didn't realise was, being that old fool I mentioned, the entire thing had been set up to entrap me. What they didn't realise is I was brutal enough at the end to cut it off – literally – and destroy them.

Katherine has just turned to a page of portraits in this thrice-damned book we are following. One is of Anne of Cleves. It shows a demure, sweet faced woman who somehow has a capable look about her. This is what I was presented with, what I expected to find when I met her. The reality was different and to this day I do not know why. The portrait did not overly flatter her; it did not distort her features, taken overall it was a just interpretation of a quiet meek lady. Therein lies the problem. A flat portrait on canvas is no substitute for a living, breathing person who gives off their aura, the person they are. I wanted vitality, energy, youth, exuberance. Until my last Queen, Katherine Parr, and I assure you that the repetition of names was not of my doing, we just didn't seem to have that many names at that time, I was not prepared to be content with meekness and demure outlook and attitude.

I have this day found the metaphor I sought for my reaction to Anne of Cleves. I have sought long for this, now it is here. Katherine sometimes discovers and prints off the words to songs which she has on what she calls CDs. The words are flat, uninteresting, lifeless without the music and the singer to bring them alive.

The difference is, Katherine seeks the words after she has heard the song, so she has some idea of its melody, its timing, its life, before she reads the words she sometimes has not been able to make out. Now, if I had met Anne of Cleves before I saw the portrait, it might have made a difference, the disappointment would not have been so intense, as I would have had an idea of her character before seeing the representation of her. Does this make sense to you? The personality did not match the portrait. The words do not always convey the beauty of the song. It is the whole: the moving, living, breathing person who gives off their own aura which matters. The song is a combination of music, words and voice. Without those things, the portrait and the words are flat. I was taken in by the portrait but not by the whole. I think I have adequately explained that now, Katherine…

The second portrait is of my fifth Queen. I have to say had this been presented to me as a possible wife and Queen I would have rejected her. She looks older than her years in this portrait and it is by that master painter Holbein, so what did he see that I didn't, I ask myself? She has a calculating look, one that I did not see for a long time, well, a few months anyway, maybe a year. This is where the portraits do not do justice to the person, for Katherine Howard was full of life, vitality, sexuality, promising much and giving much whilst still promising more, as if holding out would give her more of what she sought: wardrobe of fine clothes, boxes of fine jewels, chests of fine linens and shoes of all kinds. Celebrations, dances, feasts, positions of power for her family… all came at a price that I was willing to pay – for a while.

But I go ahead of myself there. It was just the page of portraits that caught my attention.

Katherine Parr is the last one on the page. A gentle lady, quiet, unassuming, devoted, loving and calm. Just what I needed for the final years of my life.

But back to the intoxicating minx, the inviting, delighting, dancing, frivolous, colourful, lively, enchanting…

Katherine, I have run out of words. This was different from the Great Love I felt for Anne, this was pure unadulterated lust on legs, if you like. She cavorted and pranced, she teased and tormented, she kissed and ran, she did everything to ensure she was The One I took notice of. And I did. God help me, I did.

I followed her like a callow, lovelorn youth. Bad legs, what bad legs? Council meetings? What council meetings? If Katherine was in the garden, I was in the garden. If Katherine was walking the corridors, I was walking the corridors. And then it turned. If I was in my rooms, Katherine was there too, leaning on my arm, whispering in my ear, passing me pieces of fruit, tasting my wine and commenting on it, sometimes adversely, sometimes enjoying it a little too much for my liking but I could not withhold anything from her, such was my delight in her summer freshness compared with my autumn heaviness and advancing age. But I never really thought of myself as being old. Do you? Do you count the years and set them off against how you feel, or do you think you are still young, capable of doing anything, anywhere, any time you want? Only the physicality of not being able to lift something, move something, dance as long as you did, sing as long as you did, shoot an arrow as accurately as you used to, reminds you that anno domini is an ever advancing monster that cannot be evaded. With Katherine Howard I knew none of that. Somehow she lifted all the aches and pains, dismissed the disappointments and hurts, took away the bitterness and the gall of living with an infirm body and made everything sweet.

For a time.

Oh Katherine, that time was special!

Came the July of that year and the annulment of my unfortunate marriage to Anne of Cleves. That mistake was quietly and unceremoniously ended and, in a show of magnificence, Katherine Howard became Queen of England. And the Howards stood in the background and gloated and rubbed their hands and smiled at one another and slapped each other on the shoulder and kissed the women and congratulated themselves on a job well done. Would that I had seen it at that time! Maybe I would have done, had I not been so besotted.

Much surreptitious work was being done.

You have a modern – I believe – expression that I like very much, 'taking your eye off the ball.' I did just that, being too busy playing Happy Husband to take real notice of what was going on around me. And so, before I knew what was happening, Norfolk and Gardiner had control of the council, Cromwell had been executed and those who were heretical with him were dispatched as heretics must be.

Did I regret his passing? Not really. The occasional twinge of 'should I have signed that warrant?' but they were small twinges and easily ignored in the glorious time that was my life right then. Capable he might have been, clever definitely, essential to my government? Not really. Plenty of others to take his place. Because, whatever anyone's capabilities, whatever their standing, their intellect, their understanding, all decisions were ultimately taken by one person.

Me.

Did I really care? I did not. The fact that Cromwell was capable was neither here nor there for me. No matter what the historian thought who wrote the book, no one – no one – is indispensable and he certainly was not. Capable, yes. Heretical behind the king's back, yes. A bad judge of character, definitely. No man in his right mind would have offered me Anne of Cleves as a suitable bride and if that smacks of my being what the historians call a womaniser, so be it and let it stand. I defy any man in England who had the power, the position, the wealth and the 'gift' of a crown for a woman to find himself married to one who did not please him. Katherine of Aragon did please me, for many years. I fell into the old 'middle age crisis' trap that you speak of so easily these days without realising what it was. I just grew discontented and irascible; I do so like that word, and needed diversion which she could no longer give me.

So, to revert to Cromwell for a moment, if I must, I have to say whether he was capable or not, it didn't really matter, did it, not in the great scheme of things. His removal, in every sense of the word, cleared away a problem – I had lost faith in him – made room for others – always someone waiting to take over – and handed me a load of land, estates and such-like to give away.

I showered my new Queen with gifts: pearls, furs, titles, land, estates of all kinds, my beautiful Jane's estates, well, someone had to have them, together with Cromwell's, he having had the Henry Tudor speciality cure for headaches. This all went to show her how much I appreciated…

Katherine knows what I appreciated. We talked of it last night; or rather, she caught a glimpse of it in my thoughts, sharp little person that she is. I wondered then, I wonder now, how much to tell you.

I will tell you some of it, but not all. I appreciated the youthful body coaxing an aged body into sustained life. Oh, the lust was there but the staying power, if I might so phrase it delicately, was not. The nubile body did wonders in that department. A body – I believed – unsullied by others, revealing itself garment by garment before my eyes until I could wait no longer. And then the smile, the knowing sexy smile, which capped it.

Enough!

Ah, how many men do you know who are like that, how many leave their wives for younger women because it is more interesting, more exciting, more challenging, than staying where they are? You all know them; they abound in your time as much as they have done in every time throughout history. Maybe the peasantry did not indulge in disposing of or replacing their wives through lack of interest, I believe they replaced their wives because they wore them out with breeding and work and harsh living conditions. My wives had everything they could have wished for, except long lives, it would seem… Ha! A small Tudor joke, possibly in bad taste but we will see… for now let it stand, Katherine, let it stand.

Katherine reminds me that the readers will want sex and scandal. There is very little scandal to report; that only leaves…

But in some ways, yes, there was scandal. There were those who were scandalised by my choice of queen, for the branch of the Howards Katherine came from was somewhat obscure, not very highly regarded, not really suited for the life of court and high powered positions. They also knew much about my Queen that I did not at that time. That rebounded on them later when it all came to light. I chose to ignore all early warnings, all hints and rumours and simply put it down to jealousy. Oh yes, there was talk from the start, but I have noticed from your newspapers that the moment anyone of a certain age begins to be seen with someone of a much younger age, tongues wag, vicious, petty, jealous talk abounds and rumours circulate. It is best ignored by the parties concerned, do you not agree? Mostly, anyway. I should have listened, but for the men reading this, I need to ask you this question: would you have taken notice of the gossip if you were out and about with a delightful young woman hanging on your arm, a pretty, vivacious, overtly sexy and charming young woman at that, one who flattered and cajoled, who smiled and danced, who flirted and capitulated to your every request, no matter what it was? I defy you to say you would.

The whole relationship made me feel good. I watched the faces of those who desired to be in my place and smiled inside. I felt young again. I felt as I did during the early days of my marriage to Katherine, the first Katherine, when Spain was everything and Aragon a place of intense exotic beauty and Katherine and I laughed and consoled one another in our bedchamber and she thrilled me with the pregnancies and then disappointed me with the births. Ah, but I see now how the marriage slowly failed, for I sought that level of thrills and pregnancies but with satisfactory births throughout the marriage. I longed for that nursery full of children. I sought it still, even at this 'late' age.

For you this age is not 'late', for you it is normal but in my time that was verging on old age. Good living does that, but so does harsh living. None of us lived that long; those who made it to the great age that you take as normal now were considered exceptional. Of course I aided a few people in their unequal quest to reach an old age, if you see what I mean…

It's a King's prerogative, that, to stop people growing old if they so desire. One of the perquisites of the position, if you like.

And power like you would not believe. There is no greater aphrodisiac.

Chapter Twenty Five - My Sex Life
(You wondered if I really would talk about it, didn't
you?)

Katherine has just read the most ridiculous and appalling statement on my sex life that I have ever seen and I have seen some comments… what behoves a man to write of another man's sex life in such derogatory terms, I ask myself? Someone who is looking, once again, five hundred years into the past, picking up flimsy bits of evidence and creating a whole out of it that would not stand up to the merest prodding of a little finger.

The book intimates, all but casts the slur, that I was not a gifted lover. That the marriage bed was for heirs, not games. That Anne Boleyn found it easy to resist my advances. For shame, sir!

It occurs to me that the statement is in direct contradiction and contrast to first; those who see me as a womaniser and second; the ghastly series on your television (which Katherine has wisely avoided) where 'Henry' is apparently depicted as leaping in and out and on and off a bed with every woman who passes by his avid gaze.

Let us dissect this once and for all, Katherine.

Marriage was important to me as I needed a legitimate male heir. It meant that I had to have a wife I could impregnate to create that child, there not being any other way for one to arrive. Not in my time, anyway. To that end I sought a fertile woman. Tell me which monarch did not at that time. The succession had to be secured at all costs. Or so we thought, anyway, those of us who held the crown of England in our hands and had it placed on our heads. Therefore it follows, does it not, that if one wife was infertile to some degree, as poor Katherine was, another has to be found to take her place. And if that one proves to be inadequate, another is found and so on. The line of succession should have been secured. Six wives but only three children is not a good equation. No doubt if we had lived in your time, the clever physicians would have been able to work out what went wrong with the women I chose. I knew it was not me, I was able to beget a child on other women. It just happened that those other women were not married to me at the time. A small but very important detail, that.

Apart from my wives, I had women. Lots of them. I admit this freely, for they were there, available, welcoming, enchanting, warm and comforting. I loved some of them, used others and cast them aside, just as you would expect a medieval monarch to do. The question is, was I any good at 'it'? Now I could ask Katherine to look into her past life and answer that, but it would be impolite to do so, especially as I believe Katherine, my first Queen, will one day write her own story of her life and thus will have the opportunity to reveal the truth about how she saw our sexual relationship. But I will say this: she never spurned my advances – of course not, you are saying, why should she, she was queen and was your wife and needed the heirs as much as you did. Let me tell you this, dear reader. You males know full well that if a woman does not desire you, she has ways of putting the 'request' to one side, does she not? There are other methods of satisfaction, there are other ways of releasing tensions, if I may put it that way, which do not involve –

Katherine, I am getting into deep sexual waters here, help me out!

Katherine has a trick when she does not wish to answer something or I am not prepared to answer something… she leaves her desk and gets water or attends to something. This time she got herself some water. In which case, I take it I am not getting any help. Right, well, I wrote myself into that corner, I needs must write myself out of it again.

Women are devious, deceptive, sexy, enticing, enchanting, infuriating and ever demanding creatures at the best of times. Those who crave the highest position in the land are twice as devious, deceptive, sexy, enticing, enchanting, infuriating and demanding. My first Katherine knew little of the arts of enticement at first but quickly learned for she was a young woman with a young woman's desires which were activated by our coming together. We disported many a night long, the two of us. I say this and know that any future book from my beloved Queen will confirm this. I also had women beside my queen, intriguing women, different women.   Because they were there, in case you wondered, because they were there. Now I ask you, what manager or boss has not desired his secretary or co-worker, even if happily married, because they are there, because they have enticing bosoms and legs and flaunt themselves without realising they flaunt themselves? Is it not the same for a king, one who has the entire country in his hands, with the corresponding gift of honours, wealth and fame to go with it?

For that historian's benefit, let me say that Anne Boleyn found it easy to hold off my advances because she had a greater goal in mind, the crown. Anyone could hold off a suitor if they were aiming for a ring and a crown, believe me! And, as I later discovered, there were consolations for her anyway… to ease her time of waiting. And believe me, when I finally got her into bed, I found her disappointingly mundane. I hoped for erotically exotic, I got normal. Now that was not down to me. The onus was on the one who desired the crown to make herself indispensable to me, in bed and out. Let us not cast aspersions on my abilities here, but on hers! Her sister was a better bedmate by far. I chose the wrong Boleyn when it came to sexual antics and when it came to loyalty, too. Lovestruck Henry made the wrong choice, but how many men have done that in the millions of years since Man evolved enough to know he needed a woman?

Jane was a delight. She was sexy but quiet, demure, so her sexiness came as a complete shock as she changed once in bed. She taught me to see beyond a face and demeanour and the pity is, I did not take notice of it once Anne of Cleves was presented to me. I see that now. I pity Anne and have to say again I liked her a lot – when I was not bound to bed her.

Katherine has just picked up the one comment I have not made – size. It was mentioned briefly earlier in the book but she has referred to it again. She is being honest here and said 'as I recall, big man, big body parts.' Well, we are being blatantly honest, are we not, explicit enough to keep the most jaded reader reading to the end, at least of this section – I wonder if this will be the only section reviewers will use in their quotes? I have noticed they tend to pick the most 'interesting' pieces, as it were. I will be equally honest and say yes, Katherine, you are right. And whilst you cynical readers will say, of course he will say that, I know from Katherine's memories that she knew one man who was body was very large but whose 'body parts' were very small. It doesn't always follow. With me it did.

I also know that big does not equal good. I might have lacked experience when a young man but I talked a lot with others of my age and learned of their experiences (or were they boasts?) and knew that simple fact, big does not equal good. But hell, it goes a long way toward it. I went to Katherine of Aragon as a virgin and delighted in the feel, the sense, the scent, the whole act of making love. To me it was magical, earth shattering, life changing after all those years of – how shall I put this – one handed fun, that will do. To have someone reach for me, react to my touch, writhe under me … all right, if I am being too explicit for the tender eyes of some of my readers, I apologise. But truth is truth and Katherine demands truth. She wants to know if my women thought I was any good or whether they were saying yes I was because of who I was. Would any woman dare to deny I was capable, or more than capable? You did not offend the king.

Chapter Twenty Six - Back to my Fifth Queen

I never thought of her that way. You do, for you have that kind of salacious interest in my marital status at any given time. Sheikhs had harems for thousands of years; I had six women, all legitimately married to me - one at a time. I get books written about me. Loads of them. Something is awry here; I haven't yet worked out what it is.

But we will return to the life I had at that time. A life with Katherine Howard as my queen.

All you men who are reading this – and I trust there will be men reading this, it is not exclusively for women, you know – will no doubt envy me. I was more than middle-aged by the standards of my time and I had a young woman as my queen.

I can almost hear the shouts 'tell me about it!' Even if I can't exactly hear you, I would tell you anyway, for who could resist boasting a little in their own book?

Katherine Howard was beautiful in a lively, impish, erotic and overall youthful way.

I have to admit that yesterday Katherine and I lost the entire work time she had allocated to the book. The words did not flow. Katherine did other work. It is because I was and am reluctant in the extreme to write about this period of my life. This is because I know how much of a fool I was and that knowledge, even now, hurts so much. I know I need to write of it, there is no point in trying to write about my life if I am determined not to mention one of my queens. Maybe if I write of it, the hurt will finally leave me and I will find some kind of peace of mind over that particular episode.

The reason it hurts so much is that I was so besotted, so lost in lust and admiration and gratitude that someone like her, so young, so pretty, so actively sexy, should want to spend her time with me, that when her true nature was revealed it was like a hundred knives slicing into my heart. Nowhere else. Just this big heart of mine.

The pain was physical.

The anger was all consuming.

The reaction to the anger, the heartbreak, was real enough and painful enough that I cried. Me, crying! Believe me, I did it. I was ashamed of the tears and ashamed of myself for being made such a fool of by someone so young whilst knowing full well who was behind it all, the thrice-damned Howards. I cursed myself for not listening to Charles, Will and all the others who tried to tell me. Katherine, I did say earlier, did I not, there is no fool like an old fool?

But before that happened, as I also said, I had some intense moments of pure happiness. Those were the golden moments among the blackness which laid itself down on me when I found out the truth. Blackness I thought would never leave me. For a long time it didn't. It took the third Katherine's kindness and consideration and care to prove to me that not all women are evil. It is something I knew well, for you were not, nor was my lovely Jane and Anne of Cleves, well, she was gentleness itself and held not a bad bone in her entire body. Written out like that, I wonder why I was so foolish to consider the time after Katherine Howard to be so black but it was a combination of all those things, the anger, the self-pity, the self-indulgent misery which I put myself through, the loss of what I believed in for a while – you know it, you've done it. That I know, for we all have at some point or another. If we hadn't, the world would not be full of books on lost love and lonely lovers and I know, from Katherine's music, that there are endless songs on the same subject. It's a perpetual state of the human being, I think, to love, to lose and then to love again, if you are fortunate enough to find the right person.

So, let us go back to the time when it began, when she was my new Queen and my new love and the world sparkled and shone with all the radiance of which it is capable, known only to those who are newly in love. If I once again mistook lust for love, I ask you, how many men have not done that in their lifetimes, at least once, maybe more than once, maybe never learning by their mistakes? I didn't, as Katherine knows full well. Of a surety she tried many times to tell me from the other side of life but as always, then and now, I didn't listen.

Truth: I was elderly, overweight, had bad veins and ulcers which made walking difficult, was unfit which made digestion difficult, was easily tired which made conferences and long involved meetings difficult, was lacking in stamina which made extensive love making difficult. It also made it hard to enjoy the things I used to enjoy and so the court had become a duller, more sedate place than before.

Fantasy: I was young enough to dance again, of a size to enable me to fit into some of my favourite clothes, to ride and walk, to dominate meetings and to make love all night. The court was alive, vibrant with laughter and mimicry and enjoyment.

Somewhere between those two was the reality of my life at that time. If you believe something hard enough it can happen. I found myself with vigour and desire for life. I could walk into meetings with all the dominating air I needed to impose my will on others without their even realising I was doing so and for a while even the ulcers dried up and I could ride without pain. The digestion continued to plague me, there were – problems – in that area which no amount of good thinking could overcome but I lived with it and so did those who served me, whether they found it offensive or not. Their problem, not mine. At any time they could ask to leave my service but none of them ever did. To be close to the power source is everything when you are in court and no matter how difficult the conditions at times, they stayed. All of them.

I had a sex drive again. Who wouldn't with a young, enthusiastic, pretty, exciting woman bumping up and down on your body … need I say more? She came to me with all the enthusiasm and shining eyes of a lover. I came to her with all the experience that my women, many of them, had taught me. Together we made love. She shrieked in pleasure at my touch, I yelled in pleasure at the way she brought me to fruition. We were noisy and we were uncaring and we laughed and we kissed and I loaded her with gifts, pearls and diamonds, gold and silver, estates and homes, the more the better. And if she turned and smiled sweetly at any Howard close by, I thought it kind of her to remember her family. If she turned and smiled sweetly at the young men who clustered around her, I thought her a temptress and a tease and laughed in our bed at her comments about them, for they were sharp, almost vindictive and very funny.

In the heights of my happiness, and believe me, Katherine, they were heights indeed, I decided to go on a Progress to the north of England, somewhere I had never been and had long wanted to go. I felt fit enough and strong enough and indeed young enough to do it. Katherine Howard had removed years from me by her very sexiness.

It was because of this I granted her every wish. She wanted George Boleyn's widow to come to court and take care of her, it was granted. She wanted someone called Dereham to be her secretary, it was granted. After all, a Queen has letters to write, does she not? She wanted someone called Culpepper to be her companion, along with a Paston, who was I to disagree with her choices? If they served me and if they served my Queen - in a variety of roles, some of which I did not know about at the time - they were welcome in court. Places were found for them all.

The court was basking in a holiday season of partying, hunting and jesting. I heard someone comment that it was like the olden days and it felt like that. I seemed to be perpetually smiling, unheard of for me but welcome, so very welcome. I was happy to have it like the olden days because it turned back the years for me. I might have been an old, irritable invalid to some, but in my mind, I was young again, able to dance, ride, hawk, do all that I used to do, without so much as a twinge of pain of the old joints. Oh, sometimes I suffered when I got up in the morning, but Will managed to get me going. At times he was better for me than all the physicians I employed, all the nurses and attendants that fussed around me. Many a time I dismissed them all, sent them packing to do something else, to let Will do the dressing and the shaving and the many tasks which got me ready to face another day.

I have to say meetings went easier, too. We had a lot of them throughout 1540 as we planned the Great Progress, where to go, who to visit, who to invite, where to stay, what to build when stopping anywhere, what festivals would be created to entertain us, what beds and comforts we would need on our journeying, what food we would want, what ale and wine we would drink. Much of this was left to those who had charge of the whole operation but some of it had to be yea'd or nay'd by myself and my Queen, such as which clothes we wanted to take and where we wanted to sleep and who we wanted to see. It was planned muchly as a holiday more than a 'let the people see their king' progress but it served both intentions in the end.

The planning was almost as interesting as the Progress itself. I had complete control over everything but the weather and that was in the hands of the Lord God Himself. If He chose to send His sun to shine on us, so be it, but if He chose to send His rain to make us all wet, equally, so be it. I was going to be travelling my country to see my people.

The weather was His concern. The people were mine.

We held Christmas in great style, for I was happy and content feeling youthful and showered everyone with gifts and money. I recall some exceptionally good mummers who visited us that year and had us in fits of laughter with their jests and their mummery. I recall Katherine's laughter and flirtatious attitude with the young men and smiled in a forgiving way at her antics, glad she found some happiness outside of myself, for I had no idea then that she was doing more than that. I thought she looked for a little diversion and welcomed it. Diversion inasmuch as light relief from being by my side, nothing more. She danced a lot and seemingly drank a lot too. Sometimes she came intoxicated to our bed but drink released many of her inhibitions and she was frankly more erotic like that than she normally was. Now there's an admission for me to make about my Queen! Only later, much later, did I work out why she drank so much at times. More fool me for not seeing it at the time. But there is none so blind as he who will not see, is there?

After the New Year was duly celebrated and the twelve days of Christmas came to a close, we got to work with serious intent and tied up all the arrangements for our Progress. Then it went wrong for a while.

Katherine's book reports that in March of 1541 the ulcer closed up. It mentions weeks of black gloom. Yes, that is right, but is slightly exaggerated. I longed to go on the Progress, I knew I had strength to do it then and I knew I might not have had the strength to do it the following year or the year after. All the plans had been made, all the arrangements were in place and the thrice-damned ulcer decided to close up and cause me all sorts of pain, suffering, complications and problems. Will saw me through it, as he did every time. He was my saviour at that time.

What my Queen thought was anyone's guess. Did she resent having to play at nursemaid and pretend to be unaware of my mood? Did she genuinely try to get me out of it by her flirtatious attitude and her constant laughter and jests? I know she did her best and for a long time some of it worked, too.

Don't ask me to say more, it was a troubled, unpleasant, unhappy time I wish to forget.

I got over the condition. I was fit to travel, according to the physicians, but seriously, what did they know? I had to go by how I felt, not by what they told me and I thought I could do this, make this journey, do this Great Progress and really see my country for myself. Well, all right, part of it. Had we been gifted with the forms of travel you now have, Royal trains and planes and cars, I would have seen a good deal more. But, on the other hand, it seems to me that your Royal family in your lifetime spend a good deal of time travelling here, there and everywhere, shaking hands, being polite, listening to eulogies and endless speeches and attending banquets and being bored out of their skulls at times, surely they are! Would any of them admit it, outside of the outspoken Prince Philip, that is? Would your Queen admit to being bored? She has a set face and she keeps it in place throughout the many visits, the shaking hands, the taking of gifts and flowers, she smiles, she speaks but does she reveal anything of herself? No. And that is how it should be, there has to be mystery, there has to be distance between the people and the Royal family. Why should this be? Those of us who are elevated, and I say this without conceit, for it is not conceit but fact, we need to be seen to be different. The beautiful Princess of Wales, if I may mention her in this book, broke that convention by being more accessible, more 'normal' by talking about her marriage, her feelings, her life, to mere mortals. It was a good thing in some ways, a bad thing in others. I have to say my heart broke for her, for she was so unhappy at the end. Enough, if time permits and she is truly willing, she will tell her story, too. Then you will see it from her point of view and maybe have a greater understanding of what she went through, as much as you are having the chance to gain a greater understanding of what I went through, an understanding not coloured by historians who come with their own biased view. My Katherine is the only person who writes with truth for she writes what I give her, not her own thoughts and interpretations of my life. She is sometimes surprised, sometimes amused, always attentive when we are working and it is good. I feel as if a great load is being slowly shed from my very big shoulders and I am growing in stature because the weight was crushing me, taking inches from my height. I did and do so like being tall enough to look over the heads of those around me and see what is going on which would otherwise be kept from me. Ever on the lookout for anything that would be of interest, even now…

Chapter Twenty Seven - Journeys

Finally, after much planning, last minute hitches, confusion, chaos and irritation, the Great Progress got under way.

It was a cumbersome, creaking, noisy procession of pack horses, carts, people, armed guards, banners, pennants, outriders, messengers, an incredible amount of humanity needed to transport one king and one queen from one place to another in the most luxurious and comfortable way possible. I watched it all unfold as we camped or stayed over in some castle or stately home, I watched it all fold up again when we moved on, watched with great wonderment that I, Henry, could order such a magnificent majestic Progress and have it happen. I wondered at times how it could have been done, what work went into the preparation and the actuality of it, knowing all the meetings we had and the discussions which took place were but a fraction of the real effort which had been involved in arranging and carrying out this huge enterprise.

More than anything, I smiled secretly with the smug knowledge that it had been arranged on my word, that it had to happen because of that word and that, in itself, was a marvellous thing. One I took for granted most of the time. By the end of the Progress I was taking that for granted, too, despite the fact that as time went on and we moved further and further north and then turned to head south again, problems were arising with people becoming sick, getting injured, getting tired, causing fights and problems, none of which were presented to me to resolve. I just had a wonderful time. I admit it, why not? My reign, my people, my country, my Progress!

We went, as I remember, to some wonderful places. I recall thinking that York was a glorious place and wondered why I had not been there before. Lincoln captivated me, the welcome was overwhelming and I almost wanted to stay longer than planned. Pontefract had its charms but I knew, from early lessons, that blood had been shed there and I was not as comfortable as I might have been. I say nothing against the people, just the place. Henry being sensitive, I hear you ask? Yes, there was a sensitive streak in the old man. Are you surprised? Even after all this time and all these pages, you may not consider me anything but a tyrant and despot and generally nasty old man. I hope, though, that I have done something to lift that impression of me.

The problem is that good but ghastly portrait, is it not? I appear in that to be the man you think I was, a scowling tyrannical king determined on getting his own way regardless of who might stand in the way. Does it not look to you like that? I see that portrait and the others where I am equally severe looking, frowning almost, staring at me from the covers of Katherine's books. I see that the unfortunate impression has continued into some of those books. Like the one whose closing line referred to my cruel piggy eyes.

The one portrait I am content for you to view is the one that was recently discovered, the one where I have Will in the background and my children with me. I am sorry to say that is a 'put together' portrait, various paintings combined. They are all out of time, we could not have all been there together at that time. It wasn't possible. But I like it, because there I look like a loving uncle or grandfather, full of bonhomie and tenderness and ready to give a hug to any child who might come to me. There I look like the person I always thought I was. The person I thought lived inside the bulky accursed body which was busy failing me and which I was happy to shed at the end. I did not see the tyrant, the despot, the nasty old man, the irritable irascible invalid this current author saw when he wrote of me. I thought I was just Henry, the same golden prince I was before I grew bulky and ill. Oh, I knew I was snappy at times but when your legs are screaming columns of pain and there is pus and goo and other unpleasantness oozing out, for someone who desired to be clean all the time that in itself was a hardship almost beyond bearing, let alone the pain, so I think I was entitled to be snappy. But the rest of it? Was I that bad?

Of all the things I am asked me to write about, this is the worst. You know it as well as I, but I also know that you are right, we cannot write of my life and leave one Queen out, no matter how the hurt bites into me, no matter how I resent having to display the horns of a cuckold to the world. You all know of it anyway, it is not as if I reveal a state secret with these words. And yet, do they not tear the very heart out of me to write them?   Katherine knows this and shows all her compassion in not asking me to write on when I do not wish to write on, when it becomes too much. My dignity, my ego, my standing in the country was seriously damaged by one foolish sex-mad girl and I did not see it for an age. Because I did not wish to see it. What I knew from my experiences with Anne Boleyn stood me in no stead for this one, because I did not wish to see it. With Anne, as I have said, the great love burned out and I sought any excuse, provided it was valid, to remove her from my life. Ah, call me tyrant if you must, you are getting the unvarnished truth here from the greatest Tudor of all, in my eyes, anyway… but this one all but killed me, rather than my arranging to kill her.

Back to the Progress. I keep diverting, do I not? I keep finding things I want to say!

One of Katherine's books says that the weather was bad.   I know not where the author found that information.   Katherine's reliable book of weather records shows a drought. My memory of that time is vivid, as it would be of any major achievement, like taking over a thousand people with me so I could visit parts of my country. So we will go with my memories and not the research of yet another historian … apologies to the lady concerned, but she is probably going to secondary sources like the rest of them. There are three sources of information:

Secondary sources, where you borrow freely from other historians' research;

Primary sources, original medieval documents which, remember, can also be biased;

The person who went on the journey. Ask yourself which is likely to be the most accurate…

She is right about one thing: the King of Scotland didn't show up in York. A deliberate snub which annoyed me? After the ganging up of the whole of Europe against me, should I care about the king of Scotland not turning up for a meeting? I did not. Marked, noted, memorandum made for retribution in due course and I went right on with my adventure. Historians, again I plead with you, stop putting words, emotions, reactions into my mind and mouth when you know nothing of me! In truth, at York when he didn't arrive, my reaction was 'who gives a ****?'

There are two books on Katherine's desk. One says the Progress began in the spring, the other that it began in the summer. The only thing on which they agree is the year. I despair.

Regardless of what others may think, then, the Lord God looked kindly on us. The sun shone on us from the moment we set out, a glittering parade of arms and jewels, a cacophony of hooves, harness and carts, rumbling wheels, grumbling people if we went on a little too long for them. I was excited, stupidly, as if I had never left London before, but the places we were going were new to me and that always provoked a sense of excitement. I also had the Good Feelings brought about by being with my delightful Queen.

Unfortunately the weather held too good, if I can say such a thing. There was a drought for the second year in succession and I heard tales of rivers drying up and cattle dying. The dignitaries of the towns we passed through were quick to relate their tales of suffering when they got the chance. Where I heard of real want, I left money for the poor. I was not that hard hearted that I could see my people starve. I wished I could have done more, but to do more would have meant taking land and money and estates and rents from those who supported me, the barons, the knights and the aristocrats of this land. You see, there is a dilemma here for those of us who are high born, we want to appease the suffering of the poor but also need to appease those who are supporting us. As much as I knew of the bloodletting at Pontefract, when the future Richard III disposed of three people who he said were enemies, I knew of kings who had been deposed by devious and often overt means and I did not intend that to happen to Henry VIII. I had determined that I would live out my time as king of England naturally, letting the Lord God decide when I was through, not some ambitious man and that, I am proud to say, is something I did. It was done with difficulty at times, there were moments – Katherine, I lie, there were weeks – when I thought that end had come too soon, when I choked and fought for breath and went black in the face and frightened those around me - but I did it. No death by stealth, no death by starvation, no death by an assassin's knife for me! I take nothing from my predecessors who came to their end that way, how could I? They lived their lives; they took their chances with those who also sought the crown. My problem was those who sought to place the crown on those who were married to me. But the revelation concerning my fifth Queen was still in the future, as far as I was concerned.

Before then, I travelled the country in great style and richness, with all the luxury that a king could command. I had at my side the most beautiful, lively and sexy woman imaginable, someone who cast smiles at me whenever I looked her way and I did, often! She reached out for my hand whenever we stopped anywhere, she walked with me, she even let me lean on her if the leg hurt a little and Will was not close by with the inevitable walking stick. Not that I leaned on her very much, for she was very young and seemingly fragile, her bones were obvious under her fair skin and I was afeared of hurting her. But the offer was made and that in itself meant everything to me. I gloried in the happiness I felt, the contentment that I had found a partner who meant a good deal to me and, seemingly, I meant a good deal to her, too. The smiles reached her eyes. You will recall, no doubt, I mentioned this at the beginning of my book; it is something I looked for, something by which I judged a person. It was always there – at the beginning, anyway. She seemed to be enjoying the Progress as much as I was. People wanted to see her, she wanted to be seen. She had a startlingly varied and beautiful wardrobe of clothes to show off and she did, in great style.

Wherever we went, the population came out by the hundred, or so it seemed, to line the streets, to wave and cheer, doff their caps, throw flowers at my Queen and pitch in to help build whatever was needed to ensure we were comfortable and entertained during our stay. The local aristocrats whose task it was to help us have a Good Time, as it were, did their level best. It must have cost them a lot in time, effort and real cash to make a Good Show for their monarch for I truly did have the best of everything. Were there weighing scales for people in my time, they would surely have shown I went back to London weighing considerably more than I did before I departed on my Progress! Yet the clothes I took with me still fitted without discomfort, unlike earlier times when the weight gain was such that the clothes threatened to cut off my supply of air. Perhaps I didn't gain more than a few ounces then. It felt as if I had consumed so much and drunk so much that I had to be twice the size I was before we set out. Katherine never mentioned any change but then she saw me daily and would hardly notice any increase, would she?

We had entertainment, choirs, minstrels, musicians, players, dancers, we had dances and banquets and formal balls. I had meetings and discussions and quietly checked out the loyalty of northern aristocrats and barons whilst I did so. We went to Mass and heard long sermons on how wonderful England was and how wonderful and benevolent the king was – I would rather have heard sermons on aspects of the bible but still, flattery was nice and always welcome, after all.

And finally we turned south and began the journey back to London.

Chapter Twenty Eight - Revelations

I had no inkling of what awaited me in London.

Full of happiness from my reception around the country, my seemingly devoted Queen's attentions, the good weather, the good food, drink and company, I returned to London the all-conquering king. And Cranmer handed me a letter. At first I thought him a fool not to speak to me, then I read the letter and laughed. He looked crestfallen, poor man, perhaps wondering if I was about to get rid of him, or something, or – that I had lost my senses. Who knows? What I do know is, I sent the informant, one Lassells, to the Tower to cool off. How dare he make insinuations against my Queen!

So, full of self-righteousness, confidence and renewed energy, I came back into London and back into my Court.

And walked into the biggest disappointment and heartbreak I had ever suffered and the good Lord knows I had suffered a lot already.

Evidence piled up, lots of it, more than I could dismiss as being flippant, fantastic, irrelevant. I had to take notice so I authorised investigations into the allegations. That sounds very elaborate, I merely set the counsellors to find out more in any way they could.

While the investigations got under way, I began to notice a distinct change in my Queen. She lost her exuberance, she became – furtive is the only way to describe it, furtive and perhaps fearful. She did not take the lead with me sexually any more, but instead was overly submissive and coy and her protestations of love and loyalty did not sound the same in my ears.

Katherine is asking, was this because investigations were under way and suspicion had already been dripped into my mind, thus colouring the way I perceived her? There could have been an element of that but for the rest,

I was very sensitive to the whole persona of Katherine Howard, I knew when she felt off colour, when she had a headache, when she had her monthly flow – an ongoing disappointment in itself, for I longed still for that heir to the throne – and so I was sensitive to this, too and knew of the changes. Small they were, but they were there. It reinforced all that was being discovered.

Mr – the person who wrote the book of my life which Katherine is using, you are, I have to say, completely and totally wrong. Wrong, wrong, wrong. I was not humiliated. I was shocked. What was discovered shocked me and I am usually virtually unshockable.

Let me put the facts before you and you decide for yourself.

The investigation revealed that throughout our comparatively short marriage, my queen had been cavorting sexually, if I can say that, with Francis Dereham, her secretary, Thomas Culpeper, her friend and Manox, her music teacher.

Whilst we made our Great Progress around England, that fool Boleyn woman, Lady Rochford, had conspired with my Queen and the men with whom she consorted to use every means imaginable to make a fool of me even as she paraded herself by my side for my people. Can you not begin to imagine how this felt? Can you not see that it was not humiliation which took me, but shock? The real effects of the discovery came later, when there had been time to assimilate the evidence and decide what to do about it. Self-rage, tears, bitter, bitter disappointment, disillusionment, you name it, I felt it.

Being cuckolded would be humiliating for any husband, let alone a king, but with me it went beyond humiliation into outrage because it became clear it had been going on for some years before our marriage and the thrice-damned Howards had kept it from me – and from the world. So, for those who would understand my feelings - and there are seemingly no historians who seek to do that - look at it from my point of view just for once.

I was elderly, yes. I was slower than I was in my youth, yes. Crippled, definitely not. Grey, of course. But I had given my Queen a good many bedroom sessions when all was well. You should know, you historians, how many men have fathered children when in their 70s and even older. Why should I, at my much younger age, not be capable of doing the same?

If my Queen had begun her amorous affairs during the marriage, you would have rock solid grounds on which to say it was my fault for not keeping her satisfied. I would refute it but with more difficulty than I now refute the whole thing. Then I admit you might be justified in your conclusions. But in view of the fact that the affairs had been going on long before she was so conveniently planted before me and encouraged to captivate me so as to ensure honours, wealth and high rank for the Howard family, does away with that conclusion in its entirety.

It seems obvious to me – in hindsight - that she was coached to be in the right place at the right time, to cast me one of her saucy smiles and then for the guardian to 'summon' her away from me so that I would see her run, see the dancing prancing youthful body and desire it. The Howards had gauged my reaction well. I was in need of a queen. I had been very disappointed by Anne of Cleves, why not present me with something – sorry, someone – I could not ignore, someone who would rouse all my languishing desires for sex and love and companionship. Someone who was skilful through long experience in the art of encouraging and promoting a reaction from me to her. Someone who knew many erotic skills, learned the only way you can learn it, from being with different lovers. The fool that was me did not think this through. That was my problem. That is my shame over this. Not humiliation, please note, for who can be humiliated when the entire thing has been an elaborate charade to promote one family – again.

Humiliation would have been had I chosen her, not she set out to choose me, if I had cast my desires in her direction and then found later I was making a complete fool of myself over a whore. Then yes, the world would be right to condemn me as an old fool. For myself, I call myself an old fool for being taken in by the despicable Howards and allowing them to make a mockery of me. And for falling for the wiles of a carefully coached and guided and outrageously promoted young woman. Ask yourself how many men have been led astray by what Katherine calls 'sex on legs' which some women appear to be. She has seen marriages and relationships shattered by women who walk into someone's life, flaunt themselves, smile and beckon and the man goes running. Later he realises how much he has been taken in. By then it is too late.

My tears - and I freely admit to them - were not for myself, not for my humiliation, so-called, but for the dream which had been so rudely and unbelievably shattered by the machinations of three or four people who should have known better. Did they really believe they would not be seen, discovered, denounced for what they were, co-conspirators in an adulterous situation? Or did they thrive on the danger? Did that add an element of spice to an otherwise dull life? Did the adultery need that edge, that very, very dangerous edge? If so, they got it – and suffered the consequences.

In a mood of utter cold rationality, I signed death warrants.

Francis Dereham and Thomas Culpeper were executed before Christmas. Lady Rochford and my Queen followed them to the execution block in the New Year.

I was cruel in my pain. Dereham suffered the traditional hanging, drawing and quartering. Culpeper had to endure days of waiting for the axe to fall. It was enough at the time. Did I know what I condemned them to? I could imagine. I did not have to see. I did not care.

I locked Katherine away, shut her up in a room in Syon House, a comfortable room but a prison for all that. I did not want to hear her excuses, her lies, her protestations of eternal loyalty. I did not want to see her pretty face creased with misery, her eyes wet with tears, see the wringing of hands and the longing written all over her to be taken back into the court again, to be at my side again. I aged ten years overnight, I am sure I did. I felt as if I did although none around me opened their mouths to say such a thing. I signed the document which said she was no longer Queen.

That Christmas was the dullest, dreariest, saddest and most heartbreakingly lonely I had ever suffered and I had been through a few which almost matched that description.

All revels were cancelled. I sent messengers out to ensure no mummers and players came anywhere near me. I had no mood for jovial people; I had no heart for anything. I went through each day as if I were not myself, as if I were a puppet playing a part and someone else was pulling the strings to make my legs move, my arms move, my head turn, my mouth open and shut. I know words came out but what I said is anyone's guess. I have no memory of them. I know there was a Christmas feast but whether it was swan, suckling pig or goose I have no idea. I went through the motions, nothing more. Will haunted me, a welcome yet unwelcome shadow, waiting to prop me up when I rose from a chair or from the table, ever ready with walking stick, an arm, a shoulder. Friends tried to console with expensive golden gifts but there was no pleasure in any of it. I drank too much and slept too heavily to be refreshed. I woke sodden with drink and misery.

How others saw me at that time I do not know and to be honest with you, Katherine, I do not care. What you call depression is a condition of the mind, a heaviness, a gloominess that nothing but nothing can lift. From glorious sexual heaven, being admired, adored and pandered to I was brought down to an empty bed, empty heart, empty place beside me at table and in court. Is it any wonder I was depressed? My son was ill with some fever at the time which was another worry to add to the many I already carried. Depression, oh yes, blackness, deep despair, intense loneliness and dismay at what my life had become.

Empty. I had a son and two daughters, no wife, no consort, not even a casual bedmate at this time. I had friends, a few I trusted completely, others who were not trusted friends but there. I had little else, apart from incredible wealth, still, despite my spending, and the crown of England. For some that would have been enough.

Those I truly loved had been taken from me, sometimes by my will, sometimes by the will of others. My Jane had been taken from me through the butchery of the surgeons, my first Katherine had been taken by ill humours or cancer or something, none were certain of the condition which caused her death but she had gone from me. Anne was taken from me by her own actions and my warrant, Katherine was about to go the same way. I was glad she was not in the same building as me, I could not have stood it. I was in a fit state of mind to go find her and kill her myself, but that was not seemly and would cause more problems than I already had to deal with. I went from maudlin self-pity to violent rages in a breath, in a heartbeat and none knew how to deal with it – or me.

Katherine has found this section very hard to write, for I have been hesitant, unsure, unable to say some things, wanting others changed.

I need to complete it, to ease my mind.

So I will.

In February I had Katherine brought to the Tower. I was told she had gone through her own emotions, from frenzy to acceptance, and had asked for the block to be brought to her so she could practice lying her head on it. She wanted to depart this life with a degree of dignity. I was saddened that she could not have thought that way whilst she had the chance, whilst she was Queen of England.

The 13th February was a cold, still day.

I swear even to this day I heard the sound of the axe.

Twenty Nine - Counting the Days of Sorrow

I had a most disbelieving look from Katherine when I gave her this chapter title but it is true. The old king was getting maudlin in his old age but more than that, it was true. My son was not entirely over his fever, so I carried that worry with me. My heart, mind, bed and life were empty and I missed desperately the lively, enticing, enchanting Katherine to an extent never thought I would. Whilst she was at Syon House, whilst she was briefly in the Tower, I could think of her and if pushed, and it would have been some push, Katherine! I could have rescinded the Act which took away her title of Queen and, at the end, could have refused to sign the Act of Attainder. Until the end she still lived and breathed and wore those enticing beautiful clothes which she had ordered for herself. I could have gone to see her, I could have ordered her to come to me. I could have gazed on her one more time. Once the axe fell there was no going back. She was so young! And yet, not a sign of a pregnancy. It would have made it worse, far worse, if there had been, I have to say. At the time I mourned that as well.

In the dark lonely hours I dissected the time we spent together, the months of happiness.

Katherine asked if I remember exactly when I met my fifth queen, as it has been proved I well remember how.

I disremember the date but I believe it to be early in the summer of 1540. It had to be either May or June, for we were married in the July. She was dead by February of 1542. Days more than months, months more than years. A short marriage, a short life. But, it would seem, one filled with more sex than even I got through – well, that is a slight exaggeration, I admit – and I guiltily revelled in the memories of the lovemaking even as I mourned her death.

It would seem to me that some historians dismiss her as of no consequence, calling her immature, promiscuous, all manner of things. She was not of no consequence, that is rubbish. She should not be dismissed for she was a queen of England for a time; she held the highest honour in the land. More than that, she gave this ageing monarch considerable pleasure, revived his youth for a while, gave the court much pleasure and gave the gossip mongers enough material to keep them happy for many a long year. It has also given historians much to chew on over the intervening years.

This part of my story, the life and death of Katherine Howard, has been written by me through Katherine's fingers with reference to only two books. I have not asked her to look at or even take from the shelf the books which are on Henry VIII and his Six Wives, nor any book relating just to my six wives. If there is anything here which contradicts anything there, then the fault lies with the historian for you got it direct from the king's mouth. As I said above, three sources… all the other books which Katherine owns and has not looked at since buying them, are written from mostly secondary sources.

My prediction for the future of historical writing in England: there is no source outside of the original one and the original one is sourced by one person only.

You won't like that, all you historians studying your papers and each other's work, I am sorry about that (not really, that's a small lie) but it is the truth. Wait and see.

It would seem half this book has been personal observations and half this book has been 'why did he write that?' It may not be strictly true; it just feels that way. If Katherine had all her books out on the desk, this narrative would be three times as long as I worked through and disputed 7/8ths of the statements made by those out there who profess to know me. 'Rubbish' is about as close as I can get in print to declaring my feelings about that statement and your work, historians. You know nothing of the mind and heart of Henry VIII and you never will.

Ask yourself these things, have you seen me, hugged me, heard my voice, felt my touch, been aware of my presence when I walk into the room, as Katherine does?

As I write this, or rather as I dictate this to Katherine, who has no idea what words are coming until they appear, I am standing next to a young man, a singer, who has come to be with her. We might be 500 years apart, if you consider the lives in which we represent ourselves to this special one, but we have met before, in past lives, even as we know Katherine has met with us, been with us and shared time with us in her past lives. No one comes to her by accident. We are joined at this time by love for this one who works so hard for us and gives us so much love in return. We are also joined by the knowledge of what will happen when these books appear, for many will think they are fiction, yet more will know they are channelled and yet more again will deny that and call her fraud and other names. We also know that it will make no difference to her, the work is the work and she does it. The truth is, spirit people are here with her, dictating to her, she hears, accepts, she writes.

The rest is down to you. But reverting for a moment to the historians, the reason for yet another rant by HM Henry VIII, you can shake your head over these words and the words in the book but you cannot deny them, for they carry the ring of truth. If you do attempt to deny them, then your own work is in doubt for you will show an inability to accept the truth when it is put before you.

That reminds me, I need to sort out that Chapuys person and ask him what he thought he was on about by saying I was crying for myself. Fool…

Chapter Thirty - Thrice-Damned Scotland

Well, at that time anyway. The Scots seem reasonably civilised today, Katherine, something must have changed in the meantime.

So, where were we? Or more sensibly, where was I?

This damn fool author seems to think my onslaught against the Scots and great plans to mobilise forces in France were due to my need to recover my youth. I wish the man had half the common sense he was born with, before he got any experience of life, I mean. I am totally bewildered as to how he could come to that conclusion from the evidence, so-called, that is before him, or must have been before him when he wrote the book. It is one Katherine can dispose of as soon as this book is finished and approved, along with many of the others. Katherine, it is worse than useless, this one! I know, she replies, but would you prefer I used the one from the historian you hate the most?

I would not. I will tolerate this one – for now.

Our old enemies, Emperor Charles – what a stupid title that is! – and King Francis, a fop at best, an idiot at worst, were busy destroying their lifelong pledges of eternal friendship and peace and were equally busy fighting once more. Did they seek to regain their youth, I ask this author? I doubt he will have an answer. My messengers/spies/informants were kept more than busy rushing back and forth across the Channel, bringing news of this manoeuvre and that, of this broken promise and that shattered treaty and as always, the poor people of the country were the ones to suffer. They did every time.

I wanted to join in, not because of a last grasp at recaptured youth, at my age and in my condition I knew full well that would have been ridiculous, but because it seemed like the right thing to do at the time. No more than that. Sometimes decisions are made for the craziest of reasons. How many wars have been started over not much more than that, I might beg to ask? Sometimes there are serious reasons for going to war, I have seen that over the years I have observed your side of life but also there are wars started over very small things but all have one thing at their source: greed. Land greed or power greed. I have to say that was in my mind, too. I would have liked to control Scotland then, but it was not to be. It was almost a great victory, though, wasn't it? The fool Scots got bogged down, literally, and we won a major battle, loads of prisoners, giving us lots of what you call 'the feel-good factor' – something I can identify with. Silly fool went and died though, didn't he, the Scottish king I mean, leaving that baby to run the country, when she was old enough. What can I say about someone who gave my daughter years of problems? Nothing. Both queens will tell their own stories, later.

Treaties were proposed, treaties were broken. The Scots agreed with one thing, disagreed with another. It sent my advisors and counsellors absolutely crazy with ill-suppressed fury and then it was all thrown out anyway, they signed up to fight alongside France.

I have to say, was there a more ill-considered move than that?

I lost it about then, lost the hold on the Tudor temper, let it go, let the whole thing go. I told my commander Lord Hertford, trusted man, trusted friend, to demolish Edinburgh, St Andrews and one other, Leith? Yes. To knock all the stones down, nothing to be left standing. Yes, I knew full well it would enrage the Scots but they had in turn enraged me.

He did just what I asked. It was a resounding success, as far as I was concerned. My name may well be mud in that part of Scotland to this day for the damage done but do I care? I do not. It matters not to me what they thought. It was an object lesson in breaking treaties and turning away from me. Whether they learned the lesson or not is their problem, not mine.

Chapter Thirty One - My Sixth and Last Queen and an excursion to France.

In many ways the last Katherine – and I note that At Last at least one historian is using the correct spelling of the name! – was a mixture of all my queens and the perfect partner for me with whom to live out the rest of my life.

Katherine is searching for a hint of where we met. She will not find it, so I will tell her – and you, dear reader – instead.

Hampton Court had ever been the place where I felt most at home, despite my love for all the other palaces I had, from Whitehall to the slowly-being-created Nonsuch. Greenwich was still home, so was Richmond but Hampton had an atmosphere, an air about it which made it the home I favoured most of all in my later years. Yes, I appropriated it because no one should have a bigger, better, more beautiful home than their monarch, but I appropriated it as much for its beauty and charm as for the fact that I could.

It is the home I have now in the Realms and it is as enchanting here as it was on your side of life, if not better, for here the flowers bloom all year round and birds sing endlessly and even though the grass does not really need cutting, it is cut at times so I can enjoy the fresh pure smell. There is nothing like it.

Hampton Court was where I held my 'informal' banquets, even though they had an air of formality, of course, as all the courtiers were keen to observe the rituals of obeisance before their king. I liked 'informal' as it gave me a chance to speak with people who would otherwise be further down the hall from me and I would see them from a distance, wonder who they were and never have a chance to meet them. We would eat and then wander in the gardens, then retire for a while for a rest, then eat again and then dance, or hear choirs or minstrels whilst talk flowed easily from one to the other. I enjoyed these times very much.

It was at one such informal gathering that I met Lady Latymer, otherwise Katherine Parr, and observed her from a distance after that. She was a mature lady, previously married, which meant she had experience, she had a quiet and goodly nature, her smile was pleasant and meaningful and she did not quail at the sight or the smell of me. My legs by then were very bad and if it were not for the shock to the system, I would happily have had them amputated and ceremonially burned in front of my (cruel piggy) eyes.

I asked about her, consulted those I trusted to bring me information. I was told she was being courted by Thomas Seymour and I envied him, for he was a younger, fitter, good-looking man any widow would be proud to marry. You may say I decided to take her from him because I could. You would be right. You would also be right if you said something about the woman attracted me but I could not say what it was. I could not pin it down and say to you, it was her looks, her manner, her knowledge, anything. I cited her maturity, her quiet nature, her smile and the fact she did not seem nauseated by my 'problem.' It was all that and it was more than that. It was not the thrill of the chase, truthfully, for I was too old, too crotchety and too ill to do that any more. I was tired, very tired all the time. I needed comfort and companionship. Some have said, I know this, that I needed a nursemaid. If I did, I would have hired one; there were enough around. I didn't marry to get a nursemaid! I married for companionship and affection and what this Katherine calls T L C which I understand to mean Tender Loving Care. I had all that and more from the wonderful lady who seemed pleased to be courted by me. We spent time together, a goodly amount of it, she laughed at my jokes, appeared to be fond of my Fool Will, she liked my friends and they in turn liked her. I found no reason not to make her my queen and when I asked her to marry me, she smiled her delicate smile and told me she would be delighted. I mentioned my weight, my age and my ill health. She said none of that mattered, she just hoped she could bring some tenderness and comfort into my life. We spoke of my past queens, she told me she had been aware of the rumours about Katherine Howard but had said nothing to anyone, hoping they were untrue for she had seen and appreciated my happiness, my youthful-seeming zest for life whilst she was my queen and had also seen, she was honest about this, the way the whole disastrous end to the marriage had aged me and hurt me and diminished the brightness that was my reign. I flourished under her sympathy and quiet understanding. I keep using the word 'quiet' in relation to Katherine Parr. It was this quietness which was the essence of her, it calmed you, it consoled you somehow.

We were compatible, it seemed. We got to know one another. We came to an understanding. Fittingly, we were married at Hampton Court in a small ceremony attended by close friends and a few courtiers. It was enough.

This Katherine, my third, it was good that I liked the name very much and the connotations it had for me, isn't it? was - and is - a treasure. She gave me much pleasure in so many ways. Religious, caring, devout, loving, elegant, learned, able to hold her own in conversations and discussions with our many high-ranking visitors, she was everything I sought. I no longer needed or looked for bedroom games; I was past that, past caring about that, too.

As soon as she could, my new queen quietly took on one of the roles of my much loved Jane and brought family to court, arranged for tutors, arranged get-togethers and generally made everyone feel part of the one rather than individuals left out on a limb on their own. She brought in tutors and fine thinking people. She began to exert an influence that was felt by all and it was appreciated. The court relaxed, I was in better mood most of the time, people seemed happy around me and that in turn reflected on others, so the whole atmosphere changed – for the better.

And so, from the security and comfort of my new marriage, with quiet contentment and great pleasure, I arranged to get involved in the problems in France.

The army was due to go to France. The king decided he wanted to lead the army into France. This, for those who don't know, was July 1544. Ah, now perhaps I can admit that there was a yearning to return to the days of youth when I could ride triumphantly into someone else's country and wage war. The old war horse, me, still wanted to do that. Instead I went on a litter. How shaming was that! But, whatever I may have thought about it being shaming, I went. I went and I insisted on being a part of it.

Before I went, I made Katherine Regent. Now that was a compliment to my sixth queen if ever there was one! To leave the government of England in her hands whilst I went to war, or at least a semblance of war anyway, was a tremendous decision for me and one I did not make lightly, as you can well imagine. I had always held the reins of government in my own two hands, even if at times it looked as if others were busy doing their bit. They were, but with my unspoken permission. They knew the tug of the royal hand if they strayed too far.

Also before I went, if I can say that … I arranged the Act of Succession. It had to be done; I had no idea if I would return. My health was not good. My age was against me. I had to look into the unknown and decide what was to happen. So, I decided if my son did not provide the country with heirs, my daughter Mary would succeed to the throne, if she had no heirs, then Elizabeth would, even though I cringed inside at the thought of women taking on the mantle of monarchy. It was very much a case of making do with what I had and, at that time, that was what I had. Oh, if only my first Katherine's children had survived, none of this would have been necessary, but – if onlys litter our lives and we can do nothing about them except obsess about them in the dark hours. I was, at that time, experiencing a lot of dark hours, Katherine, they were not very pleasant and were very likely to leave me in a very bad mood come the daylight.

France, then, and the warrior king getting involved in war once again.

The problem was, and I am not getting into politics, Katherine, there has been enough of that in this book to satisfy any casual reader whilst knowing it's not entirely what they want to read, that damn fool Charles made peace with Francis, after declaring war on each other and then turned on me, but I regained Boulogne. If nothing else, I regained Boulogne and I had eight long weeks of campaigning in France. I had a great time. They tried to stop me, those who were supposedly running this war but I mounted a horse (with help) and went out there and I rode around and I supervised the siege and I oversaw everything and everyone had to admit the old war horse knew what he was at after all. Ill I might have been, consumed with fever from time to time, definitely, in pain from the thrice-damned legs, definitely but determined to get out there and just BE. Which I did, in style and in great elegance and in great pain which was worth it for the glory I got from being there.

The whole campaign cost me lots and lots and lots of money. All my money, in fact. More money than I thought possible. The book says two million pounds. Calculate that at today's rate and see what I spent on a useless war. But honour was at stake, the honour of England and England's king.

I will say this. France needed England and England needed France, but not as much as the other way round. History would later prove that France needed England more than England ever needed France or even cared about France. The trouble is, the big trouble is, they are too damn close to England. Not as close as the Scots but the occasional battle with the rampaging Scots usually pushes them back to the other side of that ruined wall and in their own wild country. And for a time they even stay there.

The French are different. They are connected to the rest of Europe and keep getting involved in arguments with the rest of Europe and then end up needing England to sort them out, when they are not fighting England. To this day I am not sure France knows where it truly is or who it truly looks to as an ally. With God's help, great leaders seem to come along when required by England to help win the battles against the foes. France should take note of that lesson, too…

Although I have to say England is in need of a leader at the present time, Katherine, and I don't see one anywhere, not even on the horizon. Politics in your time is a morass of grey men and women who do and say stupid things and cause endless problems and no one, no one, appears to have the strength of mind, character and initiative to stand up and say 'listen to me and let's sort this out.' So you all go on getting deeper and deeper into debt, into misery, depression and blackness. I have to say this: you need another Wellington or Churchill to bring you out of it. I have to repeat, unfortunately I don't see one.

Back to my life.

I needed money. More money than the country could stand, even if I did force loans and taxes and all manner of things from those who could afford it. Land was sold as well.

Now, I ask you this; is the man correct when he says I did not love England and its people outside of it - and they - being a reflection of my glory?

My answer, because you have yet to read this book and I am here writing it, is that there is an element of truth in that which hurts a little, because I had never looked on it that way. To me the monarchy was everything, for it was the way I had been brought up, to revere the king and obey his commands. I expected everyone else to do and be the same. Autocrat. Charles I was an autocrat too and I know, yes, look what happened to him. A great sadness, a great shame on this country at that time - and ever since. Katherine has a tremendous fondness for that unfortunate young man who went so disastrously astray with his life. He has much to come to terms with, much as I did. This has been a revealing book, for me at least. What you will make of it, dear reader, is anyone's guess. What the historians will make of it is something neither Katherine or I give a damn about, in truth.

Chapter Thirty Two - The Final Act

Back in England, with the glory of France behind me, for all that it cost a fortune and all but bankrupted the country, I began to be ill again. Fevers took me, burned me, drained me and worried those around me. They were forbidden to speak of my dying, that was treason, so they mouthed platitudes and no doubt began their power play games to ensure they had a part in the life to come, that of a royal minority. It was a worry to me but not one I could discuss with anyone. I knew by looks, by overheard snippets, that they, courtiers and counsellors alike, thought my end was near and they could start their manoeuvring. They thought they could take a little control, they thought they could out-guess me. They were wrong…

There were enemies. Tell me when there were not? Enemies of my queen, of the religious regime she was establishing, those who spoke against the fact that few heresies were being reported and dealt with. I wondered why for a very long time. I had broken with Rome, I had instituted the Church of England, I had condemned Catholic and Protestant alike without fear or favour, I had walked the middle road, as it were and held the country in my hands. But there was talk and there were murmurings and there were those who thought my queen was responsible for all this freedom of religion.

Ever were people looking to bring someone down, to change things so it suited their way better. My queen was not exempt from that, unfortunately. But they forgot, or simply overlooked, the simple and basic fact that Henry Misses Nothing.

My queen held daily Scripture meetings with her ladies. Was there something amiss with that? She spoke with me on many matters relating to the Scripture and I delighted in her learning, having had much experience of it in my life. I knew there were rumblings in court, I knew full well that there were people trying to find cases of heresy amongst my wife's attendants and even with my wife herself. I knew all this, for the spies I paid well were busy at all times.

After some time spent considering this from all angles, I decided to pounce. I casually mentioned to Stephen Gardiner, Bishop of Winchester for his sins, one night that my wife seemed to be teaching me and I begrudged it.

Fool that he was, he fell for it. He accused her of all sorts of things, heresy particularly. I agreed with a grumble and a scowl and he smiled. He had papers drawn up for her arrest. I signed them and he smiled even more. I can tell you that a smile from Stephen Gardiner was like looking at the smile of the wolf before he tore your throat out. I distrusted and disliked the man but he never knew it.

Then it was a simple matter of ensuring there was a warning for my wife on her supposed 'danger'. I got round this by 'letting' her see the documents which had been written as if by accident. This enabled her to 'throw herself on my mercy'. I forgave her very publicly. No one could have failed to have seen it or reported back on it but still the plotters went ahead. Some men are so stupid it is quite unbelievable. But I had gambled on that, my plan was to make a very public denunciation of the plot. I knew my people well enough to know that conceit would override common sense. And it did.

The next day we walked in the gardens in the summer sunshine, myself, Katherine and her ladies. She supported me for I pretended my legs were really bad and that I was nothing more than an invalid. I acted the ageing king with great pleasure; it was part true and part deception to add to the deception. Katherine had the ability to be blank of face when needed, all she showed that day was concern at how slowly I walked and asked, with great sympathy, if my legs pained me very much. Those in the gardens with us would have heard and seen little but wifely concern and husbandly consideration as I held her arm and talked with her.

The gardens were invaded by Gardiner's messenger dog, Thomas Wriothesley, accompanied by forty men at arms. I asked myself several times why they sent forty armed men to arrest one hapless middle-aged dowager queen. Were they so frightened of her? They should not have been frightened of me, it had apparently been arranged with my consent, so why the overkill? No one ever explained that. Absolute nonsense. I thought it then, I think it now.

They charged into the garden to arrest my queen but, after a good deal of abuse from me, I was able to throw them all out. The whole plot had been thrown into disorder, shattered into pieces; Gardiner had to walk very carefully with me after that. So many people made the Big Mistake even then of under-estimating my ability, they could not see past the 'old man' face and realise that the mind was not old, that if anything the years had sharpened my instinct for deception, for plots and what almost amounted to treason.

Different historians have interpreted that happening in different ways. Some seem to believe that my queen truly was heretical, others that I schemed and planned to make Gardiner look a fool. My chance to set the record straight, again.

My wife was no heretic. She had a clear and precise understanding of the Scriptures and I actually delighted in discussions with her, despite the fact that at times she could out-think me. I was by then somewhat infirm and my grasp on many things had slipped a little, perhaps. Did it matter? We were all in this life to learn and I was learning from her. It was easy to draw in those who did not see it that way, it was good to plan and scheme and involve many people without their realising they were involved.

Henry Misses Nothing and Henry could and did out-scheme many of them all the time. More fool them if they thought they could get one past me, as it were. They did not realise I revelled in my ability to dissect any plot or ploy to damage my way of life, to take from me that which I treasured, to disrupt my court and my reign. I found tremendous pleasure in devising ways of exposing such plots for what they were, an attempt to impress someone else's thoughts and reasoning on mine. It never did work. They never did learn.

Quietly and efficiently I set about destroying the men who had tried to implicate my queen. Norfolk was in disgrace, for a start, for helping Gardiner with his scheme. All his supporters were scattered; he found himself without anyone to stand up for him. Eventually his son had my patented cure for headaches, which suited me. I almost removed the duke himself. He was lucky, by the merest whisker of Fate he was lucky. But what really mattered to me was that the Howards were finally no more. My revenge was complete. They owed me that, for foisting that chit of a whore onto me, deceiving me to gain power. It was the ultimate revenge for me and I revelled in it.

Then I removed Gardiner from the Council of Regency. I issued a short statement which basically said 'get the hell out of the council, Gardiner!' without saying it. He knew he had lost my goodwill, my patronage and my small amount of trust. My son was too important to me to entrust his care to the hands of someone who would stoop to such deceit and attempt to remove my much loved queen from my side. And the future of England and the monarchy was way too important, too. Did he think he could gain some element of control over me? He must have known my time was drawing to a close but he dared not speak of it. If that was an effort to wrest a little control from me, it failed very badly indeed.

For myself, I knew my life span was limited. I knew it well from contemplation in the dark hours and the fevers which began to affect me very badly from time to time.

I made plans. I had to make plans for I wanted to ensure there was no return to the dominance of Rome. I had fought long and hard to ensure those shackles were thrown off, I did not want them put back on again. This is why, from the Realms, I watched with utter dismay and horror as my daughter tried to bring it all back and rope England to Rome once more.

I made plans by drawing up my Will but for a time I did not sign one copy of it. Ha! Katherine, how they flapped and hinted and fussed and harried me to accept the fact I needed to sign my Will, without saying I was dying. They were terrified I could die intestate which would have caused a power struggle. But … in the first place I did not want to give them the satisfaction of seeing me sign my Will and acknowledge I was not long for your side of life and in the second place, I was rather enjoying my games. The court might have thought I was trying to avoid thinking or talking about dying, as I had done in the past, but on that one they were wrong. I thought about it because I knew it was coming. For the first time in my entire life I did not have the spectre of the bony hands reaching out for me. Instead, He, the Grim Reaper, was coming as a comforter, because I was tired, tired to my very bones, of weight problems, health problems, thrice-damned leg problems, of the back biting, the deceit, the endless power play, the talk, the pressure of being king. I wanted nothing more than to lie in my bed, thick pillows at my back, my calm tender wife visiting me with fine wine and succulent pieces of fruit or sugared comfits for my ailing appetite. I ate less food and wished I had done that much earlier in my life.

I felt my heart pounding hard, hurting me at times. I now know it was working too hard in trying to send the blood round my very large body. The legs hurt less when I didn't try to stand or walk so I did that as little as possible.

And I made two copies of my Will, signed and dated. I gave one to Hertford and one to my wife. The other copy, the unsigned one, I left to tantalise and torment those who clustered around trying to get my attention. My wife had instructions to destroy her copy once the other one had been proved. She also had my blessing to marry Thomas Seymour if she wished. I rewarded her with jewels and estates aplenty as a dowry, for she had been a good wife and queen and I was sorry to be leaving her.

Throughout the whole of the Christmas celebrations, somewhat muted by my ill health, the murmurings went on, the power play gambits went on and I quietly watched and waited and dropped hints here and there to stir the mud a little and then sat back and enjoyed the result.

I did say earlier that Norfolk was lucky. He was. The warrant for his execution was drawn up but was never signed. I didn't have the strength to sign anything at the end.

My physicians were in a state of panic, thinking they were committing treason by not keeping me alive. But they knew, as I did, it was over.

Cranmer was called for but didn't make it in time for me to confess any sins. Heaven alone knows how much time that would have taken anyway … I doubt the poor man would have had the strength to hear me out. I had no problem with that, God and I had been on good terms all my life. I saw no reason for confession.

I never really relinquished my grasp on the reins of power until the early hours of the 28th January, when I knew it was no good holding on any longer. The Grim

Reaper stood at the foot of my bed, wearing what can only be described as a benevolent smile.

I surrendered myself to his care and let go.

Epilogue

On the 28th January 1547 the physical life of Henry VIII of England came to an end. The story has come down through history that he died of syphilis. There is no evidence of that; the truth is more likely to be that his heart gave up, no doubt through furred up arteries and complications due to his extreme weight through addiction to food and wine, both of which he freely admits. He was/is one of England's great monarchs, attracting attention to this day with his lifestyle, his wives and his 'reforms', not to mention the many people he had executed. Historians seem fascinated by him, there are many books on his life from different aspects and viewpoints but all have to eventually centre on the man himself, for he was the centre of England's life for over thirty seven years. Henry seems bemused by the amount of attention he has generated through his having had six Queens, his contention is that we should focus on his political life instead, but as he asked in the book, 'what would people prefer, politics and power play or sex and scandal?' and we all know the answer to that.

His Majesty King Henry VIII first came to me on the 3rd April 2006 when I was sitting circle with my friend Mary. I did not discover who the visitor was until the following morning… he gave us enough clues but we didn't pick up on them at the time. Recognition came in a blinding flash the next day. For the past two and a half years he has been a constant companion, definitely a larger-than-spirit-life presence. I described him to a friend this way:

'The more I work with Henry the more I realise what an amazingly talented, skilled man he was/is and why he was/is such a giant of a figure in history. He is funny, perceptive, loving, sarcastic, sharp, comforting and big, in personality, body and aura.'

I have loved the work, loved the contact with this great man and am looking forward with pleasure to sharing the rest of my natural life with him.

You may well decide not to believe that this is a channelled book direct from spirit, that I am a good author and wrote an interesting work of fiction, in which case I hope you enjoyed your read. If you choose to believe that I channelled the work, then you will have had an insight into a period of history usually only seen through the distorted eyes of historians. There are more such insights to come from a great variety of people who have approached me with the same request, to tell their story and put the truth in front of the world.

My next book is the life of someone seen as the ultimate traitor, Guy Fawkes. The same criteria applies: you can take it as a work of fiction or you can accept that it is channelled from Guy himself. Either way, I hope you will look out for it and having bought it, you will enjoy his story.

Thank you for buying this book and for reading it to the end. If nothing else, you should have a different opinion on the giant of a man known as Henry VIII, which is what we set out to achieve.

Dorothy Davies,
Isle of Wight, 2014